Diary of Murders

by Sarah Cook

For more information, email: sarah@sarahcookwriter.co.uk

First paperback edition August 2023

Edited by Andrew Jones and Steven Cook
Cover design by Beth Morris

ISBN 978-1-7393470-0-0 (paperback)
ISBN 978-1-7393470-1-7 (e-book)

www.sarahcookwriter.co.uk

For the John I once knew
and the Miriam I used to be

CONTENT WARNING:

If you do not wish to be spoiled, please feel free to skip this content warning.

Dear Reader,

Diary of Murders has been a passion project of mine since its conception. Writing this story, and these characters, has been the greatest experience. I hope you get as much out of reading this book as I did writing it.

Diary of Murders, whilst fictional, is partly a retelling of my story. Unfortunately, that does mean grappling with the darker and sadder elements of my life.

With that in mind, I do feel it is my duty to inform you that this book contains scenes which may be upsetting for some readers.

This includes graphic depictions of consensual sex, BDSM, murder, blood, injuries, domestic violence, alcoholism, drug use, PTSD, panic attacks, miscarriage, and sexual violence.

Please practice self-care whilst reading.
If affected, there are helpful resources at the end of the book.

All My Love,
Sarah Cook

"Before this ends tonight, I wish to tell you a story. It is about a diary. One that I found not too long ago…"

Chapter One

I write this in the hope that I may be purged of my sins.

A confession before God.

I pray for absolution for my crimes.

For my intent is true and just and that should surely prevail.

Wednesday 13th May 1896

The work has to be done.

If we are ever to rest again within this household, that thing - that grotty man – has to be cut. I have no doubt. He has eluded the beak and no honourable man wished to pursue the case. The gallows beckon him with a ferocious cry. Hell has unhinged its jaw and from the fiery gullet has produced a scream that wails through the streets of London. I have heard it nightly.

Every waking moment the devil has not claimed back his fiend is a travesty of the highest order. I have taken it upon myself to answer the call. The work has to be done, indeed.

Harry Wright has to be cut.

I am new to this career of bloodshed, yet I know that this will require all my strength. Work of this manner is a science. It requires the tools of patience and skill. I guess that part is easy. After all, I have waited weeks for him to face the rope.

But having the gumption to take a life is hard. That is a mettle I have yet to discover. I hope that the steely resolve required will come when asked.

Through years of training, I am skilled at cutting flesh but to use one's scalpel to maim intentionally takes a tenacity that medical training has lacked. To take another's life - what kind of person can do this? Can I?

Alas, the slaying of Harry Wright is a necessity for this world and a task at which I cannot bear to fail. As with any profession, killing must take practice. He shall slither and slink through this world - like the filthy pig he is - a little while longer until I have the means to slaughter.

Since his vicious deed, Wright has been smart to evade the Law for this long. He has gone underground, and those foolish flatfoots have not the sense to find him. Justice is a fickle mistress. No matter, I have faith that he will resurface soon to do his grim bidding on the streets of London again. That is when I shall strike.

Until then I must perfect my craft. This is gruesome business, after all

See, that bastard did not work alone. No. There were others. Accessories. Villains who aided and abetted the crime, releasing horror and nightmares into my world. They are all responsible in my eyes. They walk around Soho even now - a scourge of these streets. Their punishment merely a stern word and rapped knuckles.

Fear not, they shall meet my knife too.

Oh yes, Harry Wright will die.

And the others shall cry for clemency.

But I shall not give it.

Friday 23rd August 1895

The drawings were rudimentary. Black pencil scratchings like a child would do; if said child were privy to body parts, blood, and guts. The sketches dotted the worn pages of a well-used journal, so tatty that it was nearly falling apart. They were bodies of all shapes and sizes. Men, women, and sometimes infants sprawled with their anatomy on display. Crude organs and bones next to countless words that would strain any eye that tried to decipher it. To a layman, this book was damning and shocking.

To Miriam, it was a bloody good read. She carefully pawed at the journal as she sipped from a glass of champagne. She had placed her deep red boots on top of the wooden desk, centimetres from a skull that she wasn't quite sure was fake, and nestled the book against her legs, which she had crossed to stop the dark-blue skirt from falling all the way down. The small desk lamp flickered now and then but still served as a sufficient tool for such a fascinating study.

So engrossed, Miriam took another sip of her sparkling wine, not noticing that the glass was empty. She sighed and kept on reading. Miriam gazed over the book with such an excited curiosity that she didn't hear the door open. She barely registered the footsteps coming towards her. She scarcely took note of someone standing before her. A loud cough sounded out above her, followed by a soft male voice, from the other side of the desk, saying, "Excuse me, what are you doing in my office?"

The sudden interruption caused Miriam to jump and drop the glass in her hand. The shattering sound made her freeze like a hunted animal; almost as though if she did not move then the man who loomed over her couldn't see her. When he rushed forward, Miriam suddenly dove to the floor to start cleaning up the mess. She was thankful that the wine had gone.

The man seemed to disapprove of her actions. There was a tut and a sigh. "Oh, please no, leave it be. You'll hurt yourself. I shall fetch someone to clean this up."

Miriam did not listen. She shook her head in an attempt to avoid eye contact, unsure that he wouldn't explode at her in anger if she met his gaze. "It is fine, I have done this plenty of times, glasses are tricky creatures, ha ha, and— ow!"

It was almost as though he spoke it into fruition: Miriam had cut her index finger on the glass. She put it immediately into her mouth and sucked. Closing her eyes, she winced at the pain, and as the blood glazed over her tongue, she could still feel his gaze upon her. Footsteps walked around the table. A woosh of air came before the man grabbed her wrist and yanked her finger out of her mouth. "Please, let me have a look. I am a doctor after all."

Opening her eyes for the first time, Miriam finally saw the man who had spooked her. The man whose office she had trespassed into and whose journal she had read was now squatting in front of her, tentatively hovering above the broken glass.

He tended to her wound like it were second nature. He pulled out a white handkerchief from his pocket and applied it to the cut, adding a small amount of pressure that made her wince. Muttering an apology, the doctor then reached into his desk drawers and pulled out gauze. In a flash, he had removed the handkerchief, now splodged with blood, and began wrapping the finger up.

All this had given Miriam time to inspect the doctor. Even from this angle she could tell he was a handsome man. He must've been older than her, but he was young for a man of medicine as his skin was pale, fresh, and soft. Though he was slim, his face was round with a slight dimple in his chin and a small, snub nose. Just a few wrinkles decorated his piercing icy blue eyes which he flicked at her every now and then. He wore his dark brown hair short in fashionable waves from a right-sided parting and there were small whisps of grey within the tousle. Upon his upper lip sat a handlebar moustache that he had twisted thin at the ends.

The man had on a black suit with a white shirt. It was nothing of note except for the navy necktie, the same colour as her jacket. In that moment, Miriam thought they perfectly matched. There was the usual aroma of lavender and mint that stalked most doctors, but when he removed his handkerchief, Miriam smelled a familiar puff of chamomile. Every sense of this man exuded a strange calm that, in turn, started a small chaos within her.

His face was familiar but in a faded way, as though they'd passed on a street or sat beside one another at a theatre show. An echo of a person in the back of her mind. When he had finished with the bandage, he gave her hand a squeeze and looked directly in her eyes, causing her stomach to flip. He smiled; "There, Doctor Clayton, all better." There was a pause. Miriam looked alarmed as the pair stood-up, staring at one another. Though the man stood taller than her, by a good couple of inches, he suddenly turned sheepish. "Did I say something wrong?"

"You know who I am?" She said with a nervous chuckle, looking around the office, trying to deduce what kind of man stood in front of her. Yet his personality remained unpacked. She could not discern him yet.

The man laughed, "We are stood in the Clayton Hospital, are we not?"

"A fine observation."

The Clayton Hospital was built three years ago. It stood at the corner of Regent's Street and Shaftsbury Avenue, behind the Ham Yard pub. It was triangular; three white-stone buildings with a courtyard in the middle. Each served a purpose: Men, Women & Children, and Students. Soho had been revitalised over the years and was steeped with artists and immigrants and jostled with entertainment and prosperity. Yet the poor masses and the unfortunates still clung to its streets. The hospital became the line between the upper classes in their lavish town houses who frequented shops and theatres nearby and the scruffy poor and bohemians who overcrowded homes and pubs on the other side. Much like the area, the building was brilliantly alive with patients of all sorts and classes.

That was Miriam's father's aim. Sir Fredric Clayton had taken most of his inherited family wealth and poured it into the creation of the hospital. The amiable Sir Fredric was not of his traditional upbringing but moved with the decades – especially the fast innovation of the 1890s. He had such a ferocious conviction for charity, even if he found it hard to sway the other members of the board to his thinking. Sir Fredric thought hospitals belonged to everyone and used any money from the wealthier patients to help the needier ones. That kind nature was already celebrated widely amongst the staff.

Perhaps Miriam had passed this man in the hallways of the hospital. How strange that they had not been formally introduced yet. How strange indeed. Miriam looked at him with an intense curiosity. "And you called me *Doctor* Clayton?"

"That is your title and qualification, is it not?

This man was right. Miriam had followed in her father's footsteps fiercely. Training at the London School of Medicine for Women, under the impeccable tutelage of Dr Sophia Jex-Blake, Miriam had become a devoted physician. Whilst she could have continued at the Elizabeth Garrett Anderson Hospital, Miriam wanted to forge the spirit of the institution into male-dominated hospitals.

When her father opened a new one, Miriam took the opportunity to dedicate her new career to creating women's wards and bringing more women onto the staff. The instant she put her foot in the door, she began to reshape the medical field. This was much to the chagrin of the men on the board who saw her as nothing more than her father's troublesome and hot-headed daughter.

"Yes it is, but no man in this blasted hospital actually calls me that," she said hesitantly.

"Those men are damned fools, the lot of them. I have seen your work and you deserve the same respect as them. More so, even."

"You've seen my work?" She said, confused as she had never properly encountered this man before.

The man laughed again, paused, then replied, "I am on the Board."

"... Ah." A smirk flickered across her face. That's where Miriam recognised him.

"Your name does proceed you. I was duly warned when I arrived here a month ago. Still, seeing you in action, the way you take those men to task, it is electrifying to watch."

"You flatter me."

"Oh, I doubt it. You know full well the effect you have on the board." He winked at her causing a sudden skip in her beat. "They are down-right scared of you."

"Scared of my father is more like it."

"As rich and powerful as he may be, it is you, my dear, that gives them nightmares at night."

"Perhaps that is why they would like to lock me in my basement." She smiled, "Would you like that also?"

"Me? Heavens no!" The man placed a hand on his chest earnestly. "I am merely an ardent admirer." He then extended his hand. "Doctor John Bennett. Deputy Head of Surgery."

She hesitated but took his hand regardless, forgetting that her finger was still sore. "Doctor Miriam Clayton, Head of the Women's Wards - as well you know."

They shook politely, creating sparks as they locked onto each other's eyes. As they stared, a surge passed between them. A shock of energy. Electricity. They wondered if this sudden rush raced through the other too. They pondered on whether the other could feel the earth shift slightly. Could they sense the sweetening of the atmosphere? Their hands weren't even moving anymore. They just held onto one another for a moment.

In an instant, a nervousness washed over them both. Miriam was the one to break the hold and coughed slightly. John flashed a smile and Miriam could not help but return it. He said softly, "So what brings you to my office, perusing my journal?"

"I find these types of functions to be such a bore." Miriam gestured towards the book that she had left open on his desk. "And I find surgery so fascinating."

"We think alike on both counts. And how did you find the book?"

"Risible. Like reading a book on executions if drawn by a simpleton," she paused briefly, "Tell me, do you attend all of your lectures blindfolded?"

"Here I was thinking you saved your mordant tongue for the more Neanderthal thinking men at our hospital." He chuckled, "but yes, I must admit, my hand is not great. I am sure it matters not in this line of work. Come now, let us get out of this mess."

John took her hand and guided her cautiously. Glass still crunched under her heeled boot and, for the briefest of moments, she admired the sound. When she had hopped over to him, she let out a small giggle causing him to beam brightly. His thumb glided over her fingers before he let her go.

"I do hope you are not taking me back to that ghastly party." The function they both seemed to be avoiding was somewhat of a trustee benefit in order to secure funds from the rich elite. Miriam took no pleasure in parading herself around for the upper echelons of society. Even though her father had ordered her to stay, and smile and be polite, she had slipped away at her earliest convenience. Both the thought of heading back and the idea of staying here alone with this new handsome man caused her cheeks to burn.

With a mischievous grin, John shook his head before gesturing to two olive armchairs by a bookshelf, causing relief to spread throughout Miriam. "Will you do me the honour of joining me for a drink?"

Miriam cocked her head at him out of confusion. Cheekily, he winked at her before he walked between the chairs. Bending down at the base of the bookshelf, he pulled out the bottom drawer which was bigger than any other. She heard a faint tinkle of bottles.

"Here we are," he said in a jolly manner. He stood up and in his hand were two crystal tumblers. "Which do you prefer: whisky, brandy, or gin?"

The peaty smokiness of the whisky that Miriam sipped on warmed her gullet and made her bristle with delight. There was nothing finer than a glass of scotch in the evening. Bubbles were fine for conversation and circulation, but whisky was tastier, and instantly slipped a little bit of relaxation into the evening.

That said, Miriam was still uneasy. Adhering to social decorum, she sat upright with an uncomfortable rigidity at the edge of the armchair, sipping daintily at the golden liquid. She had sensed that Dr Bennett would not begrudge her if she slid back into the green, velvet seat. Yet Miriam had had many talks in offices such as this and she had learned that not everyone was so keen on a reclining woman. It was not proper; women in society should be stiff, silent, and still. That was not Miriam at all.

At her father's insistence, she had to pretend, and she did try. She really did. Most mornings she would start her day primly, striding into the hospital with her father, trying to be as timid as a mouse. By midday she was already helping with the wounded, ushering in the poor, storming the streets in protest, or yelling at the other doctors. Miriam did not have the constitution to stay in her place.

As Miriam took another timid sip, she watched him from the corner of her eye and quietly begged him to release her from this position. Unlike Miriam, Dr John Bennett sat using the whole of the chair, crossing his legs. He had closed his eyes and sniffed at the whisky, savouring its scent before taking a huge gulp. It was as though it were the first and last thing he had ever drunk. This soft, near passionate, way of being was so familiar to her. In just that instant John had revealed part of himself. He opened his eyes and snickered at her posture. "Please Dr Clayton, I invited you to enjoy a drink with me. You have my permission to relax."

"Do you really mean that?"

"Whatever makes you comfortable. I insist."

"Oh, thank goodness for that."

Miriam breathed out the air she had been holding in her lungs. She took off her plain dark hat which caused strands of her hair to protrude messily from the tight light brown waves on top of her head. Miriam's hair was a simple style – she had gathered all her unruly hair and fastened it into a bun on top of her head just over a week ago and also curled the fringe tightly, so it stayed away from her face. Over the days, as the strands spiralled out of control, Miriam had begun to cover the mess with a hat on most occasions to feign some semblance of beauty.

Most people forgot that Miriam was pretty in some sort of manner. She had sparkling dark blue eyes. Her gorgeous face was round and chubby, pale with rosy cheeks, though her nose was triangular and wonky. Miriam was taller and more voluptuous than the fairer society women that she knew, with a biggish belly and thick thighs from a healthy appetite. The scatty and spirited nature inside of her made her unkempt, untidy, and unbecoming of a young lady.

Miriam began unbuttoning the large silver buttons of her navy jacket but suddenly froze in shock. "Drat! It slipped my mind."

"What did?"

Miriam spoke her excuses fast; "Look, I was very hurried this evening and I had forgotten about this entire event, and I was already here at the hospital, and I just shoved the jacket over my blouse and thought nothing of it but…" She opened the jacket to reveal a huge reddish-brown stain upon a white and blue striped shirt.

John recognised it immediately as blood. "My goodness!"

A furious flush flooded her face as Miriam frowned, speaking just as fast as she had before. "There is this right bastard – Harry Wright? Have you heard of him? Oh God – you will. Anyway, he punched this woman Marie square in the nose. She bled all over me, the poor dear." She seethed a bit before saying. "Oh, how I'd like to get my hands on him."

John looked dumbfounded. His eyes wildly gazed over her with intentions she could not be sure of. Taking another nervous sip, feeling that familiar warmth slip into her stomach, she had the courage to look back at him. His eyes flickered, clamouring for thoughts and words. As she met his stare, he smiled and said somewhat temptingly, "Dr Clayton—"

"Miriam, please."

"Hmm. Miriam, you are unlike any woman I have ever met."

She laughed loudly at him, reclining to the back of the chair. The jacket stayed on around her arms but, unbuttoned, she was a little less constricted. Even with a bodice underneath. John frowned at her, confused. Noticing his bewildered expression, Miriam rolled her eyes, "Oh John, most women are like me. We're merely meant to hide it, lest we wind up spinsters or old hags."

"No, my dear girl, you misunderstand me." John leaned forward, looking at her as though his hands were reaching down her throat and swiping the air from her lungs. She gasped softly as his eyes pulled her from the depths of an icy ocean. A lighthouse beacon illuminated in his stare, searching for her. "I am a doctor too, am I not? I know women are not as refined as our society ludicrously wants them to be. But you, Miriam, there is something about you. I cannot quite solve it but trust me, I will."

Those last words were quite hushed. It was the final few days of August, summer's long evenings were ending, and a cool chill had entered the city at night. The pair were already mostly drenched in darkness. The only light was the oranges emanating from the gaslights above them. The little fires smouldered in the dark. The blaze of red and yellow flames now created shadows on their faces and allowed their figures to dance across the walls.

All the while the two doctors stayed still and stared. Quiet. Ruminating on this heat between them. Caught in that timeless space again. Neither wanted to move for fear of making a singular sound. The hushed roar of the lamps was the backbeat to their heavy breathing that they were both trying to control.

A feeling in her stomach spread like wildfire: A similar sensation with new spikes that sliced into her soul. His words were fervent and tantalising, wrapping around her insides which caused her pulse to quicken. She was exposed. It was as though he saw her in a way she thought was only reserved for her own reflection.

In a gentle, pensive whisper, she said, "Who are you?"

John flashed another arresting smile but matched her tone as he answered, "I am just a sawbones of meagre means who has wanted to talk to you since you stormed my very first board meeting a month ago. As I said, I am an ardent admirer. In fact, when I could no longer see you at the party, I resigned myself to going home as the person I was most interested in talking to had vanished. But here you are."

"Here I am." She replied, using her hands to present herself like a magician's assistant. In all her time here, she'd never thought that her sharp tongue and fast words would attract someone as interesting and as handsome as Dr John Bennett. His blissfully blue eyes moved slowly over her like wishful hands. A bigger feeling flowed through her: She wanted his actual hands upon her. Musing on this craving, she smirked and continued: "You have to forgive me, Dr Bennett, I thought I knew all the intriguing people here."

"You are forgiven. After all, this face is new within these halls."

"Well, it is one I am unlikely to forget now."

"I certainly hope you do not."

There was a pause again. Miriam couldn't stand the silences any longer because she could almost hear her body screaming out for him. She wondered if he could hear it too. Goosebumps rose all over. Her thoughts plunged into a desire. Within that need flowed scintillating images of him beneath her, nude and undone. As this excitement found its way in the dark, she could not stop herself from saying, "May I ask you a sordid question, John?"

His eyes widened from the notion. *Did he know what she was about to say?* Still, even if he did, he nodded, "Of course, my dear Miriam. Anything."

She sat up and leaned on her arm. It was not the first time she had been so bold to ask this question. In fact, it was a useful tool to disarm a hot-headed opponent. For the first time, however, she knew that she was going to get the truth. "You say you have noticed me before?"

"Indeed, I have."

"So then, Dr John Bennett. My question is: Has your mind ever wandered… to fantasies of me? Thoughts of me writhing naked below you as you have your wicked way with me?"

"Yes."

The lack of hesitation both scared and pleased her. "How often?"

"All the time," John whispered, putting his glass down and edging slightly closer to her.

The air moved before him and she instinctively bit her lip, knowing another question lingered on her tongue. Part of her wished to keep it guarded but it was impossible. Soon it rolled from her mouth. "And tell me John, do you ever touch yourself when you do?"

There was a distinct pause as the weight of those words landed upon him and he clutched his hands together. He thought hard on his response, perhaps wondering how fickle Miriam's affections were. Maybe John was wondering if this was a ruse. He looked away as though the answer were across the room. It must have been because when he turned back, in a hushed voice and a small chuckle, he said, "The mere suggestion of what you asked could get us both in trouble."

"The mere presence of you and I alone in this room together could get us both in trouble John," she giggled, "but I wish to know. I implore you to answer."

Taking a sharp breath, he finally said, "Yes Miriam. Sometimes I do. Does this please you?"

"More than anything."

He then leaned forward to kiss her. Miriam pulled back before he could. Not because she was frightened or didn't want to. *Oh, how she wanted to.* But she knew that her refrain would explode inside him. The fast, irritated breath that came out of him told her that she had succeeded. "You are tricky, Dr Clayton."

"Hmmm," Miriam leaned down to the drawer and topped up her glass with more whisky. Sliding back in the chair, she hung one leg on the arm. She did this purposely to unveil the skin of her lower leg. She even tugged the skirt and petticoat back, hoping that he didn't see her purposefully arrange her garments, and thought it was a happy accident that her bare flesh was now on display. Again, he did not waver. He looked upon the exposed area with a growing intent. A lion prowling for a taste. "May I tell you a story John? One that would tell you who I am in an instant and reveal more about myself than you would ever have guessed."

Reaching down to grab his glass again, John replied, "I would like that immensely."

Miriam told her story in a deliberate and almost deviant way: "As a young girl, I never understood the role of women in our society. Especially with my family's wealth. They tried to teach me to be ornamental. Relatives. School. Men. A pretty plaything that you could admire, then have, and then place upon your shelf to gather dust.

"But I was raised by my father. He taught me passion and adventure and courage and intelligence. Also, generosity and kindness. This all boiled inside me like with raging purpose. Me! That tall, plump girl with crazy, unkempt hair. So, I did not belong to the dolls and dainty dames of my schoolmates. I loved them no less for this, mind. They never tried to treat me any differently. It must've just happened naturally, I guess. Of course, when one grows up, one learns that most women are all fiery and impassioned. They simply conceal it much better under society's gaze. They have more resolve than me.

"We lived, until over a decade ago, in a small Manor house in Northamptonshire. It was rich but quaint, with a huge, rolling lawn that my mother adored and tended to whenever she could. Her favourite place was a rose garden. It sat at the very end of the land with a stone bench at the centre. It was a place of quiet reflection and startling beauty, quite like the woman herself.

"Or so that is what I am told. Sadly, my mother died not long after I was born. Please, no need to say anything, I've had years to cope with the loss. By the time I turned fifteen, what had started as a small rose bush, had grown into this thorny lair. Dangerous branches that twisted high over wooden arches. It still bloomed, strong and vibrant flowers, but they were now intimidating. My father had left it alone, instructing the gardener to 'let it grow as it wills' – hoping that my mother's spirit had found solace in those crawling vines. He never visited it after she died though.

"It had, however, grown to be my favourite place. At first, I thought it was so I could be close to my mother, and in some way, it was. But that wasn't it. Not really. You see the stone bench was now hidden, as was anyone who sat upon it. With its distance from the house, you heard not a sound. It was my fortress. My solace. My throne of wickedness if you will."

John's eyes grew wide at this revelation, almost incandescent with the news.

Miriam's face cocked a smile, knowing she had him under her glorious spell. She continued; "Contrary to popular belief, women enjoy pleasure too. At my age, bored in that manor house, feeling different from the other young women around me, with a profound interest in anatomy, I simply had to explore. Some mornings, in just my nightgown, I would walk to that rose garden. I'd lie on the stone. I'd hitch up my skirt. And I'd please myself with no one the wiser. Alone yet with autonomy.

"One morning, doing this deed, I was startled by a noise. A sudden rustling. An intruder snapping branches and climbing through the walls of my solitude. I looked to see a boy staring at me. My age. The gardener's son, I found out later on. How long he'd been there, I did not know. But I knew it was enough. I stayed immobile, unsure whether to run away forever or stay put.

"Yet I saw a flicker in his eyes. It raced through me. I was elated and excited and frightened and fearless all at once. He said nothing but I knew his intent.

"'Do you like what you see?' I said to him, frozen yet filling with need. He nodded without saying a word. 'Are you hard right now?' He nodded again. 'Would you like to take me?' A pause but then a nod. 'Then you may.'

"I then grabbed the hem of my skirt and hitched it up, revealing all of myself. I looked away and placed my feet on the stone. He walked over, unbuttoning his trousers. I let him penetrate me. It did not last long, as quick as it would for two heated teenagers, grunting and groaning for mere seconds. He soon spilt inside me, and we collapsed near breathless together. We straightened ourselves up and finally I ran back into the house, hiding my newfound euphoria in my room. My father and I moved to London shortly after. I never did see that boy again.

"But in that hot, panting moment at the first light of day, I found myself. My true self - free and desirable and whole. For the first time, I let someone into my body and my secrets. All at my behest. All at my command. All at my control."

The last sentences rolled off Miriam's tongue and simmered in a now seductive silence. The tale clung to the air like droplets of blood on the edge of a knife. Miriam had never really told that story before but something about John made her want to spill her secrets into the night. She wanted him to know her at her core; the need and sex that ached within her. A brazen mistress that was so sure of her body and desires.

Unhurriedly, she pulled her skirts up again - just a few millimetres to reveal even more of her skin. It was a beckoning. A call. An invitation. He now had permission. "Do you like what you see, John?"

The doctor nodded without saying a word.

"Are you hard right now?"

He nodded again.

"Would you like to take me?"

A pause but then a nod. John's penetrating gaze wished to rip into Miriam. Those ravenous set of blue eyes feasted upon her carcass. What alarmed her is how much she wanted him to tear into her flesh, to carve himself into her body forevermore. She heard nothing but the drumming in her ears.

"Then you may."

For the longest moment, John stayed silent. Then he rose from the chair without saying another word. She half-expected him to leave, disgusted by her proposal.

Instead, he walked leisurely over to her. Leaning down, John placed a hand on Miriam's exposed leg. She tried to stifle a moan. The touch was warm and soft.

Steadily, the doctor then dragged his fingers under her skirts, pulling them up over the knee. At the same pace, he brought his face closer to hers. Their eyes met, boring into each other's wicked ideas. The way he moved – carefully, studiously, attentively – was as though he was enjoying every new cell he'd uncover. He coveted her, intently watching and etching her eternally into his mind. Every morsel he touched and every freckle he looked upon was just to keep her this way – memories that he could revisit for the rest of his life. He said no words, but she knew them: All his wishes and wants flowed from him to her with that deliberate and gratifying caress.

A heat raged within her, and she agonised for him. Yet Miriam held herself carefully. She did not wish to give away the electricity that pulsated through her. Ravaged, unkempt gasps stalled in her throat. John's lips were just a moment from hers. Their breaths were now entangled. They were so close to knowing what each other tasted like. And his hand…

Oh, his hand, his hand, his hand.

"Miriam?"

The pair froze.

"Miriam Clayton?"

The second deep boom of her father caused them both to jump and separate. Miriam stood up and buttoned her jacket hastily whilst John breathed out, annoyed. He sat back down in the chair, his face a picture of defeat. She pushed her skirt down and straightened herself up. Picking up the crumpled hat, she wiped it down as though she were wiping away the last few moments. Ragged in a different way, unspooled like a ball of wool, Miriam said, "I—"

"Miriam, where the blazes are you?"

"Father calls." She said instead, in a way that was apologetic to be leaving yet thankful for their time together – however brief it had been. Before she turned to leave, she hesitated, hoping that John would say something. When he didn't, gazing at the door as though it had betrayed him, Miriam nodded knowingly.

As she stepped away, John suddenly grabbed her hand. It was an urgent plea. Miriam froze, looking back as he placed his lips on her hand. John gazed up, knowing the touch had radiated through her. "I shall think of you tonight, Miriam; in all the ways you wish me to."

"And I shall do the same, John."

Chapter Two

Wednesday 3rd^d June 1896.

The stains of this evening rouge my fingertips even now. I have bathed and scrubbed in excess and yet my skin still echoes the carnage. I fear that perhaps it is my mind conjuring the stains. It has been written that the guilty can be driven insane by hallucinations of one's deeds. A heart beneath the floorboards, a red spot upon the palm, a painting in an attic. Have I procured the same vivid images from my own misdoings?

These are now the hands of a murderer, after all. I worry that my mind has already handed down a punishment of its own creation. I fear that I am to be outed by this lunacy. Depraved by my own depravity.

I am ashamed for targeting the blonde bangtail first. Though her actions were not entirely innocent, I am sorry for her continuous plight. Yet she has become the first chapter within this bloodlust. The quintessential step to revenge. The grave intention that paves my road towards hell.

London may profess itself to be the seat of culture. But the royalty and the wealthy walk these cobbles of Soho, a far cry from the gold-painted pavements of Piccadilly and Bond Street that lay nearby. For entertainment, no less. They use and abuse the poor to relieve their agonising tedium. How boring their sad little lives must be, that they may judge and scorn the pathetic in such a heinous manner.

I have to wonder: where does my privilege lie? That I can enjoy the spoils of the elite yet still see the plight of those deemed worthless. The drunks. The pinch-pricks. The grotty children.

Alas, then, it should come as no surprise to me that acquiring a woman of this sort was far too easy. Especially if it looked as though I came from money. The lavender suit was one I had not seen for a while. It was a happier time then. It was somewhat baggy on me, and as I tightened the braces, I was hit with a pang of haunted memories. However, in this suit, I was transformed. I looked like any posh toff would, prowling Soho's brothels for his bit of rough.

I knew in the soft colours that I would look harmless and perhaps they would not tell me apart from any other gullible man. I gelled my hair back, put make-up around my eyes, and stuck on a fake beard to alter my appearance. A purple top hat completed my disguise. It felt strange hiding in something so familiar.

I had to learn a few things about these fiends during my planning. Alice Haddon was a middle-aged woman, thin and gaunt, ravaged by gin and circumstance. I knew little beyond that, except she knew Marie in kinship. A friendship that relied on their rooms being close together in The Furnace, I suspect. Acquaintances through their work.

Now Alice and I were to be acquainted through my work.

The blond-haired Alice was known for soliciting on the streets. She'd earn a bob or two prowling for strange men and taking them to dangerous corners. She was one of the few, with the permission of Wright, who would leave The Furnace as though she were hunting for prey.

From a distance, I kept an eye on her wobbling. Propped up against the red wooden windowpane, she swaggered and leered at all who would pass. As I made my way over, she smiled and placed her hands on her hips. A refined gentleman who she could swindle and rob.

Would she recognise me? No. I suspect that her near drunken stupor made it unclear what type of being was approaching her. Desperate for coins, she practically threw herself at me, so I gruffly asked for us to be alone. She obliged and took my hand, wobbling as she dragged me down dark corridors and alleyways. I recognised this place. I knew it well. It was where my life fell apart. It filled me with rage.

When she settled on a wall behind a pile of wooden barrels, far from the rowdy crowd, she fumbled at the trouser buttons and braces. I grabbed her hands to stop and look at her, as a cat would when pawing at the mouse it was about to feast upon.

Before she had time to say anything in her bewilderment, I clenched down upon her wrists, making sure my fingernails cut deep into her flesh. She yelped in pain and looked up to my menacing stare. I was sure in the moment she caught my eyes that she recognised my face. Out of my pocket I took the knife and showed it to her. She begged and twisted in my grip. Tears filled her eyes as I raised it into the night, the blade glistening with the moon.

Alice cried. A look of fear crawled on her face. I hesitated, nervous at what I was about to do. In that moment, Alice kicked me, and I accidentally released her. She rushed away, fast. But I was faster. I leaped upon her and pinned her to the ground. Without a second thought, I sliced her throat. Blood spurted at me. She gasped, unable to scream.

Suddenly, I was without remorse. I took the knife and plunged it over and over and over again until I was tired.

Spent, I wiped my face and marvelled at the crimson river that now flowed from her. There was no time to think, I had to run. I fled into the shadows.

Oh, I am sick and elated. Alice's cries now the overture to the grand spectacle and symphony that I am creating. Her agony still courses through me. It is as though the blood that had streamed from her now races inside my veins. I am jubilant and feverish and, dare I say, aroused. At the same time, I am remorseful and nauseous, and guilt ridden.

Can these two parts of the soul really race together like the hounds of hell?

Have I become God Almighty and Satan all at once?

So be it then.

For this sword is now unsheathed and bound for the demons and the scum that crawl within this city. May they feel my wrath and burn in my flames.

For I am no longer a person. I am Vengeance in all its might.

Thursday 29th August 1895

In the inner pocket of John's jacket sat writings of the most sordid nature. Salacious verbs, racy nouns, and shocking adjectives were scrawled in a feverish manner on whatever loose pieces of paper the writer could find. They burned with lurid content, laying heated against his chest. John kept them close, worried that another stray would wander into his office and find them. However, every time he took off his jacket for surgery that day, he'd be fearful they'd spill out.

He couldn't possibly leave them at home. He liked them close to him so he could occasionally smell the waft of her perfume which clung to the pages – a dazzling combination of bergamot and lemon. He would remember the remnants of them on the small bit of skin he coveted the other night. On Miriam, the popular scents tasted fresh and otherworldly.

The letters had been slipped under his office every morning since their last encounter. Five or so notes of the most devilish content. Details of her body. Musings of his. Fantasies of them together in such rousing trysts. John had thought of her in this way, but her wild and wicked mind was very inventive.

The images she conjured would dangle around him for an entire day. As he worked, as he cut, as he made his incisions, all John could think about were the words sprawled on the page. Then he would think of her… sprawled…

Only when he was alone, in his solitary room at the top of a large Camden boarding house, was he able to do something to relieve the urgency and rushes he was feeling.

It is not as if John didn't try to write back. He compiled similar letters, lamenting the ache at missing his chance to kiss her properly. He wondered in ink on how long it would be until they met one another again. He wrote and wrote and wrote about his need for her. Then John would briskly walk through the hospital looking for her, but it was like she had vanished.

Even trying to catch her delivering the notes was a futile endeavour. Once he wasted an entire morning waiting for one to arrive in his office. When the note slipped through, underneath the door, he opened it straight away with a loud "AH-HA," scaring the poor young nurse who had been instructed to deliver the envelope.

Early on Wednesday evening, as the year was turning away from August, and the sky was stretching out the final minutes of daylight, John was leaving and caught a glimpse of her messy, brown hair. He called after her, but it seemed to hurry her more. He bounced down the corridor, nodding his goodbyes at anyone he rushed by, bemused at his haste. Marching quickly out the entrance of the hospital, John suddenly halted. Miriam was climbing onto a bike. He caught his breath at the door, resigned to the fact that he could never catch her. However, she stopped as she mounted, looking up and straight at him. Their eyes met across the courtyard. She grinned and wiggled her fingers at him before speeding off with a sly giggle.

Miriam Clayton was a tricky creature indeed.

However, John Bennett was sure to bump into her today. For today was another board meeting, and Miriam was certain to attend.

Eagerly, John turned up early and placed himself at the table, in the chair nearest to the door. Looking quickly at everyone who entered, John was like schoolboy with a crush, instead of a thirty-eight-year-old accomplished surgeon. As droves of Doctors, Governors, and Trustees came bounding through the entrance, taking their places at the table with their morning mumbles and grumbles, John grew more dismayed. Miriam was nowhere to be seen. When her father Sir Fredric Clayton, the Director, and

Chairman of the Hospital, walked in alone, John became somewhat frustrated and mystified. Miriam couldn't be trying to evade him so much that she'd miss her chance to argue with all these rich, powerful men?

Still, as Sir Fredric's booming voice said, "Good morning gentlemen," John knew that the meeting had begun without her.

The morning was now as lifeless and dull as it ever could be. The focus was on poisonous fake medical cures and the charlatans who peddled them to the poor. There were insidious comments, jabs and jibes, and boring lectures. They all melted into one droning hubbub. John leaned back in his chair and massaged his temple. A headache was forming. Especially as he watched Sir Fredric fight for some sort of empathy from the more callous men in the room.

The door swung open with a loud bang, John was so fed up with the morning that he did not jump or moan as the others did. Instead, he closed his eyes and winced. The bang reverberated around his sore head. It wasn't until he opened his eyes that he saw everyone standing. Looking up, confused, John realised Miriam was right beside him. He scrambled to his feet.

"Oh Goodness, Dr Bennett. Please, do not let me keep you from your nap." She said, her eyes crawled over him with a spark of glee flashing across her face. He flushed; embarrassed, annoyed, and excited all at once. He did not care that she had taunted him in front of his peers. He did not take heed in the slightest that they all laughed at him. He did not care at all. He was finally beside her. With her gloved hand, she reached over and kindly squeezed his shoulder. He tried not to show that he was blushing and bowed his head apologetically. She courteously nodded back. "Sit gentlemen, please."

Miriam dragged her hand away from him and walked around the table. John caught a waft of her perfume, which was entirely new to him. She smelled like violets. It was adequate as she was a vision of that very colour.

The dress, though simple, was more refined than her usual attire: It was smart and sophisticated. It was mostly purple with cream frills in the middle of the dress above the cinched waist. Matching cream lace anointed the long, puffy sleeves and also the collar. She wore a small top-hat-shaped fascinator which matched the shade of purple she was wearing. Her hair was tighter and neater. John suspected she had had to make some sort of effort for someone

As if she read his mind, Miriam announced her own apologies as she began to sit down. "Please forgive my tardiness. I was having tea with my Aunt. You'll be ple—"

"Oh, welcome, *Miss* Clayton." The shrill voice of Dr Michael Jenkins, the hospital's pharmacist, interrupted her. The lanky thin man with dark-blonde hair and green eyes was the only board member who was around John's age. In fact, they had been friends long before John's employment at the hospital as they were on the same cricket team. However, sometimes Michael's views on women and society were as archaic as the elder men who surrounded them. He was also almost always annoyed by Miriam's behaviour. He let out a little hot breath of irritation. "I am glad you could pry yourself away from all that serious talk of fashion and cakes to attend to more frivolous hospital matters."

Miriam paused and tightened her lips. The room went quiet as most braced themselves. Sir Fredric tried to stifle a smile. At John's first ever board meeting, the puffed out and portly Dr Peters – Head of Surgery and John's boss - had similarly thrown an insult Miriam's way. For a moment, John had wondered why Sir Fredric didn't rush to his daughter's defence and stayed as he was now – deathly silent with a playful glint in his eye. It didn't take long for John to find out why.

Letting out a small laugh of contempt, Miriam rose so she could stand and look down at Dr Jenkins. "Oh, do forgive me, *Mr.* Jenkins. I was about to announce to the room that I had secured a sizeable sum from my Aunt that we could use for, oh let me think, new training for the female physicians and nurses, perhaps the latest medicine, or maybe cleaner wards for our patients. Come to think of it, I could just open a tearoom where me and all my little gal pals could titter about you wretched men over cups of Earl Grey – if that's all you think women do when they are alone together. Or better yet, perhaps I should invest in an invention that could pry that syphilitic head of yours out from your arsehole."

There was a chorus of gasps and a ripple of laughter.

"Miriam, enough." Sir Fredric said in a faux sternness, coughing to cover his own chuckle.

"I'm sorry Father." She sat back down, looking pointedly at Jenkins. He was beetroot, staring at the notebook in front of him. There was no doubt that he would not talk again during the rest of this meeting. Or the day, perhaps.

John, however, had the biggest smile in the whole of the room.

Though the board had all risen together, Dr Jenkins bolted quickly out of the room, ahead of everyone else. John chuckled as he rushed by before glancing back at Miriam, who was speaking with her father at head of the table. She had not looked over at him again since entering the room. He was dejected and felt somewhat foolish. Especially because it seemed that both Miriam and Sir Fredric were about to leave, too engrossed in their conversation to notice that John was waiting.

Adrenaline raced through John. He had to think fast. Scooping up his notebook, he laid it open in one of his hands. He took the envelope filled with his notes to her and put it on the blank page. He breathed in, steeling himself, and said loudly, "Oh Dr Clayton?" The sound of her name caused her to pause and turn to him. "A word before you go, if you do not mind?"

"Of course," she said with a polite smile.

Miriam began walking over. John scribbled hurriedly on the journal. When he looked up, she was again stood alarmingly close to him, brushing up against his side. Curiously, Miriam took off her gloves and leaned over to inspect the journal. As she did, she breathed out. "For a moment, I feared you were about to let me leave."

"You may not know me well. Yet." He replied, low so that no one could hear him. "But you know me better than that."

John tapped the page and Miriam began to nod as though they were discussing hospital matters. He had written:

When can we meet alone again?
I am at your behest.
I am at your command.
I am at your control.

Miriam continued to nod, making agreeable sounds whilst John waited patiently for her to respond. Instead of replying to him, she turned around to Sir Fredric. "Oh father, Dr Bennett has had the most marvellous idea on what we can do with the money. A secret women's refuge run from this very hospital. It is going to revolutionise how we treat their suffering."

"Oh, Dr Bennett has, has he?"

The back of John's neck burned as Sir Fredric's gaze fixed

upon him. Dr Bennett timidly replied, "I… erm… yes."

"How wonderful darling!" Sir Fredric boomed. "Perhaps he should come along this weekend to the Manor where we all can discuss the proposal further?"

"Father, that is a splendid idea! Yes, John, you must come to the Manor with us!"

It was as though John was in the middle of a bad play rehearsal. His cheeks flushed again, mortified. Had Miriam discussed their meeting at the party with her father? Were they truly that close as father and daughter? Or maybe Sir Fredric had no idea and was simply meeting her whims as he had always done? The pair, however, looked at him for a response. "Oh… I… erm… yes, that sounds… charming?"

"Then it is settled." Miriam said, matter-of-factly. "Meet us at Euston Station no later than 10.30am tomorrow. Pack light. I've your ticket already."

Oh, my dear, you are playing a sly game, John thought.

Lightning bolts sparked through her blue eyes causing thunder to storm within him. She smiled a big grin like a cat who had a plaything between its paws. Practically purring, Miriam winked, turned, and began to walk away, "Until the morning, Dr Bennett."

"Dr Clayton wait, the proposal…" He took his envelop of dirty notes and extended it to her. "… in case you wish to peruse it further."

"Oh, I think I shall!" She took it from his hands but extended her index finger, running it down quickly yet deftly over his thumb. As the touch sparked through him, John realised that this is why she had taken her gloves off.

They shared a secret, knowing smile.

Friday 30th August 1895

If John were not a man of science, he would suspect that Miriam was a witch. The spell she had cast over him in little over a month would be enough evidence to prove she were one. Every hour, he'd lay in bed, and admonish himself for being so pitifully obsessed. He told himself that he would regain control. But every time he closed his eyes, he would see her staring at him, and his stomach would flip again. The very thought of her crawled on his skin and through his mind.

In a sleepless daze, he found himself once again early, waiting for her to arrive. For his trip to the countryside, John Bennett wore a white shirt with cream trousers and matching waist coat. Over the top, he wore a light grey tailed jacket. With it, he wore a similarly coloured bowler and carried a small walking cane and brown suitcase. It was not just that he was anticipating the warm weather and long strolls; he had hoped Miriam could see him as someone beyond the hospital.

Still, he wore the same navy neckerchief that he was wearing the night they met. It matched her eyes, after all.

John paced back and forth underneath the clock at the station, waiting for her to arrive. He'd huff and sigh and check his own golden pocket watch again and again. It was not even 10.20 and yet he was agitated. Puffing out his annoyance, John Bennett said in a heated breath; "Dammit man, pull yourself together."

"Well, someone is not having a good morning," came a familiar voice from behind. He froze on the spot before turning around to see Miriam smiling at him. She had her arm linked through Sir Fredric's. The pair looked content, as though they had just been sharing a light joke with one another. Miriam was wrapped in white with dark blue flowers dotted over it and lace frills. There was a light wicker hat, which she fastened underneath her chin. She held onto a cream parasol and a small, navy bag. In that moment, John thought they matched perfectly.

"Dr Clayton," John smiled and tipped his hat to her politely. He turned to her father. "Sir Fredric."

The elder gentlemen replied in kind. "Good morning, Bennett. How happy am I to see that I have a punctual doctor on my workforce!"

"One would not want to miss a single second of this trip, sir."

"Indeed. The trip." Sir Fredric said in a knowing tone and took his stick to point; "We should head to our platform."

"Oh, yes, absolutely. Shall I take your bags?" John said but found the pair did not have any.

"We have enough belongings at the Manor but thank you for the kind offer, John." Miriam smiled before imitating her father's deep, booming voice. "Onwards, father, we've a train to catch."

It was a mere ten minutes into the journey when Sir Fredric fell asleep on John's shoulder. John exhaled as he stared out the window and watched as the green scenes blurred by. Miriam sat opposite and observed him. He tried desperately not to look at her, acting, in vain, as though the views outside were lovelier than her. When she placed a gentle hand on his thigh, he could no longer hold his gaze on whatever lay beyond the glass window.

As John turned to her, Miriam dragged her hand across his knee before leaning back in her seat. The sun from the morning stretched across a blue sky. It climbed into the carriage with them and settled upon her left cheek as she smiled daintily at him. The dust pirouetted through that beam and his heart trembled. John could not hide it. He sighed contentedly. Miriam blushed, looking away and then back at his gaze. It was in that moment when he realised that something more was happening, so much more than that animalistic need.

"I am so glad you are coming with us, John." She said, breaking the silence in a tranquil tone.

He nodded in agreement. There were plenty of words upon his lips as he wished, more than anything, to dive into her world. Yet he was nervous. There was a fluttering so fierce in his stomach that he feared his words would stumble clumsily from his mouth. Instead, he smiled softly and turned back to the blurs and colours and shapes zooming by. Her gaze sat upon him for a short while. There was a burning on his cheeks, not just from the sun.

John did not dare look at her again until he heard a rustling sound. Finally turning to see what was going on, John saw Miriam remove a rectangle object from her bag. It was folded up in a blue silk scarf that was covered in a grey feathered pattern. Her eyes darted to her sleeping father but not to John, even though she had to have known he was watching. Then, as she unfolded, a cloth bound periodical came tumbling out.

"My word," he said in a hushed whisper, "is that The Yellow Book?"

A grin stretched across her face. She had elicited the exact response that she had wanted. She cocked her head at him, "Why yes, John, yes, it is."

There was a soft chuckle from John as he raised an eyebrow. "I do not know why I am so shocked. It would be more of a surprise if that publication was not in your belongings.

"Have you ever read it?"

A pause. "No. I have never had the chance to."

Miriam flew into excitement, her eyes flowed with a passion that John couldn't help but be drawn to. She laid the book out for him to peruse, flicking the pages quickly so he hadn't a chance to take in their details. But he did not look at what she was showing, he just stared at her and admired how fervently she spoke on these topics. Her words were fast and nearly indecipherable as she gave information in fragments; "Walter Sickert is such a fine— and oh the stories by Charlotte Mew— Oh! and Aubrey Beardsley's illustrations— and Victoria Cross! Oh!" She stopped suddenly, her voice going really quiet. "There's a story by Ms Cross called Theodora, a fragment. Dare I say it is reminiscent of our meeting in the office?"

"I definitely must read it then." He chuckled again. "I do enjoy Beardsley."

"You've heard of him?"

"I may not have read The Yellow Book, but I do know of his work. Salome is a favourite."

"Surprises, Dr Bennett. How deliciously full of them you are."

John wanted to speak more but he was somewhat stilted. Again, Miriam uncovered another layer of him so easily. Like that book, she had unfolded him from his sheath and was now eagerly flipping through the pages. Though his mind beat against it, he lowered his voice and continued; "I am fascinated by his pieces. He captures the macabre so seductively. There's a magic to them."

"Are you drawn to the darker heart of our society?"

Another pause. "Yes. I love all the stories as such. Stevenson writes of a doctor who transforms into a monster whilst Shelley speaks of a doctor who creates life out of death."

"Perhaps there was a doctor that stalked the women of Whitechapel?"

"Hmm, well, that is certainly one theory."

"Our world is full of horrors. A torso turns up in the Thames here and there. A woman kills children for money. Horrors. Fascinating horrors."

"Indeed." He could not help what he said next. "A beautiful irresistible darkness lies in the human spirit of all."

A somewhat long silence from Miriam made his stomach turn. One layer too much had been uncovered and he feared he had travelled too far to retreat. The way Miriam stared at him was as though she were cloaked in the night, instead of the blaze of a bright morning. He could also see the lamplights dancing in her eyes as they did during their first meeting. Miriam gasped a little as she said, "It is as though you read my mind and soul, John. I could not agree more."

They dared not speak about the carnal desires that were racing between them. Instead, as the train bulked and heaved along the tracks, they decided to turn the conversation to lighter topics. Instead of telling John that she ached for him to be inside her, Miriam spoke of collecting different teas and how much she enjoyed cycling through London parks. Instead of telling Miriam that he wished more than anything to taste her, John mentioned that he enjoyed sports such as cricket and football as well as museum trips in his spare time. Instead of telling each other of how they had thoughts of entwining and embracing, nude and undone, they shared their love for other books and poems, as well as an affection for the theatre and the new living picture craze that was sweeping the globe. The more they spoke, the more they connected over all sorts of things; fine wines, whisky, and an eagerness to see more beyond the smoke sodden streets of London. All whilst thinking. Thinking on those carnal desires.

They spoke so much about their interests that the journey had flashed by and soon they were arriving at Northampton Station. To John, it was as though his heart had pulled him there. He wondered if Miriam felt it too.

Both of the Claytons had fallen asleep in the carriage by the time they had arrived at their own Manor. Though John had not slept the night before and he was worn out from the train ride, he did not have the right energy to rest. His mind was awake with excitement and trepidation. His whole world was changing with each second. John was youthful and alive as though he had finally been wrenched from a dark confinement that he didn't realise he was in.

The train ride was perhaps the most he had ever spoken to just one human being in one sitting. Not even as a child could his parents procure many words from him. He was more than content with simply watching, fascinated with the world that whirled by and grew from ash and soot. Raised in Manchester, mill fever took his father when he was just five and his mother succumbed to cholera when he was ten. John was orphaned. After that, he was boxed up and shipped to a distant and elderly aunt in Gravesend, Kent. Her house was just like her, spindled, thin, and daunting. She kept herself to religious texts and wished for him to keep quiet and locked in his room. When he wasn't, she would punish him with beatings.

So, John studied in silence to escape to a dorm room in the city of London, then to a shared room, and now to his biggish boarding room with his own bathroom and office. As a doctor, he made money but all he spent it on was a fancier box for all his things. Everything else seemed ornamental.

For nearly forty years, John had slipped in and out of society utterly unaware of the darkness and shadows that shrouded him in his box. All Miriam did, when she stormed his first board-meeting, was poke a small, unexpected hole into his world. But how much brightness and wonder did that bring to the walls that surrounded him?

As John stepped out of the carriage, those walls came

tumbling down. At the end of a curved driveway, that travelled alongside a long front garden, and nestled in the middle of a small forest of trees, sat a pointed and wide, two-storey building. Ivy had consumed most of the red brick at the front, but it still looked beautiful. Maybe by upper class standards, this was a meagre manor. To John, it was a castle. In all his life, he had never spent time in a place so grand.

The size of the home had stunned John for longer than expected. He jumped when Miriam placed a hand on his shoulder. There was a nugget of shame in his stomach; he'd forgotten to help Miriam out of the cab. In front of Sir Fredric, no less. "Oh Miriam, I am sorry."

"I have gotten myself down from a carriage many times." She said with a sly chuckle. "Besides, I wanted you to see how you would react. Beautiful, isn't it?"

"Stunning." He muttered, looking at her before he turned to look at the house again. "So, it was just you and your father?"

"Growing up we had some staff – a governess, a gardener, and the housekeeper Hettie, who also did the cooking. Once we moved to London, Hettie stayed on for the upkeep. For a while, she lived here with her son and daughter, but they have all grown up and moved away. Hettie now has a small flat in the village. She could have retired a long time ago but for some reason, she still comes by daily. I believe she just likes the routine" She tugged at his hand and pulled him with her. "Come, I shall show you around."

"But Miriam, my suitcase—"

"Fear not, Father will take bring it in!"

Leaving no time for either man to argue, Miriam dragged John into the house.

They stood on the landing, leaning against the banister, and looked down upon the entrance hall. Like most of the home, it was brown with regal furniture that had been inherited over the years. The windows weren't tall, but they let enough light in and looked out on their long front garden. An unassuming grandfather clock ticked the time away beneath them.

John caught his breath from the whirlwind Miriam had spun him through. He tried to retrace their steps:

On the ground floor, there was the green smoking room and study for her father; the poky but effective kitchen; a quaint yet regal dining room; the grand scarlet parlour room full of priceless antiques; and the pink front room which was more akin to a library, with shelves and shelves of books as well as a striking royal blue paisley rug and four oxblood red leather armchairs.

On the first floor, there were five different bedrooms, each with their own porcelain basin and metal bathtub, then there was a small separate bathroom and toilet – "fitted with modern plumbing" - and a linen closet. They had popped their heads into both the attic and the basement momentarily.

John had also met Hettie, their now old but still big and jolly housekeeper. She embraced him in a tight, warm hug that made him like her instantly. It was like coming home. Sir Fredric had retired to the front room and was nursing a brandy by an unlit fireplace as the pair dashed by. He tutted with a smile and for a slight moment, John had wondered how many others Miriam had raced by Sir Fredric, enough to warrant this bemused reaction.

He dismissed it quickly as they bounced up the stairs again, only this time Miriam settled on the banister and John propped himself beside her. They wheezed together as if they had just engaged in a race. "Well, it is a breath-taking home Miriam," John said with a shrewd grin in between gasps. She nudged him for the joke.

"Hmmm, it is," Miriam whispered. "For a while this was my whole world, away from the horrors of the city. It is a remarkable safe haven."

A sadness fell upon her face. He couldn't figure out why. It was as though a memory had seeped out from the panelling and wrapped her in sorrow. John placed a hand on top of hers with a comforting intent. "Miriam?"

"It seems so foolish to have all this space and not have need for it, does it not? I wish to transform it. Make something useful out of it."

"What do you propose?"

"A true refuge." She seemed wistful. "A shelter for any woman who has suffered at the hands of a man. A chance to give them a new life. A chance for them to escape."

"Is that possible?"

"I do not know. But someone has to try."

As John turned, he looked at her - wholly - for the first time. The tight hair, the wicker hat tied under her chin, and the angelic white dress with blue flowers. It was all a subterfuge. A decoy. So, no one would suspect that she was secretly changing the world. To John, Miriam Clayton seemed to be God's greatest invention. With no hesitation, he said; "You are remarkable."

Miriam nudged him again, "You flatter me, John."

"But I mean it. You amaze me. If this is your dream, then I would be honoured to assist you." He paused. "If that is why I am here."

It was the truth. He did not care for what reason she had brought him along; he now had no intention of leaving her life.

Miriam slid her hand from underneath his but then grabbed it back. "Come, let me show you to your room."

John feared another race down the corridor, but she didn't take him far and they did not go very fast. They entered a nearby bedroom with the door seemingly hidden in the wooden panelling. She led him inside and let him take a proper look around, sizing up what bedroom she had saddled him with. It was a big room, but not overly so. It was filled with dark brown furniture, including a four-poster bed that already had his suitcase on it. The wallpaper was sapphire with floral flock patterning and the curtains were emerald velvet. There was a fireplace to keep warm, and a small table and ruby armchair beside it.

Placing his hands on his hips, John took a deep breath, smiled, and said, "Yes, this will do nicely. Thank you, Miriam."

She giggled at him briefly but abruptly stopped. The sudden silence filled the room with an indescribable heat. John slowly turned to her. Miriam's darker blue eyes met his lighter ones. She had an intent on her face that called to him. She stepped towards him, stopping just a fraction from collision. As close as they had been in his office. John swallowed, his heart in his throat. They looked deep into each other's eyes, like time had stopped again.

In this still moment, this frozen beat, she kissed him.

As she wrapped her arms around his neck and pulled him close, he instinctively placed his hands around her, giving her a refuge in his embrace.

He had imagined their first kiss in a million ways; ravaging, passionate, quick, and slow. But he couldn't have conjured how perfect it would feel. It was a firm but tender kiss, one that came from their honesty and their connection, not just an urge or a need. Their souls were now on display, melting perfectly into one another. This was a lover's kiss that could fill libraries with poetry and stages with songs. John pulled her further into him, wanting every part of her against him. She groaned which he involuntarily echoed. They were on the precipice of losing control but what was control when they had this? This... sweetness.

Miriam pulled away breathless. He went to kiss her again, but she put up a hand and stopped him. Doing as instructed, John was confused. He yearned for her lips once more. Did she not feel the same way?

"All in good time, John." Miriam said lowly, "All in good time."

And with that, she walked out of the room.

When the door closed after her, John fell to the bed; elated… exasperated… erect.

Chapter Three

Wednesday 17th June 1896

London is such a curious place to conduct this work. Having not been raised in such a wretched place, I found myself more of a lodger here. Therefore, I am privier to the insidiousness that seeps through this so-called capital. Grime clings to the air here. We breathe in evil with every breath. From the pitiful slums to the sinful palaces, this great industrial venture of ours is all a façade. A lie in which monsters and demons crawl for sustenance and commit craven acts in order to come alive.

Could a good person ever succeed here? Or would the smog and smoke and sin eventually claw at them? Could a good heart ever prevail when the city turns its tricks in the aching pain of the night?

No, I do not believe it could. No kind-hearted man or woman could survive without being turned demonic. For this city does not care about what lies within a person's soul but what lines their pockets. I have spent my adult life tending to the bleeding masses: The poor so villainised by the rich that they have to scrape by and the rich so villainised by their wealth that they'd happily keep the poor tied to their lot. The pious becomes bad and the sacred becomes profane. One can feel ebbs of sympathy for their suffering until their misery becomes malice.

Alas, maybe I do not belong with the good men and women. I am not one of the angels. I have sliced into another, and it has awakened something in me. Something I dare not confront. Not yet.

Perhaps in that respect, I do belong in this city with its terrifying towers and streets paved with sorrow. Besides, this work needs a backdrop and how fitting that London should be mine.

It is curious though. Eight years have passed since the infamous Ripper did wield his knife and yet his name stalks the alleyways even now. These streets of Soho are still gripped in fear that the murderer has returned. There were shockwaves when Alice's torn body was found, and the tremors of tattlers and tales quickly followed.

How imbecilic the public can be!

Still, I have laid low as the watchful eyes of the flatfoots and vigilante groups girded their loins, hoping to catch a villain. I wished to stay hidden for longer. God forbid I should be found before my work is done. Yet as I left the hospital yesterday, I caught sight of the other woman. Her ratty pink hat, her untidy black hair, and toothless grin so recognisable. Rose Steel. My stomach recoiled: A concoction of fear, excitement, and rage.

The smile on her face chilled me. I thought of nothing but the unhappiness she had brought into my life. I expect she thought on it no more, washing away my nightmare with the evening's gin or her latest shag. I had always believed that the women were terrorised into action. Perhaps this one relished it.

My thoughts travelled to the scars. Those tiny cuts around wrists so unforgettable. Fingernails so deep they punctured into skin. Red reminders of the misdeed. Forever etched in flesh. *Her* fingernails.

As Rose laughed, it bellowed through the Soho streets and shook me to the core. I thought on her friend that I put to rest with my retribution.

What kind of woman could be so cheery as her friend lay rotting in the cold ground? A woman who does not belong on this earth any longer, I have swiftly surmised.

I shall bide my time, however. The last killing was a layman's job. A frenzied attack of a beginner. Now I must rise in the ranks. I must be smart. Alice was afraid and had guilt in her eyes and nearly got away from my knife. She was quick to snuff it.

Tonight, my guise shall be ordinary. I shall hide in plain sight. As a passing gentlemen in a suit never worn. I shall procure my victim in her own lair. I shall ply her with poisons to keep her subdued.

Then my knife will meet with the flesh, and I will show no mercy.

And in that act, this Rose will be plucked from this earth.

Saturday 31st August 1895

Miriam sat at the windowsill. The last of the night covered the back garden. She could already see the colours drifting in as the sun rose on the horizon. As a child, Miriam had always thought that the night was a robe worn by God and as he walked across the globe, he cloaked it with darkness. The morning was just the night being dragged further and further away from her.

The older she got, she realised that the night didn't move, it just faded away. It melted into the day like oil paints, adapting into the brand-new colours; ready to face a fresh canvass.

Miriam had lost count of the times that she had sat on this windowsill and greeted a new morning. Sleep had never been her greatest ally. She would lay in bed for hours, mulling over the state of the world and the clattering clutter of her consciousness. When night settled in the Manor, she would be wide awake with restless thoughts. When it seemed impossible to fall into a slumber or if, as it so often would, a startling sadness took over, she'd climb out of bed and head to the window. Her mind was always as alive as the stars that shone down.

Here she would concoct fantasies. Never swash-buckling adventures or magical romances but she would dream of how her life should be and what steps she could take to make it so. How she would reshape the world that had been handed to her. Often, her father, or Hettie, would find her asleep, leaning against the pane.

Today was different and new to Miriam. She did not think about the usual things. Her thoughts were consumed by nothing but him.

Dr John Bennett.

Miriam did not believe herself to be above love or the men and women who chase it. It just had never crossed her mind. It had crossed her father's, her aunt's, and everyone around her, all wondering when she would meet a man and they would marry. There had been suitors, and arrangements, that, at most, had only lasted a handful of days. Miriam just wanted to live. Besides, she had never met a man, nor woman for that matter, who could turn her head from her independence.

So, when John had startled her in his office that day, Miriam did not know that he would bring the light with him. That the comfort of her night-time mind and defiant darkness would be dragged further and further away from her. That her soul would melt like oil paints, and she'd have new colours to work with. How vivid everything seemed now that he had come into her life.

Hairs bristled on her arm just thinking about it. She was hesitant to admit these new adorations, even to herself, because she was terrified. These fresh emotions brought excitement and fear all at once. She was still afraid that this was a ruse. That the minute she let her guard down or showed weakness, he would try to control her as some do. Some see new light and wish to snuff it out.

And *yet*…

The way he had happily followed her to the Manor, the way he had met her writings with equally sinful messages, and the way he had fiercely kissed her, only hours ago, told her that there was something different about him.

The night had now disappeared. The house stayed quiet. A new summer morning lay in front of her, ready to unfurl its secrets. Looking down at the garden, her eyes darted to a familiar sight. An electric idea shocked through her. She practically jumped off the windowsill with excitement and grabbed her purple silk robe, pulling it over her white nightgown.

Barefoot, Miriam quietly paced down the corridor and opened the door to his room. Lying on his back, in a long nightshirt, he looked calm and peaceful. Naughtiness filled her mind as she crept over to him. Sitting on the edge of the bed, she tenderly stroked his nose and whispered his name. It didn't take long to stir him.

"Miriam?" He grumbled, his eyes opening and closing as though he were still in a dream, ready to immediately fall back into slumber.

"Good morning, John." She smiled down at him, stroking his face gently. In his fogginess, John reached over, grabbed her hand, and held it to his chest, as though he wanted her to feel his heartbeat. It didn't escape her that he wore little clothing. She was tempted to explore the almost naked body beneath her palm, but she had a plan too good to spoil.

There was a slight smack of his dry, sleep-filled lips. "Have I overslept?"

"Nothing of the sort. It is early. The rest of the house still sleeps"

"Then what is it?"

"I had the grave realisation that I had not finished the tour I was giving you." She hung the words on her breaths to entice him more. "How could I *ever* forget the rose garden?"

John's eyes snapped opened as though a cold bucket of liquid had been thrown on him. He looked stunned but his face burst into a smile when he saw her staring down. She leaned forward and brushed his cheek with her lips, whispering; "Get some trousers on and meet me outdoors at your earliest convenience."

Skipping out the room, she could hear him quickly clamber out of bed.

It didn't take him long to appear at the front door. He had put on a pair of average black trousers but still wore his long-sleeved cream nightshirt. He had just tucked it in. Some of his wavy dark brown locks fell, unkempt on his forehead. Even his moustache was slightly out of shape. It made him look rough and rugged and only added to her yearning for him. She nodded but did not take his hand or arm. Instead, she started to walk gradually, through the garden. John walked with her, side by side, holding his hands behind his back. They were both barefoot, feeling the cold ground beneath as they strolled gently through the garden.

The land was long but only as wide as the house. There were three small stone steps that led into a stone path. On either side was green grass with bushes, trimmed round and patterned neatly. There was a small fountain to the right that was mirrored by a small pond on the left. It was all very symmetrical, beautiful, and well-kept.

This collided with the tangled mesh of flowers and vines at the end of the garden. The apprehension of taking John there caused Miriam to walk very slowly.

"Did you sleep well?" She enquired, filling the silence with words to forget about her nervousness.

"As well as I could…" he replied, "… knowing that you were sleeping mere moments away from me."

"I too was awake for that very reason."

They smiled at each other and took a few more steps in the quiet before John said, "Miriam, may I ask you a question?"

"Of course, my dear John. Anything."

"Why do are you so committed to saving other women?" He asked earnestly, hoping it did not come across as an insult.

"Must a person have a reason for wishing to help the plight of others." She replied bitingly. "Can one not have sympathy, empathy, and want to better the world?"

John nodded in agreement. "This is true, and I am aware that this drives you also. However, there was a sadness in your tone yesterday. I'd venture to say that there is something more."

"It was not my father, if that is what you think."

"I am aware of the gentle spirit your father possesses."

"Forgive me. I was afraid you'd think less of him." And with that Miriam stopped walking, causing John to halt also. She didn't want to take this pain to her sacred place. She wasn't even sure she wanted to talk about it. At the same time, it amazed her that John had picked up on that hurt. With every passing second, he saw more of her than anyone. Taking a deep breath, she said; "My uncle Charles was a brute of a man. My aunt – my mother's sister Isobel – was at the mercy of his fury and control. He was a powerful, drunken monster. Aunt Izzy is a kindly woman, much like my mother, I am told. A quiet, meditative soul but with intellect and generosity. Yet that man reshaped her. We saw less and less of her and at the times we did, she barely spoke. She had bruises and marks. She was frightened all the time."

"What happened?"

"I had discussed the matter to great length with my father, in hopes to get Aunt Isobel some help, but to no avail. Charles was more powerful than either of us – a Lord, actually - and it petrified my father. I have always wondered if it still vexes him, not to have done something sooner." Miriam looked off into the distance. "One fateful evening Izzy and Charles came for supper. They had no children which I guess added to his frustration for he wanted a boy he could mould in his own image. He despised young girls. That is probably why every time I started to join in the conversation, Charles hissed at me, telling me to hold my tongue. I could see the anger rise in my father's face. Then Izzy, in all of her nervousness, spilled her glass of wine. From its shackles, Hell broke loose. Fury raged as that thing leaped to its feet. He took his cane and was about to bring it down on poor Izzy, right there in front of us! My father and I rushed to her defence, but I got there first and shielded my aunt as Charles bought his cane down. It struck my shoulder. Hard."

Miriam brought down her dressing gown and night dress just a little and showed a red scar on her right shoulder. John made no sound as he stared, but his lips grew tight and thin. Miriam could sense the anger in him that anyone would cause her pain. For a moment, she wondered how far he might go to avenge her.

Sighing deeply, Miriam continued; "In all his wrath, my father grabbed Charles by the throat and threw him against the wall, taking the cane and lobbing it across the dining room. It clattered loudly upon the floor. Incensed, father demanded that Charles leave. As Charles stormed out, he went to drag Izzy away with him. but father bellowed 'No, she stays.' When Charles realised how deadly serious my father was, he left, vowing that he'd come back here and ruin our lives."

John swallowed. "And did your uncle do just that?"

Miriam's heart raced, excited, and anguished all at once. "No. He died in the night. They suspect it was a heart-attack. That booze and the anger ravaged him from the insides. But now, my aunt was free. Miraculously, he had left all his wealth and possessions to her. A happy ending, I'd say. However, I do not want anyone to suffer the way she did, not when I have riches myself to help put a stop to it."

The confession had fuelled a fire within her, and she did not know how to continue. The past and present collided in an agonising way. Trying to control her breathing, Miriam looked to John for a response. He exhaled sincerely, "And this is why you work tirelessly at the hospital and reprimand those men?"

"There are many horrors on the streets of Soho."

"Like this Harry Wright you mentioned?" He said, prompting

Miriam to raise an eyebrow at him to which he frowned back in response, "I do listen, Miriam."

"Harry Wright is the worst kind of scoundrel. Some men, well a lot of men, believe that life owes them whatever they wish. Women and riches, usually." There was a sly smile before Miriam's face fell. "From what I hear, Wright wishes to be above his station and in high society. He runs a pub and brothel in Soho called The Furnace. He acts like it is as the theatres in Leicester Square, but it is of a grotty repute. No one respects him and he is stuck in his place. It would be a sad story but, instead of earning that respect, he's branded himself as fearsome in Soho. The women who work for him take the brunt of his frustration. I have seen many, many in the Lady Gray Ward. I just wish I could…"

There was a sudden pause. Miriam grew silent and stared ahead. John glanced her way and breathed a sharp sigh. "This world breeds vicious men like your uncle and Wright. Good riddance to the lot of them, I say." Miriam looked at him and wished to kiss him again. What kind of man was this?, who denied his very standing and wished for the betterment of a gender deemed less worthy than his own?, where did he come from? As though he could read her mind, he said in a revered way, "I too have seen good people suffer, Miriam."

With that, she nodded in agreement and continued walking. "Oh, how I wish more doctors on our board were like you and not like that intolerable Jenkins."

"Oh, ha ha, Michael is harmless and easily persuaded. As a friend, I have found him somewhat steadfast." John grinned as he ambled beside her. "He merely forgets himself every now and then."

"Hmm perhaps. Though I suppose I do bring it out in them." Miriam giggled. "Jenkins does have the most beautiful wife. Have you seen her? Adelaide? Dare I say she's the jammiest bit of jam?"

This caused John to pause somewhat as his eyes widened, half-shocked and half-amused. Miriam winked at him, and they continued to pace slowly to the rose garden, with John seemingly more confident at solving the riddle that was Miriam Clayton. In just a few short minutes, she had allowed more pieces to fit together.

For a little while after their conversation, they paced the grounds in silence; stealing glances and smiles from one another as Miriam led John closer and closer towards her fortress. The pathway turned to small slabs in the dirt as though they were rocks in a pond. Before the pair followed them, roaming through the roving, rampant roses that covered many wooden arches in a row, they froze in awe. The flowers twisted higher and taller than them both. As John looked up, Miriam sensed his trepidation for she felt it too. It was as though they were heading further and further into her essence.

If they took these steps, nothing would ever be the same again.

A rush of memories whipped around her with the gentle morning wind. It steeled her and sent sensations down her skin. Taking his hand, without a second hesitation, she led him down the path. It wasn't a long journey but weaving through the thorns that surrounded them made it perilous. When the familiar sight came into her view, she walked that bit faster. As they entered a circular patch untouched by the roses, she looked around. The house was out of sight. It was just as perfect as she remembered.

She stopped and abruptly let go of his hand, causing him to freeze in one spot. Swaying from side to side as she walked, Miriam came alive with indecency. She sat on the bench, crossing her legs, and letting her eyes travel from his bare feet to his piercing blue eyes as though she had never seen this intruder before. "Do you recall this bench?"

He nodded. Miriam bit her lip and hoped that he was

mimicking the gardener's boy. In this fresh morning light, when John had little time to refine himself, he looked the most beautiful. Though he was older than her, by nearly a decade, there was something youthful and nearly virginal about the way he gazed upon her. Miriam knew that she was opening up something within him that he had kept hidden. A want. A need. A desire.

Something wicked that matched something dark within her.

She continued: "Do you remember what I did in here?"

John nodded again. A small smile spread on his face. She uncrossed her legs and leaned a little forward, saying in almost a whisper. "Do you wish for me to do that again, for you?"

Another nod.

"Very well," she replied. "First, the rules, John Bennett. I will lie on this stone bench, and I will show you how I pleasure myself. At no point are you allowed to touch me or touch yourself. Is that understood?"

A pause.

"I asked if you had understood the rules."

A nod.

"Very well."

Miriam's eyes did not leave his. Not as she gradually laid back upon the stone. Not as she placed her two feet on the bench. Not as she pulled her slip down right to where she needed it to be. Just not enough for her to be exposed fully to him. She enjoyed the tease of that position. The cool air of a summer morning, itself not fully awake, tingled at her. Miriam took her right hand and placed it on her knee. Then she delicately slid her fingers down her bare leg until she found her slit. She deftly glided her fingers over her mound until she slipped between her lips. Miriam delicately touched her clitoris, letting out a soft exhale of air. After a beat, she began to rub it. She was achingly wet already, which made this easier. Taking it slowly, she gasped at the motions.

All John could do was watch. His mouth opened slightly as he took a deep breath, unsure what to do with his hands. Having him in this position sent waves through her. With John frozen in that spot, his eyes darting over her body as she writhed with the movement and groaned into the air, Miriam transformed into something unearthly and magical. A witch who had conjured a mere mortal to be at her beck and call or an insatiable goddess to be adored and admired wholly.

Her eyes darted to his crotch. She wondered how hard he was and how agonising this must be. Her thoughts turned to releasing him. For a brief moment she thought about that boy, standing just as dumbfounded as John was right now. She imagined, however, that the boy was John, walking over to her and taking her in his stride. She couldn't wait for him to make love to her. As her motions turned circular, she wondered if she should just give in and set him free. She was desperate for him to be inside her. *No*, she thought, *no. All in good time*.

Pleasure rolled over her spine, plummeting through her cells, to and from the spot she was massaging. With her free hand, she instinctively grabbed her breast through her nightgown and whimpered. She sped up her right hand, knowing an orgasm would happen soon. That familiar pressure was building, and she closed her eyes, steadying her breath in anticipation. Slowly opening them, Miriam looked back to John. He had not moved. Not a hair. He just looked longingly at her as though she were a queen writhing upon a stone throne. Their eyes caught in the moment when she came. An orgasm rippled through her. She tried desperately not to call out but couldn't help moaning. Her fingers kept going until she was done. Slowing down, the feeling disseminated through her. Miriam giggled, somewhat nervously. Her cheeks flushed and she whispered; "Did you enjoy watching that?"

John nodded. He was either continuing his charade as the gardener's boy or was simply astonished. She couldn't tell by the look on his face. His eyes, however, twinkled with glee. She sat back up and composed herself. Though it was summer, the air around her became chilled. Miriam stood up and continued; "Close your eyes."

He did as he was instructed. Miriam walked over to him and hugged him. His cock was hard against her, practically throbbing through his trousers. Keeping her chin on his shoulder, she began stroking the back of his head with one hand. With the other, she found his trouser button, and prised him free. Once his prick stood to attention in the cold air, she began to stroke. Miriam was desperate to look but she kept herself calm and collected. She felt it under her grasp; it was of average length but with a thick and plentiful girth.

John moaned at her touch and grabbed her back, pulling her closer into him. Miriam wanted to take it slow and considered. Yet this was undeniably urgent for him. He buried his face in her neck, his breaths low and guttural. They tickled her and sent swells like an aftershock down her spine. She quickened her pace with one hand and slid the other into his hair, holding on with a little tug. Another groan and another and another as she stroked him faster and faster and faster.

Suddenly, he begged into her ear with a growl, "May I?"

With his words, joy twisted in her stomach. For it was clear to Miriam now that John not only knew the deepest parts of her sexual pleasures, but he relished it. In a thrilled gasp whilst moving her hand fast, Miriam said, "Yes John. You may."

Gripping onto the back of her dress, John climaxed, spilling onto the ground below. He groaned into her neck and steadied himself against her.

There they were: Two people in the aftermath of pleasure,

holding onto one another in that aching desperation, hoping that nothing would rip them apart again. Their hearts racing together, timeless and immortal.

Leaving her neck, John opened his eyes, leaned his forehead against hers, and gasped, "Miriam, I—"

"Shh shh shh. No words, my darling." And she kissed him. An intense and plentiful kiss. With it, she hoped he knew what she meant. That there were things she wanted to say, things she wanted to do, but she wasn't sure that she was ready. There she was on the edge of it all and she was scared; frightened because she was no longer alone. Was she ready to give that slight bit of independence to him? A surge of emotions rampaged through her, and she found herself overcome. They broke for air and stared at one another, caught in the thorns of all their cravings and blooming with the possibilities.

Miriam kissed John once more, gently this time, and said, "Close your eyes again and do not open them until you have counted to ten."

Chapter Four

Wednesday 24th June 1896

Blood has once again been spilled tonight.

I can still taste it. That warm metallic liquid as splatters hit my wide-open mouth. I did not expect it to happen. My tongue relished it. Fresh blood. Oh, why is it so delicious? The sweetest I have ever tasted.

This is like surgery. I create fine art with my knife and scalpel.

The operating theatre where I would work was her hovel-like room in The Furnace. It sat up some stairs from the public house. It was tiny, with just a mattress in the corner, a chair, and a fireplace. Her clothes and belongings lay strewn about. I wondered for a moment what type of woman she was. How did she find herself in these rags? Did she ever come from riches?

I wore the uniform. I entered the lair arousing no suspicions. Wearing just simple black trousers, a black waistcoat, and white shirt, I hid my features under a similarly coloured flat-cap. A common man. Not a lofty gentlemen or filth-ridden peasant. Just a man. But I must attest, and the world must witness that I am so much more.

I prepped the victim. Already I had plied her with enough gin to keep her somewhat subdued. She stumbled so I helped her to the mattress. I splayed her out on the bed as she hitched up her gruesome skirt. I waited a beat.

I gave her no chance to scream or run. I took the blade, rushed it into her stomach, and ripped her through – all the way up to her sternum. I then plunged the knife straight through her chest as she lay spread out for me. She gasped and grasped at her wounds, her wide eyes finally trembling from the sight of her killer. Her toothless smile contorted into anguish. How it pleased me so. A faint smell of urine hit my nose – she wet herself as she died. As the red stuff tumbled out of her, the bedsheets began to soak with it.

But I was frenzied with thoughts:

Fingernails. Cuts. Scars.
Fingernails. Cuts. Scars.
FINGERNAILS. CUTS. SCARS!

This was all I could think of as she lost life. Not yet, my sweet, I thought. I grabbed her hand and twisted it in my wrists. I took my blade and slid it underneath the nail. Slowly, I prized it from her hand. I heard a whimper. I did another and another and another and another until her hand was pulpy and free.

Fingernails. Cuts. Scars.

Her hand went limp. Rose Steel was gone. She would not be found until the next day. They would not recall the person who took her there. They asked no questions. They barely looked at my face when I entered the place. I am no one to them. The night has become my greatest ally in this endeavour. I melted into the shadows.

I think about the last droplet of blood that spilled from her body. Almost like a rose petal. It does not escape me how the flower has been so linked to my soul and my becoming. But that blossoming is over. I walk unguided through thorns, my body and spirit entrenched in the darkness. So impaled by spikes that I cannot be seen in all my agony.

Oh, Rose.

Oh, my sweetness.

Oh, my meagre murdered madams of the night.

I share your misfortune.

For I too have cried. For I too have bled. For I too have not been saved.

No one comes to aid the insignificant.

Crawling through my circumstance, I must untether myself from these crooked vines. My flesh must be released from the bite of its dangerous teeth. I must cut and slice and free this heart. My wounds will seep and sting, but they will not heal unless I am free from the barbs and prickles.

So, I shall continue to spill blood as I walk this path.

As it falls to the ground, I can only hope, that new flowers will bloom.

Saturday 31st August 1895

When John opened his eyes on ten, Miriam was gone.

Pulling himself together, John sighed. Not quite ready to head back, he sat on the stone bench and stared out at the bristles and flowers. How adequate a view for the array of thoughts in his mind. That morning mesh of the dark and the insidious with the vibrant and the exquisite. He was stirred, still breathless from their sunrise tryst.

He was glad that he was now alone for he was trembling. Whether it was due to the sudden morning coolness or how spent he was, John quivered for a while. It was not long until he realised that it was excitement and electricity surging through him. Miriam had awoken a pleasure in him that he had neglected: To be at the dominance of a strong and powerful woman.

John had almost forgotten how young he was when he discovered this and how his aunt's beatings would sometimes make him feel. Fearful but aroused at the same time. He often had guilt at these two natures running inside of him. Her religious manner and rough hands had caused him to edge slowly into his shell.

There had been lovers before. John had had a fiancé when he was in his twenties; someone his aunt had arranged. She was a fair and fine woman, but they could not stimulate one another in mind and body. A month before their wedding, she had run away with someone else, much to the chagrin of his elderly aunt. It did not bother John; his wants ran too wicked to be sated by a societal woman. Thankfully, his aunt died on the date he was supposed to be married on, and John was free. But he closed himself off from relationships from that point on.

Occasionally, in the darkness, he would find himself wandering London's nightlife, paying to be tied, fucked, and even spanked at times.

John shuddered at the memory of it all. He had locked it away tight. Prostitution could be wary and immoral at times – even with the most accomplished and independent dominatrix. As he became an established doctor, John saw the plight of women in that line of work, and he decided to stop. Only now did he realise that was some time ago. He had sheltered his desires and, therefore, himself away from the rest of the world.

How wonderful it was that Miriam was the key. He trembled once more at the very thought of her. The taste of her lips, the warmth of her flesh, and the smell of her sex lingered around him. He tried to compose his thoughts, but they dissolved into visions of Miriam, wrapped around him as he was finally inside her, loving her in all the ways he wanted to. They seemed on the verge of joining in that way and yet she had escaped his grasp again. She was so blissfully devious.

Walking back to the house, John was thankful that it seemed too early for breakfast, and he could get a few more hours of rest. However, when he lay back in his bed, he found himself too awake for more sleep. Instead, he pulled out a fresh journal and made crude drawings, trying to capture the lines of her body over and over again.

It was nearly midday when he arose from a surprising slumber. He cursed himself for being so impolite and hurried to get dressed, thankful that someone had put clean water in the basin and laid out a cloth so that he could refresh himself. He pulled on the beige trousers from yesterday, but instead paired them with a light brown waistcoat, the cream shirt, the grey jacket, and that same blue neckerchief. After slipping on dark brown shoes, John rushed down the stairs to greet Miriam and Sir Fredric.

However, neither could be found. What he did happen upon was a single plate setting in the dining room as Hettie cluttered about in the kitchen nearby.

"Oh, excuse me, I seem to have a slept in." He called from the dining room.

Hettie came bounding out the kitchen as though she were a comic and had a punchline ready. "Good afternoon, Dr Bennett." Her accent reminded him of his childhood. "I hope you are well rested."

"Indeed, I am. Thank you." He hesitated. "Where is Miriam? I mean Dr Clayton. I… I… mean the others."

Hettie smiled at him. "Miss Clayton and Sir Fredric have been called to her aunt's. They wished not to disturb you. She said you were tired from the travel."

"I see. Do you know when they'll return?"

"No, sir, but I guess it'll be sometime this evening." Hettie gestured at him to sit down. "I've been instructed to take good care of you until then. Please sit, I've made a nice lunch of meats and cheese."

John smiled politely and sat down, resigning himself to dine alone.

Only Sir Fredric returned that night.

As John waited, reading by the fireplace in the front room, he tried, and failed, to not look too disappointed in this fact. Her father explained that Miriam wished to spend the night with her aunt for reasons that he could not allude to. There was nothing more. No notes nor apologies. John had wasted a day. He had wandered the grounds and read books with the spectre of anticipation following him around. The anti-climactic evening immediately turned his mood sour, and he could not hide that from the older gentlemen in front of him.

Sir Fredric chuckled. "Come man! We shall dine together and get to know one another."

John nodded softly but his face was that of a wanting lament.

In a matter of hours, however, Sir Fredric had turned John's mood into a happier one. The stocky man, with bushy grey mutton chops and large moustache to match, was a fine man indeed. In spite of his station and experience, he was known around the hospital for how kind he was. That did not mean he did not have authority and could not garner respect. In fact, it was his amiable nature which helped develop a sturdy, hard-working staff force, reshaping and progressing medicine for the better. Even now in his quaint but still grand home, Sir Fredric defied expectations of himself and invited Hettie to join them for dinner.

What John had learned over the delicious lamb roast and many glasses of port, was that Sir Fredric had a wicked sense of humour too. He regaled John with hilarious tales of his youth or Miriam's as a child. Added to Hettie's indescribable cackles, the night had turned into an amusing spectacle. So creative and hilarious Sir Fredric was in his descriptions that, whilst wiping tears of laughter from his eyes, John mentioned somewhat flippantly, "You could be on the stage with the great Dan Leno,"

"Yes," Sir Fredric said, coughing from his own chortles, "Then where would the hospital be without my sparkling wit, John."

"Nowhere I would like to work, that is most certain."

As Hettie cleared up the kitchen, John and Sir Fredric retired to the latter's study to enjoy a brandy and a cigar. Though the pair were still chuckling from dinner, the mood had become more sated. They wound down the evening in two grand grass-green velvet armchairs placed either side of the fireplace. Puffing on the cigar, John could sense a deeper conversation was to be had. Sir Fredric took a long drag. He let the smoke pillow into the atmosphere. "Is there a finer taste than a decent brandy and a rich cigar?"

"No, I do not believe there is." John replied, though secretly his mind burned with the thought of Miriam's lips. "Hettie's lamb, perhaps?"

"Yes, that was delicious. I wish I had gone for thirds."

"I do believe you mean fourths."

"I believe I do" The men laughed at their silliness before Sir Fredric said, thoughtfully, "I do hope I have managed to lift your spirits this evening. Was I an adequate replacement for my daughter? "

John paused, hesitant to answer. He wondered if the old man knew that while John laughed along, Miriam was still seated in his mind. She was just a whisper away. John nodded. "I have had a fantastic evening."

"And has this trip alleviated your illness?"

"Pardon me sir?"

"Miriam told me you were quite unwell and that time off from your hospital duties, as well as this little sojourn in the country, would serve you well."

John smiled. "Ah. I see."

"Of course, I knew this was a ruse. My daughter is cunning, but I am still her father." He and John chuckled but when they drew into silence, John was still smiling, looking ponderously into the evening. Sir Fredric's eyes watched him. "Hmmm. you are quite taken with my Miriam, are you not?"

"Well… I… I guess… I…"

"Come on Bennett, I am not blind. Why else would you find yourself here?"

John swallowed a big gulp of brandy. "I am completely besotted with your daughter, Sir Fredric."

There was a slight pause which frightened John. He half-expected to be thrown into the pitch-black night by the older gentleman for being so brazen and would have to stumble blind bac to London alone. However, Sir Fredric burst into a big smile. "Good man."

Surprising even himself, John said, "I doubt I have been the first." Procuring a proper frown for the first time from Sir Fredric, John cursed his tongue.

"You are correct. Miriam has had some admirers. However, she has a remarkable nature, don't you think? No one has ever made it this far. No one until you, that is."

This pleased John in many indescribable ways. Miriam had chosen him, and Sir Fredric approved. It had been barely a fortnight since John had met Miriam in his office and yet he was slipping comfortably into this small, tightknit family.

"I would like it known, however, that I always thought you were a formidable man before Miriam even met you. This is why I wanted you at my hospital."

"You honour me, Sir Fredric." John replied.

"In some ways you remind me of myself. I too had found myself obsessed with Miriam's mother Anna."

John leaned forward with a delighted curiosity, "How did you meet her?"

"Oh," Sir Fredric replied almost dismissively. Yet his eyes, which were the same as Miriam's, glazed over with fondness and memory. "Anna and I were childhood sweethearts. Our families were of similar class and wealth. I suspect that we were betrothed from a young age, but it did not matter. We were as thick as thieves from the time we were children to the day she died. Her loss is still a great heartache. Even now."

"You have my condolences, Sir Fredric." John said humbly. He dared not to dwell on the type of pain one has when a soulmate is torn from them, let alone having to raise a child without them. That product of so much love and adoration: A constant reminder of the loss. "Was she like Miriam?"

"Oh gosh, no." Sir Fredric replied, with a sudden laughter that caused the tears that he was holding back to tumble down his cheek. He brushed them aside in hopes that John did not see them. In fact, John did and found a greater fondness for the man. "Miriam does look more like her mother, thank goodness. In quiet, studious moments, as rare as they are with my girl, it is as almost as though the ghost of Anna is visiting. However, I seem to have forged her with my own rambunctious spirit and charm. Not a lot of people would be thankful for that, mind."

"I am."

Sir Fredric smiled. "I cannot take all the credit. I believe Miriam goes beyond myself, her mother, and nature."

"Never has a truer statement been said." John said in a toast and took a massive swig of brandy. The night, in spite of Miriam's absence, had yet again been a one of revelations. His heart was as full as his stomach. His mind swirled with the alcohol that coursed within. Placing the glass down on the small table in front of them, he said with a slight slur, "I am afraid I must retire, lest the night get away from me."

"Yes, I suppose you are correct." Sir Fredric said. "After all, tomorrow is the big party."

The thought curdled in John as he was rising from his chair. He froze half-bent. "I am sorry Sir Fredric, what party?"

"Oh my, has Miriam not told you?" Sir Fredric was a good man, but he could not hide his glee at this very moment.

"No, she has not."

"Well, my sister-in-law Isobel hosts these lavish affairs now and then. Only this time, Miriam has arranged it all. From what I gathered, she wished to introduce you to everyone."

John nodded and tried to smile, but it looked more like a grimace.

Sunday 1st September 1895

The turquoise bowtie was unusual and uncomfortable around John's neck. That was nothing to how out-of-sorts he felt entering a grand mansion with equally grand people. With a matching turquoise waistcoat to go with the white shirt and black tails and trousers, John thought of a peacock wandering into a predator's enclosure. These were people of high-society, and he was a doctor from a low background who was wearing a strange suit mysteriously sent to him that very morning. He expected to be devoured instantly.

Aunt Isobel's home was another astonishment to John. The royal grand mansion towered over him, four storeys tall and extremely wide. Painted light yellow on the outside, the stately home sat nestled on a green hilltop like a prized jewel. Inside, however, a different shade of the spectrum decorated each room. The great hall, which had a majestic staircase and held most of the dancing, was deep red with golden flourishes. There were massive paintings upon the walls as well as golden cherub sconces. A large crystal chandelier dangled overhead.

As the two men stepped in, John entered an entirely different world to the one that he had known: A lavish one not meant for the likes of him. A slither of worry entered his consciousness: Did Miriam belong to this world? If so, could John ever?

He faltered still at the front door and worried about heading in. Under his breath, he somewhat cursed Miriam for putting him in this position. After all, she knew that he hated parties such as this and he thought she did too. The crowd suffocated him already, with eyes already gazing at him, tearing him apart. He could just sense their gnashing gossiping teeth ready to sink into him. Thankfully, a tray of champagne that came by. Taking two glasses and drinking one in a second, John breathed out. Liquid courage is what he needed.

Sir Fredric laughed and slapped him on the back, causing John to choke and cough on the sip he was taking. "There, there man, nothing to be scared of. We're just entering the lion's den, that is all."

"Yes, indeed, what am I worried for?"

"Come, I'll introduce you."

By the time John had reached the other end of the hall, he was exhausted, and a tad inebriated. His mind whirred with names of Countesses, Earls, Ladies, and Lords – most of whom had ailments they wished to discuss with him, which nearly everyone did when they heard John was a doctor. What was worse was when they'd badger him with their insipid ideas on how they could truly reform the medical profession. John's neck hurt from nodding so much. He was thankful to have an ally in Sir Fredric who made sure he was taken quickly from person to person and that his glass was never empty. John leaned against the grand staircase and sighed greatly. He hoped that he was somehow hidden from the crowd.

"Dr Bennett, I presume," came a muted voice from the base of the stairs.

For a split second, he was immobilized, hoping that if he didn't move, the voice would just go away. However, his polite affable nature took over. He turned and found himself facing an aged yet regal woman. She looked older than Sir Fredric but not by much. Her face was worn but cordial, with grey hair that was curled into a tight style on her head. She wore an elegant deep red dress that covered her from the neck to her feet, even covering her arms. There were feathers in her hair and she wore an ornate broach, carved to look like a bird.

As John extended his hand, he noted the familiarities, enough for him to confidently say, "Oh, you must be Aunt Isobel."

There was a small yet somewhat indignant smile on her face. Isobel extended her hand for him to kiss gently. "Please Dr Bennett, it is Lady Gray at these types of functions."

John became instantly rattled. He bowed his head apologetically and squeezed her hand to ask for forgiveness. "Oh goodness Lady Gray. I am terribly sorry."

"No matter, I suspect that my brother-in-law and niece had forgotten to inform you of my title." She gave him a slight wink and nod to absolve John of any guilt. She took her hand from him to reached for a glass of champagne. Sneakily, John finished the glass he had and took another also. They raised a welcoming toast to one another. "They are a funny pair. Love them dearly though."

"Yes," he said, laughing a little bit louder than he should've before stopping abruptly with embarrassment. He wavered over a question whilst he took another sip of champagne. The bubbles and alcohol burned his cheeks. "Where is Miriam? I mean, Miss

Clayton? Oh, Dr Clayton!"

Lady Gray raised an eyebrow at his stumbling. She took his hand and walked him to the front of the staircase and pointed upwards. Gradually, John followed her hand and nearly dropped his glass.

At the top of the stairs stood a vision of radiance. Miriam. She wore a turquoise satin dress that matched his bowtie and waistcoat. The skirt bloomed greatly, and the tight bodice made her waist cinched. Ornate silver buttons ran down the middle. The dress had a low neckline, which accentuated her chest, and a silver necklace, holding a blue gemstone, dangled low into her cleavage. Over her arms, she wore a matching bolero jacket that had a high collar and ruffles that went down the hem. The sleeves had white lace protruding from the end. Black lace decorated the shoulders and wrists. Her neatly curled hair, instead of high on top of her head as usual, descended like waves upon her shoulders.

John, who had fallen for her in a bloody blouse, was astonished at this sudden transformation. Miriam looked different yet all at once herself.

Most of all, she looked divine.

Suddenly, his world had more colours in it.

Miriam looked around the room eagerly. When she found him staring at her from below, she smiled brightly as though they were the only two people in the room. Carefully, she walked down the white marble steps. John could not catch his breath. The closer she got to him; the more John's heart thudded. This was a dream, surely. Any moment, he'd awaken on his uncomfortable mattress in London and realise that Miriam was just a concoction from an exhausted doctor's mind.

As she reached him, John put his hand on his chest and clutched it earnestly. Miriam giggled before holding out her hand for him to receive. He took it and helped her off the steps. She curtsied for what John suspected was the first time in her life. He kissed her hand as she nodded to him. "Dr Bennett."

"Dr Clayton." There was a brief pause. "You look heavenly."

"I am so glad you approve!" Miriam replied, twirling slightly to showcase her dress.

"I should walk the room," said Lady Gray. John jumped slightly, having almost forgotten that she was there, and nodded politely to her as a way of goodbye. Miriam hugged her aunt tightly before the older woman disappeared into the crowd.

For a few moments, the reunited pair stood awkwardly, wondering what to do or say next. The back of John's neck burned as he couldn't stop glancing at her, especially as her breasts were plumped by the corset. He tried not to stare at the cleavage. Alas, to no avail.

"Oh, thank goodness, champagne," Miriam exclaimed before taking two glasses. She drank both of them in haste and placed the empty glasses back on the tray. She took another two and handed one to John who looked bemused at her. She smiled and, in a gasp, said, "I do love champagne."

"Me too."

"You do? Here I thought you only liked my breasts seeing as that is the only place you can look." She nudged him slightly.

Apologetically he turned his gaze to her eyes which did not help. The setting, the dress, and the happiness that radiated from Miriam made him want her more. He wanted to be sinful right there and then. Instead, he swallowed his carnal thoughts. "I am sorry."

"Do not apologise. After all, my dear John, that was the desired effect." She then leaned forward and whispered in his ear, "Don't you just long to tear this dress off me right now?"

"Oh, most ardently." He replied before kissing her tenderly on her cheek.

"All in good time, John."

He smiled wickedly, "I was under the impression that you loathed parties?"

She swayed her head from side to side. "Oh, I do! Especially when I have to parade around talking to the bloated self-important elite and be… charming. But, Dr Bennett, I could not resist seeing the look on your face and dressing you all fancy." She played with his bowtie cheekily. Then she lowered her voice, fearful that people would hear. "Between you and I, I do love to dance. And the champagne!"

As if she had conjured them, a stringed quartet in the middle of the room began to play. A melodious tune, upbeat and jovial. It excited Miriam who had already finished her third and fourth glasses of wine. Grabbing John's own glass as well, she placed them down on a nearby table and took his hand. She dragged him through the crowd to a small section of the floor where people had begun to dance. Miriam took his left hand with her right and placed her other on his shoulder. John placed a shaky hand on her back. She flashed an exuberant smile but noticed his hesitation. "Oh God, you do know how to dance, don't you?"

"Of course, I do," He dithered. "One is a tad rusty, that is all."

It was a simple waltz. They stepped and twirled with the crowd gleefully. With each movement, Miriam's face lit up as though this were her first dance. Perhaps it was the company she was in. He ached to pull her closer to him. As they moved, Miriam said over the din, "You are a fine dancer, John."

"As are you, Miriam."

"I must admit…" She was getting a bit breathless as she danced and spoke at the same time, "… some part of this feels as if I am in a fairy-tale. As though I am Cinderella at the ball."

"And I your dashing prince?"

"Do you wish to be?"

"More than anything."

They laughed together as he dipped her. When John brought Miriam back up to face him, however, their bodies were dangerously close. They stopped the dance for a slight moment, and both blushed with the same heated eagerness. It was as though the whole room could see what wicked notions were rushing through them. They chuckled and resumed their more polite positions, before beginning to move with the crowd again. She looked him deep in the eyes as though she were saying: *Take me. Take me I am yours*. He swallowed nervously again.

"See John," she said suddenly. "See I *am* just like other women. I love fancy things, I like dresses, and I adore to dance. They escape me, that is all. I am like any woman you'd know."

"No, you are not." John chuckled at her. He nearly shouted over the music when he said, "No, you see, my darling girl, I solved it. That thing that makes you so special. I figured it out."

"Well," she replied with a cheeky smile. "Do tell, John. What makes me so special?"

Swooping her down again and bringing her so achingly close to his doting face, John said in a hushed manner; "You are mine."

Miriam grew stiff in his arms. She looked at him with an emotion that he wasn't quite sure of. Her eyes darted over him almost antagonised. When she pushed him slightly off her and stood up, parting from his arms, John grew confused.

Even more so when she slapped him across the face.

The room fell silent as gasps radiated throughout the crowd, causing the music to halt. Miriam mumbled quick apologies to everyone around her before she speedily ran through them. Her heeled shoes clacked on the floor, echoing further and further away from him.

Stunned, John instinctively put his hand to his jaw and rubbed it gently. He wasn't entirely sure of what had happened, as anger and humiliation and confusion mounted within him. John looked up, trying to ignore the room that still glared at him – their stares as scathing as their whispers. There was no sign of Miriam. Instead, he caught the eye of Sir Fredric talking to Lady Gray on the other side. Sir Fredric nodded towards the door.

The doctor needed no other invitation to leave the party.

Chapter Five

Wednesday 1st July 1896

Murder! Murder! Read all about it! Murder strikes London once again!!!

Rose Steel was butchered. Expired before her time. Copped it! SLAIN! Ripped!

Cruelly taken from this earth. Stripped off her life by a villain. Another Ripper on the streets of Soho. The devil in his furnace taking his fill of its seedy underbelly.

Headlines read that another tail has copped it. The news is all the chatter, from the lowly streets of Soho to the posh tearooms of the Strand. The wagging tongues slither from person to person until it becomes a roar.

They say that her insides were strewn on the bedsheets. They say that you could smell her before you saw her. They say the killer took a souvenir.

Such salacious secrets and falsehoods. It rippled through the city so quickly. The blonde-haired woman's murder went with some words. But the unhinged stabbing of Rose has caused more heated gossip.

Even the hospital was burning with such thoughts. It held their bodies, after all. Even in the basement, there were mournful mutters.

What a show! What a second act! What a performance!

Rave reviews, I would say. I must profess that I did not expect to be so excited by such acclaim. I have never been one for the spotlights or the stage. I did not understand why someone would want such eyes upon them. Peacocks strutting around waiting to be lavished and adored by thousands.

I have spent this life without the need for that, walking my own path without having to appeal to the public eye. I have been fine without bright adulation.

Do I want these killings to go down in history? Will these chapters be immortalised upon my tombstone? Will they theorise and debate over these slayings – tour the crime scene like they do in Whitechapel?

I worry about the connections. That people will be able to figure out the plot. The imbeciles at Scotland Yard have yet to piece together the ruins just as they have failed to capture Harry Wright. I wonder if he is a suspect. I wonder if they'll draw back the curtains and find him looking sheepish and blame him. It was his brothel where the last victim was found, after all. They were his possessions. His whores to parade and trot out. I hope the trail leads to him – to fish him out from wherever he is hiding.

Speaking of Whitechapel, I overheard a marvellous theory that good old Jack slayed his prostitutes to bring to light the suffering of the slums. How novel an idea! That killing can do good. I must say my murders were born in the gates of hell as vengeance tore into me. But what if they could do something I have wanted my entire life – what if they could reform the poor? What if we could make the rich confront their wrongdoings? What if these women did not just die in vain? Would we still be immortalised then?

I am not the Ripper though. I am a different player. I come not as enlightened as he. For my sights are set on the villains; the clawing whores, the woeful watch-out, the cradling mother, and the devil himself – Harry Wright.

The audience now watches. But what good show plays as you'd expect? Who am I to deny you, ladies, and gentlemen, from a twist?

What if we changed the game?

It may prove to be my biggest challenge yet.

Watch out! Watch out!

For my next trick is about to amaze.

Sunday 1st September 1895

There were so very few windows alive with light when the carriage pulled up to the Manor. John grew uneasy at the quiet as he stepped out into the fresh summer night. Not even the horse and the cab made a sound as they pulled away from the house. Darkness had enveloped the place. With the high emotions of the evening, it was more daunting than when he had first arrived. He had not meant to offend Miriam but the thought of doing so made him sick.

Walking to the door, he realised it was ajar. An orange beacon came streaming out. He stalled on the step of the entrance. A momentous feeling descended on him. It was not a doorway anymore but a precipice. The point of no return. A threshold which would make and break this courtship. Gingerly, he stepped into the home and his soul moved.

The lights in the hallway flickered as he arrived. The ticking of the grandfather clock was all he could hear. The room still smelled like her.

Looking around he noticed that every other room was in darkness. Yet above his vision, on the landing, just slightly down from the top of the stairs, he could see a yellowish light streaming through an open door. His room. He swallowed again, unsure what to prepare for. Another fight? Another kiss?

John's climb was measured. He counted each single step like a child would. There were fourteen steps altogether. Fourteen steps. For a quick moment, he wondered if it meant anything, but he dismissed it. Still, he knew that he'd remember that number for the rest of his life. His stomach was whipped up into a frenzy. His hands shook as he was guided into the light.

There lit only by the fireplace stood Miriam, watching him with an undecipherable countenance. He sighed at the very sight of her…

… The sight of John caused a shudder to flow down Miriam. Part of her wanted to run to him and shower him with kisses. The other wanted to hold her anger. Whatever his intent was, it enraged her that he would still think of her as a possession. No matter how beautiful he thought her plumage or how much he admired her flight, she was still a bird to him that he wished to cage and take out whenever it amused him. The very thought of it bristled in her, maiming the lust she had for him in that moment. As his frightened face fell into an apologetic one, her heart fluttered. *Damn him*, she thought.

John took one step forward. "Miriam I—"

Miriam would not let him have the first word. She stormed towards him flustered. So very quickly and so very angrily, she said, "John, I want you to listen to me very carefully. So very carefully. I am not nor will I ever be yours. I do not care what our society dictates or demands. I may be a woman, but I am my own person. Do you understand?"

"Miriam, please that is not—"

"I asked if you understood me."

John said nothing, pursing his lips, and nodding gently.

She nodded in return, and walked closer to him still.

They stood in the embers of the night, shadows crawling over their skin. They were both eager, yet their passions were stalled. They breathed heavily together, unsure what move to make or who would be the first to make it.

So, they made it together, leaning forward in throes of passion, kissing like they had wanted to kiss the first time they met. Fully and completely. Their hands gripped onto one another and held on pleadingly. Their aching bodies wanting to touch everything.

As they broke apart for air, Miriam removed her jacket. John watched the light fall onto her chest as it heaved in her corset. He wanted to rip her dress apart. He took a step forward to do so. She halted him again with a shake of her head, before spinning around and dragging her hair away from the hooks of her dress. Hurriedly, he began to unbutton but she said, breathless, "Slowly."

John did as she commanded. He gradually unhooked the garment. Every so often he would pull her close to him and kiss her neck. She gasped at each sensation. The dress fell to the floor. Miriam then took off the hoop underneath and stood in her chemise, a pair of drawers, and a bodice. Turning to face him, they kissed one another again. As they did, she reached to his shoulders and removed his jacket. She then unbuttoned his waistcoat and unravelled his bowtie.

She stopped and stood back. He went to unbutton his shirt, but she raised a hand and told him to stop. He did as she commanded. They stood, almost naked, panting for air as they eyed at one another. John waited for his next instruction as he throbbed for her.

"Your shoes."

He did as he was told and took off his shoes and socks.

"Your shirt."

He did as he was told. Deliberately, he unbuckled his braces and removed his shirt, never taking his gaze off her.

She paused for a torturous time and then said, "Your trousers."

He did as he was told. With a flicker of a smile, he stood – proud and nude - in the fire's glow. His thick erect penis was almost at her command too.

Naked, John was more fetching. Though his frame was tall and thin, he still had muscles from clear regular exercise, and a small stomach from a plentiful appetite. He was a fine man with bed of dark hair on his chest and a bountiful bush around his firm cock. In the nude, John looked more confident than ever; ready to do whatever Miriam requested of him.

The very thought sent waves through her. She grabbed at her corset and pulled it open, quickly taking off the chemise afterwards. Her breasts fell and bounced slightly. They were gorgeously large. John swallowed a little. It took all of his strength not to rush forward and honour them completely. Yet Miriam had not finished. She hooked her hand into the waist of her drawers and dragged them down her leg to the floor.

Suddenly completely undressed, Miriam became self-conscious of her form. Her squishy belly and hips and any other fleshy bits that most did not find attractive were now fully on display. She stood in the firelight and waited for his eyes to finish darting over her.

"Exquisite," he whispered, causing a warm sensation to spread between her legs. She was already aching for him and now they were ready.

And yet…

"Kneel."

John dropped to the floor.

"What am I to you?" She said with a heated whisper.

John paused, unsure how to answer. He looked up from his position. The very image of her looked infernal and haunting. It was as though an unearthly being had sprung from the flames to taunt him. Kneeling nude and hardened, he was awash with a fearful veneration. There she was entirely: A temptress. A siren. An enchantress of nefarious, unruly passion.

Trembling at the sight of her, John found himself yearning for her approval. Bowing as though she were a deity, he finally replied, "A goddess."

Miriam placed her foot upon his shoulder and said wickedly, "Praise me, John. As your goddess, I demand it."

Wasting no time, he kissed the ankle beside him, then the milky skin of her calf, then he brushed loving tender touches up her leg that tickled her with his moustache. Miriam gasped as he reached her knee. She nearly lost her balance as he headed down her inner thigh. Pausing, he looked up for her consent and she nodded softly.

Placing his lips against her privates, she shuddered. His tongue began gently flicking against her wet spots. She grabbed his hair to steady herself. She did not want to tease anymore. Not tonight. This build had been excruciating for her also. She was afraid of coming too early. All she wanted to do, now, in this night, was enjoy him.

Against her body's wishes, she said, "Stop."

He did.

"Stand."

He rose to her command. *Oh, how striking he was*, she thought. She wanted to devour him whole. Stepping forward, she kissed him affectionately, the tip of his erection pressed against her belly. In a hushed tone she said, "Close your eyes and count to ten."

John did as he was instructed, yet he was hesitant that she'd run away again. When he reached the requested number, he opened his eyes and found her lying on the bed, facing away from him. It made him want her more. Orange hues and seductive shadows fell upon her pale skin and buttocks. He swallowed his nerves. "May I?"

"Yes John, you may."

He climbed onto the bed with her. Pulling her hair to one side, he began to kiss her. First on her cheek and then on her neck. She quivered against him as his hard penis pressed against her lower back. John placed his left arm under her neck and his right hand upon her leg, as he had only days ago. He slowly dragged his fingers over her knee and thigh. Miriam giggled at first but as his caresses traipsed up her skin, joy danced down her.

John's lips found her shoulders as his wandering hand found her breasts. Gently, John grasped at them. With a whimper, Miriam began to circle her hips against him. She heard him gasp as she did so. Excitement radiated through the pair of them as her nude skin rubbed against his engorged member.

She took hold of his right hand, which squeezed and fondled her breasts, and guided it down, sighing when she settled him on her clitoris. Remembering the bench, he began to deftly circle the spot, mimicking her own movement from before. His fingers briefly spread into the wetness below to make it more pleasing for her.

"Oh God!"

Miriam began to writhe in his arms. Reaching behind her blindly, she found his hard cock and stroked it plentifully. He grunted into her as his mouth adorned her flesh. She could not bear it anymore, fearing once again that they would both finish before they had done the deed.

Positioning herself, she lifted her leg up slightly and guided him to her entrance. Miriam turned her neck and nodded at him. He furiously kissed and thrust into her at the same time. The thickness of him and the wetness of her made them both involuntarily moan into each other's lips. He paused to enjoy her tightness around him. After a beat, he began with a steady rhythm, pushing and pulling inside her. He hooked his arm under her leg, then his hand found its way back to that aching spot, and he began rubbing it with more vigour.

Miriam groaned loudly and moved her hips the best she could

to match his movements. She reached behind her and grabbed his buttocks, kissing him whenever she could. His left hand took hold of her neck lightly, coveting whatever skin he could find.

There they were, finally united. Two lovers who had tensely teased their way to this very moment. This craving for one another echoed throughout eternity. Their unison spread over their coming days until the end of the universe. Dazzling with stars and turning with the earth. It felt like the first time and the last time all at once.

But it would not last long.

For this was fire and it burned brightly.

They quickened together and fumbled for release, sweating, panting, and groaning in near unison. Animals who wandered in darkness for too long.

John pounded harder and faster as he was about to become undone. However, it would be Miriam who climaxed first. The currents began to turn within her. She couldn't hold them back any longer, not when he pleased her like this – not when she needed him so.

She called out his name as she twitched and bucked against him in a hot, breathless orgasm. He kept his fingers playing but the sensation of her insides contracting around him caused him to release himself. John moaned as he kissed her, before slowing down and stopping entirely.

Searching for air, they stayed entangled in every sense of the word. He was still inside her. They dared not move. After all, despite them having met little over a week ago, it took an age to get them here.

A minute passed and John slipped out of her, falling onto his back. He was still breathing hastily. Miriam turned onto her other side and stared at him. The bliss that rushed throughout her was flawless. She reached over and put her hands on his chest to feel his heartbeat. It raced as gloriously as hers did. Smiling, she delicately stroked her index finger upon his skin.

John watched her doing so. She was radiant in every way, memorising every freckle and every hair upon his chest as though the night would make her forget. The happiness in her eyes was an unparalleled delight to him. He never wanted that expression to leave her face, nor did he ever want to forget it. He did not want to leave this bed. There they could lie, naked and share each other, for thousands of lifetimes.

Unexpectedly, he grew hard once more.

Looking down, Miriam giggled and bit her lip. "Again?" He did not say anything, he just smiled and nodded. "Very well." She leaned over and kissed him. First on his lips, then on his neck, and then in as many places as she could as she made her way down his beautiful body to his erect penis.

Taking him in her mouth, she felt him twitch and she heard him breath in through his teeth. The taste of them both upon his member thrilled her. As she sucked him, she followed her mouth with her hand, taking moments to lick the tip with her tongue. He gasped as she slowly swallowed again, placing his hand on her head, and thrusting upwards so that his cock could slide easily down her throat.

After a few motions like this, Miriam stopped and grinned. She climbed on top of him and guided his dick into her. A small soft murmur left her lips as she slowly slid down. He placed his hands upon her hips as she began to circle them. She put her palms on his chest so that his heartbeat could race again beneath her fingertips. The way he stared at her, with awe and admiration, made her supreme. She changed the movements, bouncing up and down on him as he pushed into her. They groaned together.

Miriam quickened the pace. Leaning forward, she pushed her ravenous mouth on his eager lips, moaning against him.

Suddenly, John was fearful this would be over too soon again. He grabbed her back and flipped her over, falling out of her momentarily. As he leaned over her, John stared down at her naked beauty in wonder. He cherished the way it curved; he adored the unique blemishes dotted around; and even coveted her scar on her shoulder.

Kneeling between her legs, he positioned himself at her entrance and then, when he bent down to passionately kiss her, he slid back into that warm tender spot he so greatly worshipped. Parting from her lips, he let out a small gasp as Miriam cried out in delight.

John wished to make love to her in a more measured manner. This time, he was going to show her what she meant to him. He drove himself into her with deep, unhurried thrusts. Each time Miriam yelped and clung onto his back.

Their eyes met as he ardently moved in her, and he hoped she could hear his wordless pleas. That he knew he did not own her. But she was his. His to love. His to cherish. His to give everything he has to. And he was hers. If she'd let him be. *Oh, would she let him be?*

With that question in mind, he began to quicken slightly but still was precise and intentional with his movements. He winced and huffed again.

Miriam gazed over him as he closed his eyes for a moment. She wrapped her arms around him and pulled him against her body. He nestled into her neck. His hot heated breath rolled over her skin like mist on the ocean. On his shoulder, she showered him with affection and deftly stroked his skin.

John came back up to look at her, slowing down momentarily to enjoy the sight and memorise her in that way. In his sights, Miriam was perfect, and her heart swelled. Caressing his cheek, she began to whisper; "John I—"

"Shh shh no words my darling." He smiled and kissed her, picking up the pace again. They held each other close as she grabbed his buttocks and helped move him quicker. Faster and faster and faster, deeper and deeper and deeper, harder and harder and harder, again and again and again, until that familiar sensation flowed from him and into her. He grunted, collapsing on top of her. Miriam kissed his cheek gently and rubbed his back out of comfort.

Miriam wanted to say it whilst he was still inside her. All the commotion he was causing within her. All that adoration she had for him. All that bliss. As every single ounce of him lay upon her, Miriam had to say the words. In his ear, she whispered, "John I… I love you."

Lifting himself slightly to face her, John stroked her nose with his, tickling her with his moustache. He kissed her with glorious devotion before saying, "I love you too, Miriam."

Miriam took a brief moment to look at the night and begged God not to move. Do not take another step ever again. Keep the sky in darkness. Keep this night forever this way…

Chapter Six

Wednesday 22nd July 1896

Do you know how I did it? Could you see behind the smoke and mirrors? What illusion did I use to conjure it?

Let me tell you. Let me guide you through the trick. Let me draw back the curtain…

Forgive me. I am too elated. My hands still shake. I quiver with this… jubilation. I want to dance around this hollow home. I fear rousing suspicion though.

As I burn tonight's costume on the fire, stoking the blood-soaked rags until they are but ash, I drink in celebration. The whisky flows into my gullet like brimstone but tonight I relish it. I am not Icarus whose wings burned in the sun's rays. I am David, he was my Goliath. This was an incredible triumph of wills. I am almighty. Like I have burst through the gates of Valhalla victorious, dripping naked with sweat and blood. Alive again in the flames.

I see them glisten on me as I catch my breath. I smoke a cigarette to calm my nerves and sip at this victor's elixir.

It is a sorry state of affairs that women in this world are easier to kill. Especially women who sell themselves. This weak society drove them to the gutter and therefore any person could take advantage of their state. Women are at the mercy of men every day, with their brute strength and wandering hands and force of will. They are the biggest killers and will take women in their stride. Though the work had to be done, and the women had to go, I do still mourn for them and the circumstance that they found themselves in. I am still ashamed, though I know my acts are pure and just. I know it in the depths of my soul.

However, the largest game in this wicked hunt has been snuffed. A big hulking gormless man who would follow that vicious creature around. His undoing would be thus the undoing of Wright. For alas, Harry would no longer have his shield or protector. I have batted down a defence.

Paul Hobart was a witless giant. He towered over all in Soho with his six-foot-four stature. His frame was bound in muscles and fat. His fists could break bone. Yet it was not he who wielded them. They were at Harry's command. When the villain was absent, Paul would make sure Harry's terror still reigned from the flames of The Furnace. A thug, and like any other thug, he would speak with his strength more so than his words. He was more muscle than mettle.

So how was I to compete? How could I cut this oaf down with just a blade? How does the mountain bend to an ant's will?

Cunning. Cunning like that detective who outfoxes his nemesis. I needed to make Paul vulnerable. And in these times, what weakness plagues most men and women? Liquor.

A different disguise was necessary. I had to scum myself down. Rags ashamedly stolen from a dead vagrant at the hospital. The brown trousers, covered in muck already, were baggy around my legs and kept falling down. I had to tie them tight with rope. They reeked of piss and gin. I heaved as I put them on myself. There was an oversized yellow shirt which I suspected to be white when first brought. I matched it with a brown flat cap that shadowed my features. I took boot polish and mucked up my face. I looked as anyone would do, wandering the streets of London, looking for goodness knows what. I was now one with the poorer side of the scum that populates this city.

This would be no easy task. I had to let that filth think I was like him. I pretended to be in a stupor and wobbled over to his table in an insalubrious little pub. There I cajoled him into playing cards with me. *A gamlin man, I wos, I swear, no 'arm, no foul, aye? I jush wanned to play cardsh see!*

What a fool. He believed my performance. I flogged my money and lost, again and again and again. All the while rousing him to play, again and again and again. All the while slipping him a drink, again and again and again.

My own special brew, of course. A concoction I have used before. A slip of the hand and the libations would be laced with laudanum. The unsuspecting would be none the wiser. I am the drunken jester, after all. Only, nobody knew the punchline. Oh, how they would laugh if they did.

As the night drew on, Putrid Paul grew wearier. His opponent too clever for his own understanding of the game. Eventually, with poison growing in his veins, he slammed his fist upon the table gruffly exclaiming; "I'm finishhhhed," throwing his cards in my face.

I watched in glee as he stumbled out of the public house and into the streets to relieve himself. I counted to ten before I followed. I could have laced him with more, I could have ploughed him with the opioid until he frothed and concaved right in front of me. But where was the fun in that? I wished to see blood spilled.

Paul carried his gruff weight down a dingy alleyway, struggling with all that muck within his system. He fell into the walls, earning cheers from his city counterparts standing way down at the pub, all believing him half-cut.

Finding a shadowed doorway, Paul began to piss with that disgusting thing. Concentrating on this act, he paid no mind to the figure who crept up behind him. I waited until he was done. I then bent down and slashed his hamstring. Exclaiming loudly, Paul fell to the ground with his tackle still in hand, dripping the last remnants of piss down himself. As he fell, I hid in that now soaked doorway so those who looked down from his cries would assume he was too drunk to keep himself up. In laughter, they turned and walked away.

Oh how no one will be keeping look out for you tonight, Paul!

I stepped down as Paul winced in agony. He made a few swipes at me which I ducked, again and again and again. He flailed, knowing it was useless if he could not stand. I took a deep breath and brandished the knife. I wasted no time in slamming it into his exposed penis. Again and again and again. No more would it defile the innocent. Paul lay on the floor in agony, and I plunged the knife into his neck with unbridled fury. Again and again and again.

The work, however, was not done. I had yet to make a mockery of him. I who knew what he was about to do that night. I who knew his misgivings. I who became his judgement. In the cloak of the night, I moved down to his spurting cock – already hot and heavy with blood. I then cut it from him. Slowly with my knife, I tore his appendage from its root. It was not too intimidating. As he drew his last bloodied breaths, I stuffed it into his mouth for all to see.

There. No muscle was a match for my malicious might. David wins tonight. The very thought of it. I am glorious now.

No one has found him yet. But eventually the word of my deeds will come to light. Will they suspect the same murderer? I hope so and I hope it confounds them all.

And you, Harry Wright, will know that I have slain your man. Your muscle. Your protector.

There is nowhere you can hide. This dark Angel of Redemption is about to swoop down upon you and smite you to the gates of hell.

The spotlight is on you, my tricky friend.

I dare you to resurface now Harry.

I will have you under my knife.

Again and again and again.

Monday 2nd September 1895

Alas, God is a fickle creature.

The sun rose in a blazing manner. The pair, who had fallen into a deep sleep wrapped up in one another mere hours before, were stirred awake by the morning.

There is no shame in the trepidation one feels when waking up the next day. No matter how passionate lovers can be the night before, the morning can strip it away. This particular pair were raw in this new light: Slumberous, spent, and sticky in the last sun of the summer. They opened their eyes together, happily exhausted yet nervously content. It was as though anxiousness was crawling across the bedsheets, scaring the sanctity of the shadows away. The warmth of the day was a reminder that they had to face the world. They could no longer be entwined in each other's arms. They could no longer be as one. They could no longer be just them.

Miriam thought about this first as she lay upon John's chest. He was still drifting in and out of consciousness. Miriam listened intently to his heartbeat. It was a glorious sound, ricocheting through his muscles and flesh as it pumped life into every cell of his. It kept him so wonderfully alive: So blissfully here, in this moment, as fragile and as human as anyone else. Miriam felt as though the rhythms belonged to her. She was nearly coaxed asleep again listening to that beat, that beat, that beat. Yet when his lips touched the top of her head, she realised she wanted to stay awake and enjoy this new day with him. Even if it meant facing the world together.

John began to play with her hair which was frayed from activity. His eyelids were heavy, and it took a lot of strength to keep them open. Strength, he feared he did not have. Not just yet anyhow. He was intoxicated; the taste of her still stained his lips like the remnants of a fine wine. The scent of her upon his fingers like cigarette ash. It was a celestial aroma whipping and whirling around him lusciously. As he continued playing with the mousey-brown strands of hair, she sighed with content. Her breath skimmed the cells of his skin, causing goosebumps to follow like a trail. It happened again and he thought of how mesmerizingly alive she was, so strong and powerful like no one else. John felt as though that breath belonged to him. He wanted to spend this new day with her. Even if it meant facing the world together.

There was a faint noise of clatter coming from the kitchen. Both Miriam and John laughed, then moaned as an unrest swirled within their stomachs. It was time to unravel from each other and the thought ached equally within them. So much so that Miriam sheepishly rose, peeling herself off of him, suddenly aware of how naked she was. She grabbed the sheets and twisted them around her body. He smiled at seeing a somewhat timid side to her and even though she edged her way off the bed, he made sure his fingers stroked and caressed her. It was as though each gentle feel was a souvenir of how beautiful she was. She bristled blissfully at his touch. When she was out of his grasp, she whispered apologetically: "Father will soon be home. We'd best bathe and look presentable."

"Hmmm," He replied in agreement though the thought was ghastly. Then he ruminated a little while on what she said. "Your father did not come home last night?"

She turned to him, and a slick smile spread across her face, her spirit now pushing through the morning malaise. "I had proposed to father that, perhaps, he would enjoy the party more if he stayed at my aunt's."

John chuckled. "Miriam Clayton, you are a sly devil."

"I am merely prepared."

With a little jump, she hopped off the bed and placed her bare feet on the wooden floor. The soft pad of her footsteps sounded out as she made her way around the room, scooping up her discarded clothes as she tried to keep herself concealed with the thin white sheet. She knew that he stared, his eyes following her long after his touch did. Her face flushed from being overtired, but she became even more undone under his stare. For a moment, Miriam wondered why she was embarrassed until she realised it was just another tease. Another way of leaving him wanting. Soon she was hot and warm from that power. She allowed the sheet to slip, uncovering her thigh.

As she had taken the sheet off the bed, John lay there, happily nude in the morning. He watched as she bent over to pick up the assortment of clothes. His eyes skimmed over her as he traced her skin with memories of the night before. The leg she had failed to entirely cover had slight bruises from the tussle. Remains of his fingerprints. A swoop inside his stomach reminded him of coveting that leg with his hands. Thoughts and images from the evening fluctuated within him. Though the man had woken depleted, watching her somewhat shyly try to put herself together again excited him. He grew aroused once more. What kind of magic did this woman have? He groaned from that thought.

The sound of his moan caused her to look up. When she did, John threw his hands over his member, embarrassed. That devilish light lit up in her eyes again. She stood up straight and said, "Dr John Bennett! You are terrible. You know we mustn't!"

Miriam dropped the clothes she had found to the floor. She then slowly unravelled the sheets around her so she, too, was naked. Walking over to the bed, the sunlight soaked her in a new kind of fire. She reached across to the bedside cabinet to grab his navy necktie. As she weaved it through fingertips, John instinctively reached up his hands and clasped them together for her. In doing so, he revealed his stiff and wanting erection which caused her to shiver with delight. Kissing him deeply on the lips, she began to wrap the necktie around his wrists. Placing his bound hands above his head, she climbed on top of him and whispered. "You deserve to be punished."

And just like that, the morning's anxiousness had gone.

They had reluctantly parted less than an hour later. The smell of food cooking wafted through the house and made them realise how ravenous they both were. The air was tinged with meats and coffee, followed by the soft humming of Hettie. They wondered, together, whether she had heard their morning antics then decided it was best not to think on it. They would never leave the room if she had.

Separately, the pair bathed in warm water. They soaked off the remnants of their trysts and examined their bodies, sleepily going over the night as images drifted in and out of them. They mused on the same thoughts. They pondered on how they were different yet entirely the same. It was as though the evening had opened them up and the person who they were, wholly, came spilling out. And the other adored them for it. Together, without knowing, there was that pull of trepidation again. They both wondered if the night would stay within them or if it would be washed away as they cleaned themselves up.

As the heat of the day drifted through the house, the pair dressed accordingly: John in his light beige and grey suit, Miriam in her white lace day dress. The colours they wore contrasted with what they were feeling inside. An innocent shroud for the devilish natures that had been awoken. They thought on this with a smile before they opened the bedroom and found themselves timidly on the landing together. They met each other's eyes.

Then a sudden shyness moved between the pair. They hesitated with the knowledge that even though they were now restrained with their daily armour, they had shared nearly everything with one another. He could outline the crevices of her. She knew his dark desires. In their attire, they were scared again. More so than when they were naked. They nervously shuffled and sighed at one another.

Miriam breathed in and said in the exhale, "Are you ready?"

John nodded before gesturing to the stairs. She smiled timidly and went ahead of him. Yet as she began to descend the stairs, delicately grabbing the banister, John rushed forward, placing his hand on hers and kissing her fiercely on her cheek. She blushed and giggled as the pair hushed one another so not to alert people to their presence. Looking up to him, she caught herself in his blue eyes. Placing her forehead against him, the pair both knew that last night was not a moment in time, but they were now intrinsically entwined. Their breaths. Those beats. All muddled and tangled like rope and lace.

On top of this world, clutched in an embrace, they knew that they were to take these steps together.

Summer knew that there was little time for it now. September was allowing the night to seep in earlier and every so often, a chill hit the air. In protest, then, summer decided to not leave without a fight. The warm weather was sweltering with little breeze to cool and fan those struggling in the heat. Two exhausted lovers were no match for the blaze of the sun.

John and Miriam lay in the grass, half-way down a hill, by a small lake, their bikes discarded nearby. The tall blades kept them somewhat sheltered from the path nearby, but Miriam was insistent that barely anyone ventured up here in weather so thick and unkind. In the air were scents of dusty pollen and the dry wood of the nearby trees. A picnic basket which had been lovingly prepared by Hettie remained unopened. They were still full – they had silently scoffed huge swathes of eggs, meats, and bread rolls for breakfast, like starving beasts. The food and the bike ride to this secluded part of the countryside had tired them further. They had not said many words and they could only muster polite comments about today's activities. There was little strength to do anything else.

Miriam lay on her back, wishing that she could strip off her clothes so she could be nude in the summer heat. The patches of sweat that had formed on her neck and underarms made her feel unwashed and the bloating from the food made her feel grotesque. The lack of sleep had bushed her mental defences. She tried to will away these thoughts about herself, closing her eyes in the hope that she would catch a few more minutes of satisfying summer slumber. Yet she couldn't drift off completely as she was acutely aware that John was staring at her.

Laying on his side to face her, John couldn't help himself. Though he was similarly tired, now more a morsel than a man, he didn't want to close his eyes. He wanted to capture every moment as though he were a camera, imprinting every detail of Miriam so he could replay it to himself over and over again. He was so besotted, loving every slight movement she made as she breathed evenly in and out. Thoughts and questions were racing through his mind; tingling at his lips were words he had been aching to say since their first meeting, but dare he?

"Darling John," Miriam said with a slight croak to her voice and without opening her eyes. "If you are going to stare at me like that with mischievous thoughts running through your head, you better do or say something."

John was neither alarmed nor shocked that she had read his mind so clearly. Still, he huffed slightly, somewhat stilted in his tracks. "I thought you craved quiet, my dear."

"I do," She snapped one eye open to look at his bemused face. "Yet the rattling of your brain has proven impossibly loud. Too loud for me to ignore. Best say your piece to give me peace."

He chuckled at her tongue-in-cheek manner. Throwing his courage to the sticking place, John took a deep in-take of air; "Miriam I—"

"I beg of you, let it not be a proposal." Thwarted once more, John closed his mouth and let the question sink into the pits of his stomach. He looked indignantly at her for a long time, curiously picking apart the words that she had just said. Miriam sensed his consternation and sat up slightly, perching on her elbows. She squinted at him as the sun beat down on her angrily from behind him. Though he was blurred in the light, she could see his furrowed brow and pursed, irate lips. She laughed at him, but she didn't really mean to. "Oh John, I have upset you!"

"It is nothing Miriam," he said in a manner that suggested it was everything.

"John, I…" She hesitated.

"No Miriam it is fine. I understand." He paused. "I thought we made our positions very clear last night, however."

"I thought I made it clear that I do not wish to be your possession."

"I know but—"

"What is marriage, if not that?"

John meditated on the question before saying, "You know ours will be a partnership. I simply wish to adore you forever."

"Hmmm," Miriam replied. She had offended him, and it had marred their lovely day together. She was holding back. There was a twist in her stomach. Truth was, there was just one more facet of herself she hadn't let him see. One that she hadn't shown anyone, at all, really. Miriam had held it back for so long and she wondered whether he was the man to share it with. She closed her eyes again and said, in the softest voice he had ever heard, "John, I am scared."

"Of me?"

"No." She took a beat. "Of me."

It was his turn to laugh without really meaning it. When she stared somewhat angrily at him, John stopped and placed his hand on her soft, red cheek. "What is there to be scared of."

The touch of him sent waves through her. Suddenly, a tear rolled down her face. He brushed it away with his thumb. Miriam did not know what words to say; how could she explain everything she had ever done? "I fear that I may lose myself in you. That this dizzying affair has clouded our minds and I will be so blinded by it that we will collide. And I'd hurt you. And myself. That I could not bear."

"Hmmm," John said in response. There was a slight pause that worried Miriam. "This does not scare me."

"It doesn't?"

"No," He said with a beaming smile. "Personally, I find our collisions to be quite exquisite."

Miriam prodded him but laughed, allowing a few more jailed tears to be released. John kissed her now wet cheek then hovered over her mouth. Miriam's eyes darted over his face as he paused. His lips did not touch hers in such a tantalising tease. As the air between them brushed her now wanting mouth, she was reminded on how paired their spirits were. When he kissed her, she moaned with no repression.

The sound against him caused John to instinctively drag his hand off her cheek and place it on her bosom. As he gave her breast a slight squeeze through the layers, Miriam prized herself from his lips, placing a hand on his chest, and said in a mighty laugh; "Are you not fatigued from last night's dalliances? Or this morning's?"

"Somehow with you, I am reawakened." He kissed her again, his hand still touching her breast as she quivered beneath his palm. When they stopped, he said in a meaningful hush, "It seems you need reminding of what you mean to me, Miriam."

Pushing her gently down on her back, his eyes were as alive and adoring as they were when he made slow, deep love to her last night. Miriam gulped, out of control for the first time in their quick, heated relationship. She wasn't entirely sure she enjoyed feeling perilous underneath him. Yet as his hand leisurely dragged its way down her bodice and to her skirt, Miriam melted into his movements.

John leaned on one hand and watched her face as he began to reach underneath her skirts. Those prying fingers like intrepid adventurers, making their way through lands of material until they came to a parting, ripe and ready to be entered. Miriam gasped before the intrusion, closing her eyes in anticipation.

Slowly, John's index finger delicately brushed over her mound, tangling with the bushel of wild hair. He softly skimmed the slit with this one wandering hand. Excitement caught in her breaths as Miriam fell under his mercy. Teasing, John waited for a while, just deftly stroking her until she clenched in anticipation. When she sighed from the frustration, he slid into the parting. It was warm and wet and, oh so inviting. As she shuddered at his playful manner, John found the mark that she had loved so and studiously began to circle it with his finger. A faint whine came from Miriam as he did. He leaned forward and kissed her again, careful not to speed up, but gently caress.

The taste of her lips left him with a need for more. Miriam had begun to subtly writhe beneath him when he stopped, removing his hand from her skirt. Confused, she barely opened her eyes when he planted another kiss on her. He smiled and crawled between her legs, pushing them up so he had more room. As she looked down on him, he whispered; "You are my goddess, Miriam. And I wish to praise you."

Miriam giggled and threw her head back as he dove through her skirts. There was a soft blow of his breath upon her privates before he pecked them. She was wonderfully wet and wanton. Soon, the sensation of his tongue had replaced his fingers, circling over her clitoris in a steadied movement. He grabbed her thighs with his hands and pulled her closer to him, causing her to squeal out loud. John alternated his motions. He'd flick his tongue up and down quickly then circle her spot unhurriedly then he'd suck it. It was joyous to Miriam. Different waves of pleasure would radiate throughout her as he switched. She slid her fingers into emerald blades of grass and gripped onto them tightly as her body reacted wildly.

There was something so giving about the way he was pleasing her that there was already a familiar build within Miriam. John could sense it too, pushing his appendage harder against her with faster strokes. She began to stiffen in his arms, however, unsure whether she wanted to lose control completely. He paused briefly to say, "Let go, Miriam."

Those words, with his tongue feverishly plunging and licking at her, was all she needed. In the sticky, hot heat of summer, Miriam panted and tried not to cry out. Instead, she halted the sounds in her throat as she arched her back and came in one big orgasm. He slowed his movements as she twitched against his mouth, breathing, and sighing heavily. Everything that she had been repressing suddenly floated away like the dust caught within the sunlight. She swallowed as John removed himself from under her skirt and darted quickly to her lips so that she could taste herself upon his tongue in that sweet but strange sensation.

Miriam was open and alive once again. She scrambled to her feet and pulled his now utterly exhausted state up. Without giving him chance to protest, she took him down the hill and towards the lake. She stood him beside a large, bushy oak-tree that offered shade and more seclusion. Before John could catch his breath, Miriam pushed him against the trunk, kissing him intensely. He laughed first at her sudden insatiable eagerness but when her hands started to play with his trouser buttons, he gave himself to her once more. "If you'll indulge me as well," she said, whispering so close to his ear that it was as though her breath was caressing him also, "I'd like to pay in kind."

Dropping to her knees, she did not wait for an answer and sprung him from his trousers. She placed her hands on his member, giving a few starting touches like a greeting. Darting her eyes up, she gave him the softest wink then gradually took all of him into her mouth. Then she pulled him out but curled her tongue upwards so that it ribbed along his shaft. He groaned louder than she ever did and that thrilled her. She repeated her actions before she placed all of him down her throat. She gagged this time and was breathless when she came up for air. Taking a few moments, she used her hand to pleasure him before placing her mouth upon him once more. Now she sucked on his cock with a faster momentum, allowing her hand to cup his buttocks from between his legs, bringing him closer into her mouth. John gripped the trunk of the tree as she did so. There were many whimpering sounds coming from her as she relished every part of him. John started to moan too as he was close to climaxing.

Neither of them knew exactly how close. Miriam was licking and sucking his member then she took a moment to get air. However, the sensation of her doing so, and with her hand continuing to rub him, caused him to spill over.

"Miriam! Wait!"

And suddenly he ejaculated right into her face.

The pair froze, completely shocked.

The sticky stuff stayed still for a few moments then began to slide down. The movement of it caused her to unfreeze and yell, "JOHN!"

"Forgive me, Miriam. I… I…" And then he broke into laughter. He couldn't help it. Perhaps it was because he was still surprised at what had happened or perhaps it was the sight of her pouting as her face was covered completely by his semen. The comedy of it all rolled through him as he buttoned himself back up.

"I do not find this amusing!" But Miriam was trying to stifle a smirk. It was clear that she did not know what to do with herself. She huffed resentfully.

"Come," He offered a hand and lifting her to her feet. "Let us clean you up."

Then he unexpectedly scooped her into his arms. She squealed and protested as he did so. "John, what are you doing?!"

He said nothing but smiled brightly, walking over to the lake nearby. She wriggled in his arms when she realised what he was about to do. John carried them down the banks and soon he was up to his knees in water. As John waded out until he was nearly waist high, Miriam yelled at him, "John JOHN! DON'T YOU DARE! JOHN STOP THIS AT ONCE!"

With a scream, he plunged her whole body into the water. She kicked and flailed as he brought her back above the surface. Instinctively, she wrapped one of her arms around her neck and used her other hand to wipe the water and muck from her face.

John looked upon his now drenched lover, spluttering and shivering in his arms. The lace of her dress clung to her pale skin.

Her brown hair now looked black as it stuck to her face. When Miriam had finished wiping her face, she caught him looking deeply at her and met his eyes, wrapping her free arm around his neck as well.

The water splashed around them, but it was the only sound. As it lapped from their movements, the pair looked and swallowed at one another. The earth seemed to halt. The whole world was just for them. That near silent, timeless place again. A plane that only they were sharing. A glint of happiness shone between them.

A skip in John's heartbeat caught in his throat, pushing out the words again. "Marry me, Miriam," he said in a heated whisper. "Marry me, and I shall praise you every day. Every day until I die. And every day after. Marry me, my dark goddess."

The sentences rippled around her like pebbles on the lake's surface. His love surrounded her as she soaked within the water. There, in his arms, she was safe and secure in herself. She kissed him with all the love she had. Leaning her forehead against his, she smiled. "Yes, John, yes I believe I shall."

Chapter Seven

Sunday 9th August 1896.

The Soho Slayer!

So, I have a name!

The Soho Slayer!

They call me that on the cobbled streets and in the whispers on the wards of the hospital. Oh, what fun this is! Those fearful unfortunates conjuring up some caped demon that stalks them in the night, ready to gobble them up if they do not behave. What larks!

A strange contemplation hits me though.

Indeed, I have slain most of the foes that dared dangle their presence in front of me. They were demons and had no purpose on this Earth, having escaped the clutches of hell to wreak their havoc on the streets of Soho.

But as the fallen three would witness, these streets no longer belong to the wretched. The creatures of the night must crawl back to their basements and bars. I am the one they now fear.

The Soho Slayer.

Oh, I am gleeful at the thought of this spectacular spectre my killings have conjured.

And therein lies the rub - I *am* gleeful. I am happy. I am… enjoying this?

This was not to be an endeavour that I took upon lightly. These misdeeds had reason and rhyme. A purpose, no less, to purge London of the pitiful few who dared cross me. I am a murderer, and I should be wallowing in great shame. Yet, I feel joy in abundance, as a child does when they skip down the streets. I am eager, wanting to slice my knife through more who have wronged me.

It is as though I have waded out to a great lake, slowly through the thick river weeds as the cold-water laps against me. I fought against the undercurrent, afraid that it would drown me if I wasn't too careful. Yet now I allow it to swallow me whole. In the belly of the brook, I am submerged. The water that fills my lungs soothes me. The waves that are now cascading down my belly swirl against the fire. I am flooded with these ideas. I am drowning in a need to work once more, unsheathing my sword against all the heathens, and not just the ones in my story.

The Soho Slayer!

The thought of a lake takes me back to our proposal. I remember the excitement rippling out from us. Our sodden clothes. We were drenched but we did not care. I remember the shivering against me. The question. The answer. Not even a year has passed between us. Not even a year from what we were and look at

My goodness! What luck! What grotesque luck! I cannot contain myself. There is a part of me that wishes to caterwaul throughout this small townhouse. I dare not wake… Oh. I must not dwell.

I am already fearful that the knock has disturbed the household.

This household now knew only silence and dust, settling on once loved ornaments and fine furniture that we had little use or care for. This was our temple for one another. It held our secrets like a confessional box. We would anoint and praise one another until the sunlight beckoned us back into society. The house had passion seeping from the woodwork, drenching our bodies in shadows as we basked in the night like demons.

Now it knows nothing. The shadows only hold shame. The fire is only ornamental. This house is cold and lifeless. It is silence and dust.

No visitors had knocked on the door since Adelaide and her newly born child had been sent away. No visitors. So, a knock as darkness was drawing in scared me from my previous writing. I stayed still in my seat, hoping it was just a figment of imagination. Another procession of knocks. They were neat and concise. Authoritative. I knew at once that it was the Law.

Steeling myself, I answered the door and saw Detective Blythe at my doorstep. The very sight of him must've paled my face. I feared he'd find me guilty on the spot. I tried my best to look innocent and confused, perplexed by his appearance. He greeted me with the usual guff platitudes and asked if I was alone. Glancing up the stairs, I breathed in a heavy sigh. I nodded. "In some manner, yes."

Without another word, he breezed by me into the living room, curiously looking around the place as though there were bloody handprints on the wallpaper and a banner hung from the ceiling screaming "I am the Soho Slayer."

I nearly chuckled at his squinting saunter across my home. I offered him a drink which he declined silently. Fear not, Detective, for I do not poison. It is the knife by my breast of which you must be afraid.

Regardless he paced as though he were summoning up the courage to accuse me. He said in his usual gruff tone that he was here on a sensitive matter. "Regarding your… case." He could not look me in the eye. I tried not to look stressed, but my cheeks flushed. He did not notice in the dim gas-lighting as the night snuffed out the last of this heated summer day.

"I hope you are here to tell me that you have caught Harry Wright. Otherwise, this is quite the imposition, Detective."

"My apologies. Alas, it is not the incarceration of Wright that drives me here." He stayed still scouting the room with a degree of rumination that I feared would turn into recrimination. At this point, I half-expected him to begin riffling through my belongings. I gave him a stern look.

"Then why are you here detective?!" I almost shouted, wincing as I boomed. I was fearful that it would echo through this home. I was quickly remorseful for my tone and, in a hushed manner, said: "Forgive me. This is a hard time."

"No apology necessary. I cannot imagine what you have been through. What you have both been through." Blythe took off his hat out of respect and it repelled me somewhat. That after all that had happened and all this man had seen, he could follow this world's rotten customs.

"Are you most certain I cannot get you a drink?" I said out of courtesy, heading over to the trolley to pour myself a whisky.

"No. I will keep my visit brief."

I held my breath, trying not to wheeze out my jubilation. "Oh?"

"I am here about the murders."

I nearly dropped the bottle. I coughed and said as innocent as a babe. "What murders?"

That caused Blythe to smile. Slyly. Like a cat that would have all the cream. "You mean to tell me that you've heard nothing of The Soho Slayer? You work at the hospital, do you not?"

I tried not to hesitate. "The Soho Slayer? My, the press do come up with ludicrous names. But, alas, dear Detective, I have not been privy to any knowledge or gossip about the Soho Slayer." I emphasised the last part as though it were comical.

"I must say, I find that very strange." He muttered, causing my stomach to twist in knots.

He knows, I thought suddenly.

"Whatever do you mean?" I tried not to stutter.

"It's just, you live so close to Soho and work nearby, I am surprised you've not heard anything of this. As big as… well. You know. Whitechapel."

"We are quite isolated here after everything."

There was another cough. The type of cough that does not denote illness but awkwardness. He looked down again, clutching onto his bowler hat hesitantly. "And…"

"And what?"

"You see, the murders themselves. I mean the victims, you know. They're all… well… they are all linked to your case."

"What are you saying?" I said with a false confusion.

"The victims: Alice Haddon, Paul Hobart, and Rose…" The detective fumbled for his notebook to retrieve the name that he had forgotten which frustrated me somewhat.

"Steel." I said, quickly cursing myself after the fact. "I believe that was the name."

"Yes, Steel."

"They are all dead?"

"Murdered by an unknown assailant."

"Good riddance."

"I beg your pardon?"

"Goodness!" I said, in faux shock. "Who would do such a thing?"

"Who indeed." The detective said more confidently. He put on his hat and stood up with much more attention than before. He paused before saying anything further and stared at me as though he were creating a noose with his eyes. I tried not to show emotion: No fear, no sadness, no fright. I just stared back, hoping that the images of my misdeeds did not show in my own eyes. He took a deep breath,"This is why I am here."

I walked over to the drink station and poured another whisky. As I did, I gave a small scoff. "Surely, you do not believe that *I* had anything to do with it?"

The next blasted pause seemed to last an eternity. I was instantly aged by the fright. My heart stopped beating; I was surely dead. The detective looked intently and then shook his head.

"Of course not." ELATION! "We know very well who did this."

"Who?"

"Harry Wright, of course."

That name soured my drink. "Of course."

"This is the reason I am here. We just wanted to warn you. If Wright is going around, cleaning up his messes with murder, you two might be on the list."

"Oh, I see." I bit the inside of my cheek to stop myself from laughing. "Well, thank you for the warning."

Detective Blythe spoke very little after that. He offered a police guard in case we needed it and then left into the pitch-black night. As soon as the door closed, I practically leaped in the air, sending a wave of jubilation through this sombre home.

I must mute my excitement, but I am giddy that I have foiled Scotland Yard. I have succeeded. What luck I have had! I must be blessed by God and the universe. They are protecting me in my crimes. I am not a great person of religion, but this has to be a divine intervention, surely? They all believe that Wright is committing the very crimes that are leading me to him. Oh, what will they do when they find him sprawled and splayed out, after he finally meets my knife. I must stage it like suicide. I must.

There is creaking coming from above me. Perhaps I have… I must go.

There is still work to be done, after all.

There are two more to go…

Several Glorious Months:
September 1895

Miriam and John did, indeed, collide with one another in thoughts, feelings, and threads. They were meant to be as if there were a piece of string between them that they pulled at until they met and entangled so divinely. In such a short time, they had knitted themselves into a beautiful tapestry. A picture that would stretch out beyond their years. They wove eternity into their bones. The artists, Miriam, and John, would be bound together forevermore.

The cool crisp wisps of wind spun down the streets of the city as September settled in. This was the start of their engagement and an exploration of their bodies and souls. They tested their limits and boundaries with every fervent meeting. Even though they were betrothed, the polite society of London would keep them constrained to secrecy and the eager eyes of people they barely knew would happily gossip or tear them asunder. Especially if they found out that they'd already consummated their relationship in so many different ways.

When darkness settled upon the city, they would scurry away in midnight meetings at one another's homes. There they would indulge in passionate power plays and have wondrously wicked ways with one another as John submitted to Miriam's will.

Their days were filled with agonising waits, especially as they worked so near to one another. But every building has secret places, even in a hospital. They'd often find themselves in the locked pill cupboard or she'd venture to his office, push the door closed behind her, and unite with him... over and over again.

In one instance, they stayed behind after a board meeting. No one had noticed that they were alone; the other doctors were caught in a heated debate as their argument spilled into the building's corridors. With the realisation that there was no one else in the room, Miriam ran quickly to the door and closed it shut, locking it in haste. John had barely time to note this before she passionately kissed him with a breathless urgency. He too shared her ache, pulling her closer into his body than ever before. As they broke apart, Miriam whispered in his ear: "Turn around and bend over."

John did as he was told, placing his two open palms flat on the brown pine table. Miriam wrapped her arms around him and fiddled with his braces. Once freed, she pulled his trousers and underwear to his knees. He did not protest but the rough manner caused him to slip to his elbows. The coolness of the room hit his bare buttocks and it wasn't the only thing to do so. From behind him, Miriam gripped one of his shoulders and said, as she had said before, "Roses to stop."

When John nodded in agreement, Miriam wasted no time in slapping his rear. It started softly, with her gloves on to soften the blow. She removed them when she hit him with force. Her hand hit his naked skin with such a sound that the smack echoed throughout the room, sending waves of pleasure through both of them. His cock stood to attention quickly, uncomfortable below the edge of the table.

Suddenly Miriam paused and he could hear her footsteps walk slightly away. He dare not move unless she told him too. When she returned, John heard her breathe in and then - THWACK - a thick book hit his arse. He grunted but did not say the word. His silence often meant permission. The pain filled him with such a need. He felt shameful and sexual all at once which coursed through him like a merry alcoholic concoction, making him drunk with lust. She entered into a somewhat rhythm with the hitting and as she progressed, she too would groan with him.

When he relented with that delicate word, Miriam stroked his buttocks gently, bending over to kiss him on his now sweaty face, asking him if he was OK. She then slid her hand down and fondled him until he released, a reward for his punishment.

Then they slipped out back into the busy corridors of the hospital, composed, as though nothing had transpired between them.

October 1895

They knew that they could wait no longer to wed, longing to spend their days and nights with one another. They married on the 3rd of October, both wishing for a small affair. Still, upon her father's and her aunt's insistence, they were to be wed in a church near the Manor, where all her family had before.

It rained on their wedding day. In the early hours of the morning, Miriam had noted a thicket of clouds in the sky. They loomed ominously. As soon as the betrothed pair arrived at the church, branches of lightning stretched through the grey and petals of rain descended upon them. Before entering the stone building, Miriam jokingly said to John that it was because they were sinners and God was mad that they were coming into his house. The statement caused them to giggle like a pair of schoolchildren throughout the entire ceremony.

John wore a deep purple jacket over a light lavender waistcoat and tie, with a purple hat that fell in between the shades. Miriam wore a big, bright, white dress like any virginal wife would, with puffy shoulders and long sleeves. He gasped when he first saw her. His dark goddess looked utterly angelic and almost peaceful.

Upon their knees at the altar they spoke vows with an honesty and truth unlike any other couple that had knelt on the stones beforehand. They promised decades to one another - that they would burn as brightly as the stars that collided in the heavens.

They had an intimate reception at the Manor, much to the chagrin of Lady Gray's social elites who wished to poke and pry at this new couple. Friends and family came from across the country and just one couple from the city, Dr Michael Jenkins, and his wife Adelaide, came by. They enjoyed a luscious spread with happy conversations and dancing.

John and Miriam had found the day both euphoric and excruciating. After all, they were so close to many bedrooms that they could consummate their marriage in, yet they were stalled by all the congratulations. The pair did not help one another: A seductive hand underneath the table during their wedding breakfast or whispers of saucy platitudes to one another during speeches kept their feverish wishes heightened.

The anguish didn't last long. The day had disappeared as quickly as it had arrived. Sir Fredric had fallen asleep in the armchair in his study. Adelaide and Michael had retired to the largest guest room. Hettie drank sherry at the dining room table, flushed with merriness. Lady Gray, and other guests, had ventured to their homes as the evening ended.

In the rose garden, shrouded by pitch black darkness, as the rain pelted down on them, soaking their wedding clothes, Doctors John and Miriam Bennett finally made fast, fierce, and ferocious love on the stone bench, for the first time as husband and wife.

November 1895

It would continue to rain for most of October and November, but it did not matter. The pair were united in every sense of the word now. They had moved into a little townhouse in Westminster, by St James' Park, just streets away from the river.

It was quaint; though three storeys tall, it was thin and so they had no need for housekeepers. They tidied, and cooked, and cleaned for themselves. It was better that way. They could keep their secrets behind closed doors. It was their temple. From their bedroom at the top of their home to the fireplace in the living room, they worshipped each other in body and soul.

Every other weekend, they would visit the Manor to help rebuild it as a refuge, alongside Sir Fredric and Adelaide Jenkins, who threw herself into the project, utilising her societal connections to raise funds.

The Jenkins and the Bennetts had grown close since the wedding, even though Miriam and Michael had argued in the boardroom (and would argue many times after.)

Miriam had a fondness for Adelaide. The young woman was American but quieter than Miriam and much more conventionally pretty, with golden blonde hair curled into tight ringlets and a slight frame. Adelaide was a comforting companion, pithy when she wanted to be, and a reminder to Miriam of the girls she grew up with and had similarly admired – in many different ways. Adelaide also had an uncanny ability to temper her husband's more traditional values.

As trees waned with the season, the friendship between the two couples, especially the two women, blossomed.

In the late autumn, after exhausting neckties, Miriam and John introduced rope into their lives. John adored being bound whilst Miriam would tease and torment him, binding herself in bejewelled and colourful corsets to titillate him.

It even slipped out of their bedroom. On November 12th, John's birthday, Miriam tied John to the chair in his office. She teased him until he was utterly stiff and practically salivating for her. Suddenly, she walked out of the office, and locked him inside without so much as a word to him. Working in the hospital, she left him waiting, and wanting, for hours, telling the staff that he had taken a sudden turn and was resting in his office. They were not to disturb him at all.

Under her strict orders, he was to be left alone. Under her (assumed) strict orders, John could not cry out. Under her strict orders, all he could do was wait.

When she returned, his eyes were filled with utter rage and yet they were utterly ravenous. She walked slowly over to him, dragging out each step purposely. Tactfully, she freed him from his confinement. Then, hitching up her skirt and slipping down her drawers, she bent over the table as though she were presenting him his award.

There was a moment of stillness and silence. Enough to make Miriam fear that she had gone too far.

However, John stood up, unbuttoned his trousers, and fucked her harder than he had ever done. The hospital surely shook that day. When finished, collapsing on top of her, he whispered gruffly; "Do that again. Just do not tell me when."

December 1895

The pair adored the autumn and winter because the nights were longest. In the dark, they could play their little games by the roar of the fireplace. At times, Miriam would command John to crawl to her, even using the rope as a leash as though he were a dog. She'd sit in her fine bespoke corsets and stockings, spreading her legs for him like a treat to be won. However, by the time he had reached her, she'd slap his buttocks until he couldn't take any more. It thrilled them both: A pleasurable punishment and a raw reward.

Nights continued like this and would end in different ways: Miriam would soothe him with ointments and cradle him in her arms or they would make powerful love. Sometimes Miriam would be the one who enjoyed being whipped, but not as much as the pair enjoyed her dominating him. Through this, they were connected and complete.

The festive season, which had become entrenched in Dickens iconology, saw them willingly reach out to add more things to their pleasure.

Christmas was an opportune time for them to gift one another sordid little treats. John had bought her a selection of riding crops to heighten his excruciating enjoyment.

Miriam's gift was more of a conniving plan. On that holy Christmas night, after drinks in the front room, and a test of the crop, Miriam lead him upstairs. Waiting at the door, she told him that he could only watch. He was not allowed to touch anything, or anyone, or even talk until Miriam told him otherwise. Though he was mildly confused, John nodded in agreement.

Miriam lead him through the door. There, drinking champagne on the bed, were Dr Michael Jenkins and his wife Adelaide.

There was a momentary shock. John even stood back, dumbfounded at the proposition. Then he remembered every time he saw his wife in heated whispers with her best friend. Whilst, indeed, it was a little surprising to find the Jenkins' curled up on the Bennetts' bed, John found that he was not surprised. After all, Miriam had a wicked tendency to find someone's secret desires and coax them into fruition. Immediately, John knew that this couple were willing.

Fully clothed, John took to the wooden chair that had been placed at the bottom of the bed. Miriam reminded him of the rules. He'd have to be silent and still.

So, clinging onto a glass of champagne, Dr John Bennett would do just that – he would watch. He observed as Miriam slowly undressed both his good friend and his good friend's wife until they were all naked and giggling. He stared as Miriam used her mouth to pleasure Adelaide, soon climbing onto the blonde, beautiful woman. The women circled, bounced, and rubbed against one another until the pair climaxed one right after the other.

Lightning shot through John in that moment, and he shuffled awkwardly on the chair, his dick longing to play. But he kept on watching. He gazed upon his wife as she, on her hands and knees, placed herself at the end of the bed. He looked on her as his good friend Michael positioned himself and entered her from behind, causing her to moan loudly. Dr John Bennett watched the whole scene unfold.

All the while, Miriam gleefully watched him, staring into his wide, yearning eyes.

With his wife inches away from him, getting pounded by his colleague, John's erection became agonisingly hard. Whilst he loved being caught this way, in Miriam's grip, he longed to be the one making love to her. Adelaide watched too, pleasuring herself on her knees beside the copulating pair, kissing her husband as she groaned and writhed. Miriam and John would not take their eyes off of one another. *Are you watching?* She said silently. *Are you enjoying?*

John could bear it no longer. In a second, he wished to see her come undone. He leaned forward and whispered into her ear; "Does he fuck you better than I?"

The question caused Miriam to gasp loudly, which gave John his answer. Sitting back on the chair whilst tipping his drink to her, John flashed a sly smile as Miriam lost control somewhat. As she regained her senses, panting at the vigorous activity, Miriam suddenly grinned wickedly. "Adelaide, my husband broke the rules. He needs to be punished."

Unexpectedly, Adelaide matched Miriam's near sinister smile, climbing from the bed, and walking over to John, talking his glass from his hand, and placing it on the floor. He was expecting to play no part in this scene and yet he allowed Adelaide to lift him from the chair. He allowed her to start removing his clothing as he tried not to look down at her pert, small breasts, flicking a look to Miriam who gave him permission with a small wink back. He allowed Adelaide to take his trousers down, leaving him as naked at the rest of them. Finally, he allowed Adelaide to bend him over the end of the bed.

Whispers away from Miriam, John could feel the hot heat of her panting on his cheek. Adelaide then began to slap John's behind, hard. He closed his eyes, relishing that familiar glee of humiliation and pain. It was mixed with the new tension of having his friends witness this moment for the first time. His stomach would flip but Miriam would reward him with kisses when she could.

As the spanking intensified, Michael's hands clung onto Miriam's hips tighter, and his pace quickened. Miriam laughed loudly: "Oh oh oh ah, no, not yet Michael, I want you to see my husband fuck your wife."

With that cue, Adelaide stopped slapping John and took a similar position next to him. As John wondered what to do, Miriam said heatedly to him; "Merry Christmas, darling."

John grinned and placed himself behind Adelaide. The blonde haired, slight woman, took his cock into her hand, stroked him, and then guided it into her. Instinctively, John grabbed her hips and began to thrust into Adelaide, mirroring the movements of Miriam and Michael in front of them. John's eyes, however, would not leave Miriam's and hers would never leave his.

After the four of them were spent, Adelaide and Michael drunkenly left in the early morning in a haze of satisfaction. Though their friendship did blossom further, in more socially acceptable respects, the four never spoke of that tryst again. Nor did they repeat it. They all found out Adelaide was three months pregnant by the beginning of January.

It didn't bother John or Miriam. They were more than enough for each other.

1896

The New Year bought many glorious new adventures.

In February, they even divulged their deeds in public. Well, somewhat. There was a sordid little club in the burrows of Piccadilly. There, they attended a marvellous masquerade where people could be whatever they wanted and do whatever they desired: Sex in public, sex with others, whips, chains, and performances. Without anyone truly knowing who they were, the

Bennetts could devilishly delight in one another with an audience – companions of the night – watching their every move.

Their desires ran darker than most, but it wasn't always what they'd indulge in. Sometimes, they'd enjoy more passionate and simple lovemaking where they could express their adoration in more sensual and slow movements, much like that first time. Often, they would find themselves in quick heated embraces at work, having once again thought of nothing else but their writhing bodies all day.

Sex may have been a foundation for their relationship, but they were more than their rampant escapades. The pair delighted in heated conversations and debates, they dabbled in the arts and theatrical shows, and gentle walks in the park. They worked together in the hospital, passionately continuing Sir Fredric's work after he retired at the beginning of March. The Bennetts began developing the Lady Gray Ward in the basement and began helping women out of London, secretly scurrying them away to The Manor as it started its new life as a refuge.

To all around them, John and Miriam were pillars of the community – courteous and kind or ferocious and generous, respectively.

To John and Miriam, they were soulmates.

Some nights they didn't even make love at all, they just stayed in that silent, timeless place, holding onto one another with their equal and blissful restless thoughts. A tapestry of heartbeats and breaths. Tangled like rope and lace. The pair would wonder on the fragile perfection of their being and their unbelievable union. Their entwined bodies and spirits were made completely for one another, destined always to share the heat and flames of their love.

For this was, indeed, fire.

A blaze that was forged tremendously for these two divine sinners.

And it burned brightly.

It would not last long.

Chapter Eight

Monday 17th August 1896

What have I done? What have I done? What have I done?

Oh, the Almighty. Oh God in heaven. Please, please, please take this as penance.

I know that I have not been as diligent in faith. I am no ardent believer. But I kneel before you on these creaky floorboards ready to throw myself on this pyre. I am at your mercy. Look upon this poor wretch and give me the grace of your spirit.

I am reprehensible! I am irredeemable! I am incurable!

But am I beyond your salvation?

Please lord, please I beg of you to please come to me in these desperate times. For I fear I have crossed a line and I have become a true murderer! A monster! A fiend!

I have always believed that this sin of mine was forgivable. Like the hangman who pulls the lever. The noose I have fashioned for these criminals was weaved from their own crimes. I have felt guilt and shame, but it was cloaked in good reason.

Was it not? Was it not? Was it not?

But this new work that I have done has a hefty toll. The stains upon my skin weigh upon me. I am a sinner now. I have done the unforgiveable. I have murdered the innocent. I have…

Oh, it is too impossible to write. But I must. This may be the only way I can find absolution in the next life.

I have butchered the innocent. Not just the innocent but those who I hold dear in my heart. Oh God, I have killed my friends.

Now rouged with their blood, I can see what demon I have become. The red liquid looking black in the dead of night. This is what a creature of Hell does, crawls through the entrails of humanity and coats itself in flesh. That is what I am.

Is there a way back from this?

I do not profess to know what came over me. My hands still tremble out of confusion. I was awash with heinous thoughts and blinded by rage. Another side of me did flood my senses. A trembling Jekyll, living in the wake of Hyde's misdeeds.

It happened so fast.

Tonight, I sat alone, the shell of the person I once was, and I brooded on thoughts as I have done these past months. I could think of nothing else but those small moments. Not the vile act itself but the steps it took to get there; the clawing whores, the woeful watch-out, the cradling mother, and, until I faced him, the devil himself.

A nagging sensation pounded through my brain. It ticked away untouched for some time and, it seems, as I wielded my knife, I had untethered it from its binds.

That another face was part of this picture. That another person had played a crucial part in my undoing. That another must meet my sword.

Dr Michael Jenkins.

I had dismissed it so many times yet tonight, this seemingly irrational thought bit into my brain and refused to let go. We had shared so much, him and I, and despite our differences, there was an unbreakable kinship in that. Perhaps I felt it more than he. Maybe he had been biding his time until he could exact revenge against me. He led those women to my doorstep. At the time, I was blind, thinking he thought naught of it. But a stirring occurred in me – what if he knew?

The days and weeks after Paul's death, I was ravaged by the thought. I had a hunger for blood that I could not sate. The growling in my insides became deafening. Because I saw Michael and Adelaide happy. Their days were filled with endless blessings. They were happier than us. Happier than our household. Just happier.

Knowing what he had done became too much of a burden. I flushed with a resentment so pure and so vivid in my mind that I thought it must have been sent by a holy divinity.

And it was too easy. My lord, it was too easy. I did not need disguises or to cover myself in shit to do it. Genteel society makes people into dupes. It is a trust different from that of the poor. The poor trust in desperation: A begging to the universe that this time, he will not be rushed upon the blade. However, the rich have no such qualms. They have a naivety that nothing could go wrong.

I know that naivety well.

Those inexperienced with misery find themselves the hardest to fall. All it took was a simple knock on the door. I was greeted with a surprised yet warm hello from Michael. Soon thereafter Adelaide had embraced me so ferociously that I almost turned away from the terrible deed I was about to commit. It was late enough that the housekeepers had all been sent away for the night. The Jenkins drank by a fire. Their young babe asleep upstairs.

I could see nothing but hot, white rage. I tried to conceal it the best I could. They shared pleasantries. I could only return stilted responses, the glass trembling in my still gloved hand. The blade jingled in my pocket as though it was jumping to get out. They smiled and smiled and smiled in their angelic mockery.

How dare they have this heaven that has been taken so ruthlessly from me!

Adelaide reached over and tapped my knee when I had grown into a longing, yearning silence. It was as though she had pressed a button. I thought on how nice and quaint she was and how nothing bad would ever happen to her at all. She had never been graced with pain. I could not help myself. I brandished my weapon and furiously bought it down on her over and over again.

In a panic, Michael pulled me back, but I was too quick for him. Using my elbow, I whacked him in the nose causing him to fall back. In this confusion, I used my time well. I drew my knife and stabbed him in a gleeful frenzy. I thought about his hands and his cock and his venomous tongue and how he must've known what those women were plotting. He must've known! I reduced him to a bloody pulp. Covered in his blood, I stopped only out of exhaustion.

Dying, Adelaide slithered across the floor. Using the last of her strength, she tried to get away. In my only act of mercy, I went over and slammed the knife through the back of her neck. A quicker kill.

There I stood over them, watching as my work had entered the town houses and higher society. *How distressing for them!* I thought in my wrath. The pearl-clutching masses with high horses will look down and find their own carcasses on the floor. I did not wield my knife indiscriminately. The richer side of the scum that populates this city must know my blade also.

I heard the baby cry in the nursery upstairs.

There was a possession in my gullet that yearned for more. I did not know myself in that instance. I had been forged as someone new. I walked slowly to where the noise was coming from and found their daughter Eloise: A fair babe who'd I held in my arms until I could not stand my yearning woe any longer. Now she wailed on her back as though she knew what terrible fate had befallen her parents.

I took my gloved hand, still dripping with the remnants of Michael and Adelaide. I placed it upon Eloise's noise and mouth. I held them closed. As she wriggled, all my senses came flooding back through the void. After what was ripped from me, could I do the same to another? "No, not the baby," I whimpered.

Sharply, I took my hand back. The babe screamed loud – her face smeared with her parent's blood.

Although I was aghast at what I had done, I had to use my intellect. Ransacking the house, I demolished furniture and took jewels. Leaving the door open, I ran into the night, hoping that it would not be long until someone heard the child's cry.

Now I am wracked with turmoil. I am beyond the deeds of justice. I am a murderer – pure and true in this wickedness. The blood of my friends will forever be a blot in my ledger, a stain on my soul, and these shackles will last forever. This is a new agony, and I am grieving once more.

But was it not you, God, who infused me with such terrible pain?

Was it not you who took everything from me?

Was it not you?

Monday 6th April 1896

Miriam placed the journal on the desk gently. It was the same place where, several months ago, she had propped her feet up and attracted the irritation, the interest, and then the infatuation, of her now husband, Dr John Bennett. Taking her orange gloves off, she began to run her fingers wistfully across the deep, red leather-bound diary. Then to the worn wood of the desk. She smiled to no one but herself. Bubbles of excitement popped in her stomach as she removed a bottle of brandy and box of cigars from a paper bag and placed them by the journal. They served as gifts in celebration of such joyous news.

Sighing contentedly, Miriam sat down at his chair. The room had not changed much since she first snuck away from that insipid party. There were more books and ornaments on his shelves, and a picture from their wedding day sat on his desk where an (undetermined) fake skull once lay. It all looked neat and tidy.

However, Miriam knew that the bookshelf still held a secret alcohol stash, that naughty notes were hidden in unused books, that there were pornographic pictures of Miriam tucked somewhere in his papers, and that a piece of rope was kept in the bottom drawer of his desk. That was John entirely: He had all the composure of a gentlemen – the kindly, near-quiet doctor – but within him brewed someone positively indecent. It was one of the many reasons why she loved him.

Nostalgic, Miriam pulled open the bottom drawer and removed the rope, wrapping it around her fingers whilst she laughed to herself. Through her delight, there was another feeling brewing. Another sigh would leave Miriam's lips. One mixed with different emotions, sounding out with a register of both excitement and melancholy. A joyful hesitation sat on her chest.

Their lives were about to change completely. A new chapter in their story. While that delighted Miriam, she couldn't help but brood on whether or not their passions would alter or end entirely.

With the rope still wrapped around her left hand, Miriam opened the journal and wrote a humorous note to her husband. She chuckled contentedly to herself, knowing immediately that whatever was to come, they would face it together. She grew anxious for him to come back from surgery so she could surprise him with the presents and news.

The door of his office swung open. Miriam jumped up from the chair like an excited child. However, she was disappointed to find that it was only Matron Lockett stood in the doorway. The older woman was flushed. Hurriedly, she rushed into the office, causing the keys and equipment of her gold chatelaine to jingle a melody. Matron spoke as fast as she walked, "Oh there you are Doctor Bennett, thank goodness."

Ignoring the pebble of dissatisfaction that had sunk to the core of her stomach, Miriam replied, "What is it Matron?"

"It's Marie." There was a beat. "She's back."

"Oh God no."

Without a second thought, Miriam and Matron ran out of the office.

There was a small ward in the hospital. It lingered near the basement, darker and danker than the higher floors. Though more akin to a hovel than a hospital, it served a great purpose. It was where Miriam worked most days. It was staffed by a couple of nurses alongside the stern yet substantial Matron Lockett. No male doctors were allowed to pass through its doors. Not even

John was permitted to visit. This ward was almost a secret, especially to regular patrons, and that was how it was run.

It was called the Lady Gray Ward and it housed women who had fallen victim to violence; whether that be from their spouses or their pimps or just men who think they could do whatever they'd like, whenever they'd like. Miriam would tend to the patients, listen to their stories, and try her best to get them safely out of the city – often utilising the Clayton Manor as a safe-house for them.

Miriam and her team had helped a fair few women start again in places beyond the smog of London. Unfortunately, stuck in circumstance, bound by marriage, or simply unable to see their worth, a lot of women would fall into a cycle of abuse. And sometimes, it would end tragically.

Sitting on the small cot in the middle of the row was Marie who had regrettably become a regular in the ward. The weary woman was holding a bundle of cloth to her nose which was bleeding. Her right cheek hosted a small cut that was surrounded by a red mark. Her ginger hair was pulled out of place and her simple, bottle-green dress was scuffed with mud and blood. When Miriam stormed into the ward, Marie averted her eyes immediately and said under her breath, "For fuck's sake!" As angry footsteps made their way to her, she spoke excuses quickly, "Look, Miriam, this is nothing. I fell. I was drunk."

"This is a game I am no longer willing to play with you Marie."

The woman on the cot said nothing more as Miriam approached and sat down beside her. Instead, with clear tears in her eyes, Marie turned away. Grabbing Marie's hand, Miriam gave it a comforting squeeze and leaned forward to brush back Marie's bedraggled, ginger hair. Matron Lockett waited quietly with a wash basin and clean towels to tend to the wounds.

The pair on the bed had grown close over the past year, even before Miriam had met John. And yet, they would almost always meet in this situation. Marie McDonald, though few believed that was her real name, was a 40-year-old sex worker. At one point in Marie's life, she had more: A comfortable shop girl's job in Mayfair, a blossoming relationship with a bank clerk named Joe, and a child on the way. Over the years, Marie had lost them all. The job had made her redundant, Joe had become an alcoholic and died clutching the bottle, and disease had taken each of her children. Penniless and pitiful, Marie worked the streets and developed a similarly strong relationship to gin.

Though the years and alcohol had aged Marie and dishevelled her face, she was still considered beautiful with sparkling green eyes, red, curly hair that was beginning to grey at the roots, and a curvy body. With her vivacious nature, and regular stint at singing in pubs, Marie was popular. Popular enough to procure lodgings at The Furnace, Harry Wright's establishment, which was nestled down Portland Street in Soho.

As Miriam understood, the place was a pub downstairs and a brothel upstairs, which Marie worked in. Harry Wright's reputation for having a vicious streak preceded him. Miriam had yet to meet the man, but the stories of his insidious nature echoed throughout her ward.

He was considered the most violent character in Soho. Many wounds that were treated here was his doing and every time his name was mentioned, Miriam would fly into a rage. She would do anything to see him bought to justice. It ate away at her. There were many nights in which John had to calm her down after she had ranted and raved about Wright all evening.

Though different in class and station, Miriam and Marie could not recall what had made them so fond of one another. There was a likeness in their humour and candidness that helped an appreciation grow between them. Plus, Miriam was the only one who would listen to Marie's plight – even if Marie did not take the advice given. The younger of the two had urged Marie to leave London and stay at the Clayton Manor. "He'll find me." Marie would often say grimly. "He always does." Then she'd suddenly be gone, and Miriam would feel helpless.

In this position on the hospital bed – one that they had been in countless times before – Miriam gave Marie's hand another gentle squeeze. When Marie squeezed back, Miriam gestured for Matron Lockett to start treating the poor woman. As Matron Lockett did, Marie began to cry, "You lot must think me a fool."

"We think no such thing." Matron Lockett said sharply. Head Nurse Elizabeth Lockett, or Matron as she was known throughout the halls of the hospital, was a small, skinny woman who was harsh and commanded respect. Even Miriam was somewhat scared of her as they worked together on the women's wards. Nevertheless, Matron Lockett treated all patients of all classes with the same amount of respect. "Now stay still. I do not believe it is broken but I still wish to be cautious."

When Marie was finally patched up and the nose had stopped bleeding, Matron Lockett left to make sure that the others in beds around them were OK, leaving Miriam to confront her wounded friend. Marie's breath shook, "I bet I look a right state now."

"You look as beautiful as ever."

"Oh, you are a terrible liar, Miriam." But she offered a small smile as a thanks.

"Now Marie," Miriam said, still tackling strands of Marie's hair. "Will you tell me the truth of what happened?"

"You know I can't."

"Why protect him?"

"It's not him I protect, Miriam." Marie said softly. "If I bring up his name, you'll go do something stupid."

Miriam breathed out of her nose furiously at the accusation, even though she knew it was very true. She kept her lips pursed for the longest time, thinking on what to say next. As she tended to Marie in a gentle way, a fury was still bounding through her. She could not just sit idly by whilst a friend was being hurt in such a ruthless and brutal manner. Still, she tried to keep calm for Marie's sake. "If I promise not to do or say anything, will you be candid with me?"

There was the longest pause before Marie nodded. Through painful tears and stalled breaths, she then told Miriam about the incident: How drunk she was last night, how she didn't go back to The Furnace to earn her keep, how he had been waiting this afternoon when she finally returned, how he dragged her into the streets by her hair, and how he had delivered several blows to her face with his cane. As though he were making a spectacle of her, he jeered at the crowd which had gathered around them and bellowed; 'This is what happens to whores who try to jilt Harry Wright.' And he kicked her in the stomach. Before the ordeal was over, he bent down and hissed at her; 'Next time you skip out on me, I'll kill ya.'

As the last sentence rang out into the afternoon, Miriam breathed heavily. She was trying to keep calm, but she was shaking with rage. Standing up suddenly, Marie instantly looked dismayed. "Please Miriam, you promised."

"I know I did." Miriam said through her gritted teeth. Without a second thought, she was storming through the ward. Before she knew it, she was out of the hospital and racing down the streets of Soho.

Despite it only being the middle of the afternoon, The Furnace was rowdy. Hesitating at the door, Miriam could see groups of men and women drunkenly cheering. Her stomach twisted, knowing that just moments ago this happy crowd was watching a woman beaten bloody and blue. Those last words that Harry had said to Marie resonated through Miriam's head and instilled her with a wrath-induced determination. She thundered through the doors, shouting in a voice that she had not used in a long time; "Harry Wright!"

The crowd fell silent immediately and turned to look at this strange spectacle. As the light of day streamed through the windows, Miriam was silhouetted. Stepping further into the pub, she came into view: The clean, posh, orange day dress instantly told them what class she was which bemused many. There were murmurs and comments as she looked around. She said out loud again; "Harry Wright?!"

Like the parting of the Red Sea, the crowd began to disperse until there was a clear line to a man leaning at the bar. He stayed facing away from her. His grey hair was greasily slicked back. He stayed perfectly still which infuriated Miriam. "Are you Harry Wright?"

Harry then turned slowly. If Miriam had not heard stories, she would wonder what made him so intimidating. He looked just like an ordinary man in a polished, burgundy, velvet suit, and green necktie, sipping on a beer and smoking a cigarette. There was stubble peppered on his chin and his brown eyes were wrinkled. His hair was slicked back so much so that you could see the thinning of it. A black wooden cane with a silver dog's head leaned against the bar. Meeting Miriam's eyes, Harry smiled sickeningly; "My my, 'ello darlin'. I am, indeed, 'arry Wright. 'Ow can I be of service to you?"

No one was sure what she was going to do as she marched through the now parted crowd. Not even Miriam. So, the punch also took her by surprise. As her fist collided with his jaw, a powerful blow that knocked him back against the bar, there was a raucous gasp from everyone around them, followed by scattered titters and scoffs. The act winded her. It was as though she had jumped off a building and suddenly remembered that she had to meet the surface. Her pulse buzzed in her ear as adrenaline coursed through her.

To everyone else, Harry's reaction was quick but to her it was slow; he reached for his cane and rose it above him, ready to bring it down on Miriam. However, a tall and muscular man, with short brown hair on his head, pulled him back whilst the crowd around Miriam closed in on her. They all knew why they had to: Miriam had clout. If anything happened to her right now, the police would be straight down here. Miriam stayed still and incensed, unsure what to do next. As Harry fought against the restraints, the bartender behind him looked her dead in the eye and said, "You best leave, Miss."

"Fine." Before she left, Miriam pointed viciously at Harry, "But mark my words, if I hear you have laid your filthy hands on another woman, it will be I who kills you, Harry Wright."

She stormed out of The Furnace, exhilarated.

When she got back to the hospital, Marie had vanished again, and Miriam finally hit the ground with a hefty thud of regret.

The small office had filled with smoke. It circled around Miriam's head in a thick cloud. She was too distracted to actually take a drag on the cigarette, only smoking when truly stressed. She let it burn down to nothing. Sighing, she watched as the ash fell into her lap and she lazily brushed it off, adding grey smudges to her favourite orange day dress. Stubbing out whatever was left of the cigarette, Miriam placed her fingers to her temple and circled it gently.

The pokey room was close to the Lady Gray Ward. The

hospital had banished her here. Her father was no longer an active chairman. In March, Sir Fredric had retired to the Manor in Northamptonshire to help grow its new purpose as a refuge.

The minute her father had left, the rest of the board had wasted no time in relegating her back to the basement. It had not stopped her storming their meetings, but it did make it easier for the men of this hospital to ignore her demands. Even though her husband was still a part of the board. Even though her father's name was still on the hospital. Even though she tried and tried and tried.

What's more is that they were attempting to ignore the suffering of her patients. She had only just started building the ward, for its true purpose, and yet, in a matter of weeks, all that progress was slipping backwards. She wished she could change the tides for women like Marie but every day, it became increasingly more hopeless.

Now Miriam's temper and anger had bled into the streets. Against anyone's better judgement, she had violently confronted Harry Wright. She worried about the ramifications and feared for her friend's safety. What could that horrible man do to Marie now that Miriam had intervened? She wished that she could find Marie and squirrel her away from this god-awful city. Instead, Miriam brooded, hoping that she hadn't put Marie in truly terrible danger.

A tear slid down her cheek and landed on the grey smudges that now dotted the orange dress as she spiralled into this pathetic and powerless sadness. All she wanted was to cry and wail in John's arms.

John!

Suddenly, Miriam stood up and raced out of the office. She had forgotten about the presents on his desk which he was bound to have found by now. Today was supposed to be a celebration after all. Running up the stairs, she tried to place all those bad thoughts away, deciding that tomorrow she would finally rescue Marie from the clutches of Harry Wright.

Tonight, however, she had exciting news to tell her husband.

Rushing across the courtyard that sat in the middle of the three buildings of the hospital, Miriam tried to keep her composure. It was already dark, and a biting chill had descended. The breeze blew around her, but she paid it no mind. By now, she was filled with anticipation and eagerness.

"Oh look, there she is! Dr Bennett!"

Miriam was so focussed on her destination that she barely heard these words and could not see Dr Michael Jenkins waving to get her attention. In fact, she was nearly through the entrance when she was suddenly startled by Jenkins barking her name. "MIRIAM! WAIT!"

Spinning around, breathless, Miriam was both annoyed and surprised. Michael was stood with two women – one with curled blonde hair and the other with black hair that she kept underneath a ragged, pink bonnet. They looked distressed. Michael beckoned them to follow him as he walked over to Miriam.

"I apologise if I interrupted something pressing, Dr Bennett. However, these two women require your assistance. I believe it is urgent." Miriam found it funny that after everything they had done together, Michael could not look her in the eye.

"Thank you," Miriam replied, and Michael nodded at her before rushing off, believing his involvement to be over. Miriam rolled her eyes after he was out of sight. She turned to the women, "How can I help you both?"

"You're Miriam Bennett, right?" said the blonde woman urgently.

"Yes I am." There was a terrifying look on the pair's face which sank in Miriam's stomach. There was an ominous feeling in the air. She knew instantly who they were coming in aid of. "What has happened?"

"It's Marie, miss." The black-haired woman continued. She was missing one of her front teeth. "She's been beaten bad. Won't have anyone help her but you."

Miriam's heart panged with guilt and anger. Danger had come for Marie, and it was all Miriam's fault. Looking upwards to John's office window, she could see that it was unlit. Perhaps she did have time to help Marie before John found his gifts. A petty worry. Miriam admonished herself for thinking it. Urgently, she turned to the pair of women in front of her and said defiantly, "Take me to her."

As they ran through the Soho streets, Miriam thought only of Marie. As they turned into Portland Street, Miriam thought nothing about The Furnace even though it loomed over her. She thought nothing about how quiet the alleyways now were or how the pub was eerily silent. She was led through Portland Mews, which was thick with darkness and muck, but Miriam was not hesitant or scared; she thought only of Marie.

Behind a pile of discarded barrels, Marie was lying, bruised, and battered. Her eyes widened with shock as she soon as she saw Miriam. Shaking her head violently, Marie screamed at Miriam to run away.

Miriam did not listen. Instead, she immediately rushed to Marie's aid.

See, in all the mayhem, Miriam had not thought, for a second, about her own safety. As a blow landed on the back of her head, causing pain to radiate throughout her skull, Miriam's last thought was that perhaps, maybe, she should have.

A fog descended and Miriam fell, unconscious, to the floor.

Miriam stirred. Her head throbbed and she was unsure of her surroundings. Her eyes fluttered but all she could see was black. In a hazy second, she thought she had gone blind but as she gradually woke, she began to see figures in the low light of the filthy street. Coming to consciousness, Miriam realised that she was lying on cold, dirty cobbles. Except for her head, which was resting in the lap of someone. As she regained her senses, Miriam looked up, realising that Marie was cradling her and calmly stroking her face. Confused, Miriam went to move but her arms were pinned down. The two women from earlier were holding on to each arm. When she tried to wiggle herself free, they clung on – painfully digging their nails into her skin.

"My my, look who's finally awake." A familiar voice sent chills down her. She looked down and there he was, towering over her at her feet. Harry Wright. There was that same sickening grin on his face and his eyes glowered with depravity. "'ello darlin'."

It caused her stomach to twist in a frightful agony. However, she didn't want to show it. Instead, she frowned and breathed in deeply. She wrestled against her captors, and, attempting authority, she yelled; "Let me go."

Harry's face dropped. Lifting the dog-head cane in his hand, he slammed it down hard on her face. The bite of it cracked through her temple, followed by a brief dizziness. The claws on her wrists dug in deeper, breaking the skin. Marie hushed Miriam, trying to hold her head still whilst gently stroking her hair. There was pain from her wounds, but the terror was worst. Harry laughed then barked; "You ain't going' nowhere sweet'eart. You are all mine."

Miriam tried to look for escape, but it seemed hopeless. Keeping guard down the main passageway entrance was the tall, burly man from the pub. If she was able to get free from the women holding her down, he was bound to catch her. And she did not know what violence this man could do.

Miriam feared death. Suddenly the fright took hold. Images flashed through her mind. As they did, she lost control and started to cry. In woeful whimpers, she pleaded; "Please, please don't kill me. Please."

There was that awful laughter again. It echoed round the small courtyard. "I ain't gonna kill you, darlin'. No no no." There was a flash of his yellowed smile. He slipped his hands beneath his braces and pulled at them. "Alice, go watch the other end."

The blonde-haired woman let go of Miriam's arm. Freed somewhat, Miriam saw her chance. She punched the other black-haired woman in the face. This caused a commotion as the now injured woman fell backwards and scrambled to retaliate. Miriam tried to free herself but found Marie was still holding her down. As she pleaded with her friend to let her go, she did not notice Harry standing on her right hand. The crunch of her bones and the agony caused Miriam to call out. For the scream, he landed another whack of his cane on her cheek.

Harry picked the dark-haired woman fiercely off of the floor; "Rose, go join Alice you useless fuckin' bitch." Turning back to Miriam, Harry sneered and rolled his tongue within his mouth, "Can't get the whores these days. Now, come 'ere." He threw the cane down beside her. The strike of it on the stone sounded out and shot through her sore skull. Then, removing the putrid-green necktie from around his collar, Harry grabbed Miriam's now broken right hand and her left. Squeezing them together tightly, so another wince of pain reverberated through her, Harry tied her hands and placed them above her head. "Should've known you would've put up a fight."

Lowering himself to the floor, in between her legs, Harry Wright grabbed the hem of her orange skirt. That's when Miriam realised what he was about to do. She began to thrash and kick her legs but several hefty blows of his fist upon her face caused her to stop and snivel, "No no no stop."

Suddenly, Marie squeezed Miriam's wounded cheeks and into Miriam's open mouth, she began to pour gin. Miriam spluttered and choked with it. Marie, however, calmly said to her; "Hush, hush now, it will be over soon."

From his jacket pocket, Harry produced a small knife and began cutting through Miriam's dress, underskirts, and drawers until she was completely exposed. The cold hit Miriam's privates with a stomach-turning chill. His grubby hands pawed over her naked thighs. He cooed with a strange admiration. "Ooooo, what a delicious cunny."

The gin had mixed with blood pouring from a wound on the cheek. The way he was looking at her was grotesque like a rabid predator prowling for a bite. Nausea flooded through her. Anguished, she grimaced and looked wildly around as she tried to figure out what to do. Fighting against her restraints or calling out would certainly cause another blow to rain down on her. She feared one more crack of the cane would kill her. Yet she had to fight – didn't she? *Didn't she?*

Miriam hoped that if she prayed for help, it would come. But as he undid his trousers and pulled out his prick, Miriam knew it was too late. Her heart raced and she breathed jaggedly, not knowing what to do but sob in Marie's arms. As Harry positioned himself, Marie clasped her hand over Miriam's mouth, and when Harry forcefully entered her, Miriam shrieked into Marie's palms.

"Ohhh!" Harry said in gleeful pleasure. "What a delicious cunny indeed. I bet it 'as seen some fun. Not 'arf as much fun as it is 'aving now."

The feeling of him unwillingly inside her was cruel and cold. Pain emanated through her body. Miriam could smell him as he leaned over her and continued his vile act: A strong saccharine sweet aftershave to mask the stale tobacco and alcohol stench as well as his general uncleanliness. She tried to look away or close her eyes, but his dirty hands batted away Marie's and squeezed Miriam's cheeks tightly. Wright pushed his face closer. As he raped her, he hissed through his yellow teeth; "Oh no sweet'eart I want you to see this. I want you to remember this for every single day of your fuckin' life. I want everyone to know as you walk around this city that 'arry Wright 'as fucked you good and proper."

Harry kissed her. He tasted vile. The mixtures of scents overwhelmed her. He thrust aggressively in her, quickening up and grunting. Miriam had to see it all, his face contorting as his hot alcohol addled breath hit her cheek. Occasionally, Marie would put more gin in Miriam's mouth, as though it could help her through this ordeal. Instead, it made her sicker.

As he continued, fast and furiously, Miriam fell out of herself. Her soul had escaped her, floating away from her body. She thought about her spirit racing through London's streets to her home. She thought about being curled with John by the fireplace. She wished that this could all be make-believe, and she was soon going to wake up in her husband's arms. She hoped that all this was a nightmare ready to dissolve in the morning light.

But it wasn't. It was real. And it was torture.

He started making more disgusting sounds and sped up until he released himself inside of her with a loud groan. Collapsing on top of her, Harry had finished. He kissed her again before peeling himself off from her. Standing, he buttoned himself up, picked up his cane, and removed the tie from her hands. As her arms flopped to her side, he knew that she wasn't going to escape. "Bet you 'aven't 'ad a fuckin' like that sweet'eart." Suddenly, he violently kicked her in the side and stomped on her repeatedly, whilst hissing; "Not gonna 'it me now, are you?"

There was pain but Miriam did not feel it. She was no longer there. She was broken. The millions of pieces of her were strewn on this cold, muddy, cobbled street. Miriam lay there, her head gently stroked by Marie, who was softly crying and apologising. Miriam felt nothing. When he had finished kicking her, Harry spat down and said loudly. "Wanna go Paul?"

The big, burly man grunted in agreement and walked over to her, unbuttoning himself. Miriam did not fight, nor did she care. The damage had already been done. She wished to dissolve into the night and melt away from this new, horrid life. But as Paul knelt down to position himself, he said gruffly; "Oi Harry, She's bleeding down there."

Through the void that she was plunged in, Miriam's heart broke. All the agony and her senses came flooding back. With that rush of emotions, and a surge of pain and cramping, Miriam vomited down herself. In the anguish, she began to wail and cry loudly.

The sudden commotion frightened the gang around her. Lights in windows above them began to flicker on and shouts of concern bellowed down. The other women began to sprint out of the courtyard as Paul gestured for Harry to leave. Marie stayed still, trying to calm Miriam down but Harry stomped over and began tugging Marie away. With another swoop of his cane, he hit Miriam again, causing her to quiet instantly.

As she was overcome with the darkness again, she said in a faint whimper. "My baby…"

Chapter Nine

Thursday 20th August 1896

It was my wedding day the last time I was in a Church.

I had not thought on that until I sat at the back of the dusty pews, staring at the crucifix that stared back at me. It was a crisp day; the air had started to cool as summer was beginning to fade into autumn.

I wondered what drove me in there. Why had my feet dragged these heavy bones to this temple? Why was I sat in front of these artefacts? Why did I feel the urge to pray?

I must make penance. I would slice into these layers of flesh and place pounds of it on the altar. I would allow these streams of light to turn into hell fire to consume my meat and bones.

I was not normally a person to attend such a place of worship. Religion was more like child's play. And yet I had belief. It is a foolish person who closes his mind to the unexplained. That spirits may live beyond us. That there are places for us after we die. That there is a greater plan for us all.

For a moment, it was as though God had touched me. He had given my life meaning. A heavenly touch reached down and blessed me with a sword. In his image, I was reformed and remade in God's furnace. I came through the flames as his Angel of Vengeance, bequeathed with a mighty purpose.

What foolish thinking. I was nothing but a monster. Lucifer as he fell from heaven. I crawl in the dust and ashes.

A tear ran down from my eye. I feared more would burst the dam of my resolve. That I would break into confession, fall down upon my knees as I did nearly a year ago, and renounce my sins. That I would trade rings for cuffs. That I would trade posh clothing for a noose and swing before the summer was out.

Oh Lord, is this what you ask of me? Am I to die at the hangman's hand before Harry Wright is impaled upon my sword? I asked expecting no answer but aching for it nonetheless.

Then, I heard a babe begin to laugh. It came through my senses like the summer's sun collecting colours through the stain glass window. An angelic sound, which caused my soul to soar as though it were chasing that noise. I looked up to see where the sound was coming from.

There I caught two parents in the fog of my senses. They were familiar, but in a faded way, as though I had passed them on the street or sat beside them in the theatre. She was buxom in purple with mousey, frayed brown hair. He was older and slim, with wavy dark brown locks and a thick moustache, twisted thin at the ends. They cooed over their child that wiggled in their arms. Laughing, the parents were content, wrapped in the air of their child's laugh. All three smiled with a radiance that panged in me. That ache.

A rush of wind blew through me. The babe had stopped chortling. Suddenly it started to cry, curdling the air, and sending shudders down my spine. That cry. It was loud and piercing. It was as though its arm was being twisted all the way round. It was in pain. So much pain. That awful sound inside my mind. I could think of nothing but that wailing.

The wailing. The cry. The sadness.

My child.

The wailing. The cry. The sadness.

My child is dead.

The wailing. The cry. The sadness.

My child that never got to be.

Thewailingthecrythesadness.

Eloise. Smeared in her mother's blood.

Thewailingthecrythesadness.Thewailingthecrythesadness.

ELOISE. ELOISE. MY CHILD.. MY CHILD.

THE WAILING! THE CRY! THE SADNESS! THE WAILING!
THE CRY! THE SADNESS!

"WILL YOU PLEASE STOP THAT CHILD CRYING? I CANNOT
STAND IT!" I bellowed at the top of my lungs, winded by my own
anger.

Then the sunlight disappeared. The shadows of the evening had
already descended on the dusty pews and only darkness and
moonlight dared fall through the stain glass windows.

How long was I sat there? I did not know.

The only thought that stretched through my mind, with its grubby
little ways and grotty little fingers, was that I was alone.

Alone. Alone. Alone. Alone.
How long have I been alone?

Monday 6th April 1895

John picked up the journal from his desk gently. He sat down in the chair and admired the shiny, claret-red, leather cover. Deftly, he ran his fingers over the book as though he were a child poking at presents on Christmas morning. He wasn't sure whether he should open the gifts of brandy and cigars, or even peel open the pages of the book in his hand. *Perhaps*, he thought, *I should wait for Miriam.*

That morning over breakfast, she had cooed and teased him about a massive surprise. After a long arduous day of tending to patients, he had half expected to come into the office and see Miriam scantily clad and waiting for him. Their gifts to one another, in secret, of course, were so often salacious.

Laughing at the memories of their consummations, John turned back to the gifts on his desk. As tame as these presents were, and as random as their appearance, they were pleasant enough to satisfy. The brandy was expensive, the cigars were rare, and the journal was incredible. Feeling sneaky, John opened the diary and found a note scrawled on the first page. It read:

The Crude and Risible Writings of an Expectant Father by Dr John Bennett.

There was a massive swoop of emotions throughout him, and his heart twanged. A smile appeared on his face as excitement raced through him. Part of him wished he had waited for her because now all he wanted to do was embrace his wife. His pregnant wife.

"I am going to be a father." He whispered to himself and giggled gleefully. Miriam was pregnant. They were going to have a child together

John stood up giddily and buttoned his jacket with haste, preparing to rush out of his office. His mind was consumed with finding her. He did not think on how he hadn't seen her since they arrived that morning. He didn't think on how dark and late the evening had become. He didn't even notice the loud shouting and the squeal of nurse's whistles that echoed from down the hall. John ached for Miriam and just wanted to take her in his arms. A child! How perfect their family will be! John thought of nothing but telling her how much he loved her.

Rushing out of his office, he suddenly walked straight into Matron Lockett, who was rushing in. The collision caused them both to yelp. Instinctively, he grabbed her shoulders to steady them both and squeezed her apologetically.

"Oh Matron, I am terribly sorry. I was just…" He paused. Snapping instantly out of his rose-tinted moment, John noticed the blood that was smeared on Lockett's apron. His eyes darted uneasily over her face which was red and distressed as tears streamed down her cheeks. She was struggling to catch her breath and could barely look him in the eye.

Dread hit his stomach like a drop of poison. It spiked and bloomed within him, devouring his happiness immediately. "W… w… what is it Matron?"

"Oh John…" Matron Lockett took a couple of beats to compose herself. "… It is Miriam."

A mix of anger and sadness infused in John. He did not hesitate. Instead, he pelted out of the office to find his wife. Matron Lockett tried to stop him at the door, to calm him down, but it was useless. Running down the halls, John was overcome with trepidation that was so deep and powerful. He could not stop thinking about all of the worst scenarios and he wondered whether he was strong enough to face them. Yet he had to be, he had to find Miriam. He had to see her. After all, maybe everything was going to be fine if he just saw his wife.

In one of the private rooms, there was a congregation of three nurses and two doctors, including Dr Michael Jenkins. A police officer covered in blood was sat on the floor. Everyone was pale with shocked faces, whispering furiously to one another. Michael looked morose as though he had seen a ghost. As John rushed to the group, his heart beating wildly in his chest, Michael looked at him and leaped to block the door. Holding his hand up, he said, panicked, "No John. No. You must not go in."

"Get out of my way Michael," John said with a fake patience as his friend held him back. "I wish to see my wife."

"John… Please. You do not want to see her. Not like this."

"Goddammit man, let me through!" John bellowed, causing those around him to gasp out of shock. No one in the hospital had heard him raise his usually calm voice in such a manner. The aghast police officer stood up as though he was ready to stop a fight, though he looked like he had little energy to do so.

Michael relented. He moved to one side and let John through. John found himself hesitating, trying to muster up the courage to continue. There he was again, at a threshold, the point of no return. Everything was about to change. He closed his eyes and drew a breath before stepping into the room…

At first, John thought there must have been a mistake. He did not recognise the beaten woman who lay before him. Swollen bruises and cuts upon her face made it nearly impossible to identify her. In a brief moment, in a hopeful second, in a worse thought, John wondered if they had got it wrong. This must be someone else, surely.

Yet the more he stared, appalled at the scene, the more he could see it was Miriam. His darling wife. The horror of it all made him weak and he grabbed the doorframe to steady himself. Miriam was covered in blood. Her favourite orange dress was torn and in disarray, though someone had tried to rearrange the mess to cover her privates. The frayed skirt was soaked in dirt and blood. There were bandages around her right hand. She was covered in vomit and there was a strong stench of gin. There were small cuts on her wrists and her exposed thighs. Though a nurse tended to her wounds, Miriam was deathly still. John said quietly. "Is she... alive?"

"Yes. But she is sedated."

"What happened Michael?" John said but there was no response. There was a sea of emotions within John. Misery and malice bounded through him like hounds from hell. The very sight of her like this pained him. His heart was breaking. Something wretched had attacked his wife. He did not know what to do with the anger within him. John suddenly took Michael by the collar and screamed in his friend's face, "WHAT HAPPENED TO MIRIAM?"

Then John fell, crying, to the floor. The sobs echoed down throughout the hospital.

In his office, John sat in a stunned silence. The image of Miriam lying there, sprawled out like one of his crude surgical sketches, was frozen in his mind. He feared it would be there forever. He held a glass of whisky in his hand, but he did not drink. The presence of it served to steady his hands because he did not know what to do with them. It was a strange sensation, over-thinking the position of one's hands, especially as they shook with anger, sadness, and more. The familiarity of the glass gave John something to fixate on.

In three chairs around him sat Dr Michael Jenkins and Matron Lockett as well as Detective Thomas Blythe, a stout and clean-shaven man. They watched him uneasily; unsure what he was about to do next. John was already too tired to do much. Exhaustion ripped through him with the grief. His mind clung to the idea that Miriam would flounce through the door any minute now, laughing as though he had fallen for her grim joke. He would be mad, of course, but they'd embrace and chuckle together. John was overcome with that ache.

The detective was speaking but John tuned in and out in ebbs. "Lying in a courtyard in Soho... residents alerted the police... thought it was the Ripper... murmurs and cries... carried her here..."

John did not respond to the detective straight away. He let the words hang in the air with all the dust. It seemed like hours had passed until John whispered; "Will she be OK?"

There was a hesitation from those in front of him. Matron Lockett put a comforting hand on John's knee and answered kindly. "She will live. And we shall help her the best we can."

Detective Blythe shuffled on his chair before he continued; "Look, Dr Bennett... this will be hard to hear but the manner in which she was found, the tears to her dress, and her wounds... we believe someone has taken liberties with her."

"What do you mean?"

"John..." Michael leaned forward and said gently "... there's reason to believe that she has been... raped."

"Oh God... no." John replied, tilting his head upwards to stop a new ripple of tears from falling down. His hands shook harder as he clung to the glass, fearing it might break in his clutches. The word turned in his stomach and hammered in his mind. He could not bear that Miriam had been through all that pain. All that agony. All that defilement. Through gritted teeth and halted breaths, he said, "Who would do such a thing?"

"I have my best men looking for the culprit as we speak."

"Dr Bennett, I am afraid there is more..." Matron Lockett said uneasily. The stilted stop she took soured the atmosphere. John grappled at the seams, hoping to not become undone again in front of everyone. His emotions brewed on the surface. "Was Miriam with child?"

Turning his sights to Matron, it took all of John's strength to say: "Yes. I believe she was."

There was a dreadful, pained pause. The look that stretched morosely across Matron Lockett's weathered face told him all that he needed to know. John said nothing but threw the glass across the room. It smashed loudly and silenced all those around him. Only an hour ago was he jubilant and wickedly in love, having only just found out about his future child and wished to celebrate with his beautiful wife.

Now that had all changed. The child was gone, and his wife barely clung to a life that was to not to be the same as before.

John was now as shattered as that glass – a million pieces scattered across the cold, dusty floor.

Returning to Miriam's room, John sat in a chair by her side, and gently held onto her unbroken hand. Every so often he would kiss it, hoping that she'd be comforted through her unconscious state. He had banished everyone out of the room, though Detective Blythe insisted on stationing an officer outside the door in case Miriam woke up and could speak of the attack. The only person who he allowed in was Matron Lockett to clean Miriam and help dress her in a simple night gown. As Matron Lockett tended to his wife, John said in a low voice, "I must confess, rather cruelly, that I wish she was struck so hard that she has no recollection of her ordeal."

Matron Lockett patted John on the shoulder. "She is stronger than anyone I know."

"Strong enough to survive this violation? Who could?"

"Miriam could."

Matron Lockett had meant it as a kindness, but John was angered by it. It was not that he did not have any faith in his wife's strength of spirit or mind. It was that she shouldn't *have* to survive this. Miriam shouldn't be here - lying in this bed - stripped of her consciousness and her safety. John actually feared for her to wake, having to cope with her injuries, the loss of her child, and the memories of the attack. There was more anguish to come. At least in her sleep, she could have some peace.

When John did not respond, Matron Lockett left him alone.

The night had melted into the day which brought forth its own horrors. In the bright light that streamed from windows overhead, John could see the true extent of Miriam's injuries. More bruises had appeared over her arms and face. Her left eye was swollen shut. He took it upon himself to examine the rest of her, finding more random cuts on her crotch and thighs. Black and purple bruising covered her stomach and right side. Incensed at the wretched display, John applied ointments and bandages gently before tucking her back under the blankets. She did not stir but breathed deeply.

She had not awoken by midday when Detective Blythe had come by with new information. John took him outside, worried that any word of the crime would cause Miriam to wake in distress. Detective Blythe, the stout, clean shaven man, said gruffly; "We got a statement from a bangtail in exchange for her safety. There's been some other witnesses, including your Dr Jenkins. We've pieced together some culprits and some kind of reason, I guess, as to why… well… as to why it transpired in the first place…"

Listening to the bilious story, the details of what had happened to his wife and why Miriam was targeted, caused a dizziness to come over John. It was far more gruesome than he ever thought. By the time Detective Blythe had uttered the villain's name, a switch of electricity surged through John. Something changed – John's soul twisted darkly within him. A blinding wrath came over the once kindly doctor as Blythe said "Harry Wright."

It was a name that John had heard plenty of times since meeting Miriam. She would often pace through their home or in his office, yelling wildly about the scummy man and all his deeds. She'd lament about his stranglehold on the women of Soho. She'd wish that she could destroy him and take those women away from his clutches. John had listened to her rants and raves and comforted her. Yet he never thought that she was in danger. He should've known better. John should've known that one day Miriam's frustrations would boil over, and she would find herself in Harry Wright's path and now within his wake.

Guilt followed the rage. For the slightest second, he had blamed her for the attack. How could he? Miriam was only protecting her friend and was tricked into that violent courtyard. The remorse became further fuel for what was beginning to fume inside of him.

As Blythe went to leave, he said to John; "We shall not rest until Wright is caught and strung up, Dr Bennett, you have my word."

That sentence caught on the thorns of John's anger. He turned caustically to Detective Blythe and said through gritted teeth,

"Why have you not apprehended this m… ma… monster already, Detective?"

There was an awkward shuffle from the Detective as he looked down at his feet. "He's fled, Dr Bennett. But we're looking over the whole of Lon— Dr Bennett?"

It was not long before the Detective's words were merely an echo down the corridor. John did not think about him. He did not think on all those familiar pitying faces that watched as he angrily raced by. He did not think about the cold breeze of winter as he ran ragged out the hospital. He did not think of the shouts and bellows from people he bumped into or the loud chatter of the alleyways and streets. He thought nothing about the pub he now faced as it loomed over him. He could only think of Miriam. There was no hesitation as he pelted through the doorway of The Furnace.

The angry slam of the door caused most people in the near-empty pub to jump. John stood in the doorway. He breathed heavily as adrenaline raced through him. He looked at the faces of the small number of patrons, wondering which man or woman amongst them had helped Harry attack Miriam. Whose hands had laid theirs on her? Everyone looked at him curiously, all except a tall, big, muscly man at the bar.

"Can I be of some assistance?" came a voice from the lowly bartender over murmurs.

"I am looking for Harry Wright." John said, neither forceful nor quiet. Just in a matter-of-fact manner as though he were conducting business.

"Forgive me, sir. We ain't seen Harry." The bartender said nicely enough.

Yet this angered John; "Do not take me as a fool, man. I demand to see Wright!" John quickly paced over to the bar and slammed his hands upon the counter, causing the bartender to jump. For a flash, John remembered himself and remorsefully looked at the youngish worker. This type of rage did not usually suit him. Every second, however, it made its home. John was about to make some sort of apology when he was grabbed by the collar.

"Oi!" said the huge man with short brown tufts of hair. "He said Harry ain't here, alright?"

John was then thrown to the ground. He sized up his opponent, wondering if this was the man that witness said was with Harry. Did those hands that grabbed him also touch his wife? The thought churned in him, and he scrambled to his feet. His hand clenched, ready to fight but as soon as he noticed the stature of the man before him, John thought better of it. There were many eyes upon him. He glanced around the room as the patrons of the bar stared at him - men and women - all muttering under their breaths. Their stares as scathing as their whispers. Not knowing what to do, he glowered at the assailant before him.

"Very well," John whispered. "But this is not the last you shall hear of me."

Walking out of The Furnace, John now had a dark fire within him.

Sitting back alone beside Miriam, John was in a haze. He had not slept since the day before and he had barely eaten. There was no urgent need to do either, but the lack of them both coursed through him. With the earlier confrontation still heating him inside, John was not tired either. He just sat and mulled over his thoughts.

As the clock struck exactly seven, John heard a murmur beside him. His heart thudded in his chest with a frightful anticipation. Miriam was waking up. Dropping to his knees, he clung to her good hand. She could only open her right eye and she was still disorientated. As she blinked and blinked again, she saw him kneeling beside her, kissing her hand with all the love that he could muster. There was a slight smile at the sight of him.

"John?" she said in a raspy, quiet voice. Yet within moments it was clear that the pain and the memories were flooding her senses. "Forgive me."

With that, Miriam began to shake with tears. John climbed onto the bed and held her in his arms as together they sobbed, and sobbed, and sobbed.

Matron would find them both asleep together by the next morning.

Chapter Ten

Friday 21st August 1896

What foul trickery.

What a turn.

What lurid temptation have you dangled so precariously in front of me, God?

It has been mere days since I abandoned all thought of completing my work, for fear that I was losing control and losing myself. I walked away from the knife. I pledged that I would do better – that I would use my life to continuing doing good. To help the needy and not smite them from this earth. That I would learn to forgive and heal and move forward into the goodness of the light.

Michael and Adelaide were a tragic loss. I spent days after tortured by the thought of their bodies and their babe now alone in this world. I expected the crushers to storm my own home and take me to the gallows. I nearly implored them to, hoping that if I swung, I would be made pure and chaste again. Yet the robbery ruse prevailed. They looked at the slums and the petty thieves instead of those close by. It only added to my guilt.

The news of their deaths wailed through the halls of the hospital.

Who could do such a thing? To such kind people? To such lovely people? What an outrage! What a tragedy!

Did they speak about us in that manner? If so, I could not bear it!

I must admit that the first deaths had not made their way to my home. At least, we did not speak about them. I wondered if my love had known. That they knew this of me. We had known of the darkness within us – raging through and around us – but does my love know I have committed a sin? That I have murdered? This I do not know.

When the news broke about Michael and Adelaide, we wept for hours in each other's arms as we did that dreadful night in April. Knowing that I had brought more pain into this household still broken and sore from the last undoing further made me wish to give up the knife.

Now days before their funeral, you show me a sign.

Oh, Holy Spirit, how you have listened to my words and my deeds, and my misgivings and you have… blessed me? You have praised me. With this one act, you have shone your holy guide and given me a sign that the work must be finished.

For I have finally found Harry Wright.

I did not think the bartender would recognise me as I approached him in the poor ward. I was asked to examine his broken hand. He could not look me in the eye as I silently poked and prodded at him, his face practically beetroot as I stared.

There was something familiar in the injury – an echo of recognisable boot tracks and the pain they caused. The reminder burned in me. I breathed raggedly, tightening my lips as I said; "The bones need resetting, that is all. Who did this to you?"

I had grown used to pained silences but this one suffocated me. The bartender looked through me as though I were air as his features turned pale and frightened. He said nothing so I repeated the question with more force, trying not to spook the man with the anger rising in my chest. Still gripping his injured hand, I said; "Was it him? Has he returned?"

The bartender again said nothing, and it infuriated me. I gave his broken hand a hard squeeze. He exclaimed loudly before I dropped it from my grasp. I straightened myself and whispered; "Fine, I shall get a nurse to help you, seeing as you are refusing to help me."

I took only five steps away from the man before a quite revelation fell from his lips. An admission so shocking that it curdled the air. I nearly didn't catch it as he whispered, "He never left."

Oh, those foolish flatfoots. That asinine Detective Blythe. Harry Wright had been hiding in plain sight, like a rat crawling into its secret hole, biding his time until he saw it fit to resurface.

I wonder if my bloodshed seeped through the floorboards of The Furnace and covered him in fear. Did he bear witness to my becoming?

Oh, it does not matter now.

The possibility for glory is just within my reach. Lord, you have now bound me to this quest. In your almighty judgement, I therefore serve you. I… am Ragual. I am your angel of retribution.

I shall unsheathe my sword soon and sever the head of Harry Wright clean from his shoulders. Oh, how I wish that I could mount him on my mantelpiece as a reminder to all those who seek to do harm against my family.

Take this as my credence, as God is my witness, the days of Harry Wright are numbered. He will meet my knife.

And my work shall, at last, be done.

Sunday 23rd August 1896

The door had become a beast.

Bright sunlight streamed through the panes of glass creating square shapes on the floor in front of her. Miriam traced the edges with her eyes, counting them over and over again. They loomed maliciously, like the nasty teeth of a demon waiting to gobble her whole. The chatter of the street outside roared in her mind, distorted, and twisted. She thought about the lives that flitted through the city, unaware of this cage that she was now in; trapped by an invisible ghoul that only she knew was there.

Sighing deeply, she clung to the banister as she sat on the bottom few steps. Her breathing and thoughts were wild and unruly. She tried to steel herself and build up the courage to face the door. Every so often, she would try to will her body to move but it would not. Even worse was the times it did. A strange adrenaline caused her to stand and yet mere seconds later, she would find herself sitting back down on the steps.

The black bustle dress she wore constricted around every inch of her and she had an itch to strip it off. There was an ache to rip all of her garments to shreds. Then, when she was naked, she'd twist and tear-off her flesh and lay there as mere bones. Peace at last. All she could do, at the very most, was to remove the black, veiled hat and hold it in her hands, trying her best not to cry.

This was a new sickening routine in her life. She had finally edged herself out from the guest room and she should be proud of making it this far. Yet that blasted door mocked her. Dread and shame consumed her heart. What feeble creature had she become? A shadow of herself in black, frozen in time by that memory. Trapped in the walls of her mind.

It had been over four months since that dreaded night. Miriam had returned home from the hospital a day after she had woken.

John had witnessed too many youthful nurses peeking, and though there were well-meaning visitors, they sadly offered little comfort. Therefore, he insisted that he would continue her care privately. The world was just too exhausting for her. The pain just too raw to be consumed over and over again by curious eyes. Her wounds would never heal whilst they were teased and tickled by gossip and whispers.

Miriam, however, refused to be stationed in their marital bed. The horror would surely seep into the linen and stain the happier times they had shared there. To any other man, the request would've seemed silly, but John empathised. Even as broken as she was, John still understood her.

Confined to her new lodgings, in the small guest room below their bedroom, Miriam would often wonder if he could feel her pain like she could feel his. John had said nothing on the matter, and spent his time tending her wounds, both physical and psychological. But she knew that there was anger and hurt and shame within him too. Though he'd never look at her or treat her differently, she could sense it all around him.

After all, Miriam could read John like a book, and he was the only one to understand her. That special connection that lovers have. A deep, dark way within them. Somehow, they both knew that it was some sort of hopeful beacon. A lighthouse through the violent ocean that ebbed around them.

There were tough and bleak days ahead. The aftermath was already filled with them. The visit of her father and her aunt proved too much for anyone to bear. The usually refined Sir Fredric had apparently broken down the minute he heard word of her attack. When he saw Miriam the first time, Sir Fredric tried his best to keep his composure, as Aunt Isobel clung desperately to his hand, her lips thin and tacit. Yet Miriam could see the heartbreak in their eyes. Upon their leaving, she heard her father's angry cries as they rung out in the halls of her home and heart.

Over time, some of the physical injuries healed: The swelling in her eye became a bruise which then disappeared within a month. There was a scar on her cheek from where the cane had hit it repeatedly. It reflected the one on her shoulder from her uncle. A fine collection from brutish men who wielded their iron fists, taking their power and stripping women of their own. Her ribs, which were fractured after she was repeatedly kicked, had taken weeks to heal and made it hard for Miriam to move. Especially with the broken hand and her dizzying head wounds. She was bed bound physically until early May.

After that, it was no longer due to the injuries. Miriam simply could not move from her bed, even when flowers began to bloom, and the spring sunlight began to descend. She had made a hollow home in her confinement because she was in a different type of agony. The attack repeated through her in waves, descending on her time and time again.

The loss of her unborn child was particularly gruelling. Having her baby bled from her in such a cruel manner had left her deeply despondent. She said few words on the subject and eventually, the tears dried up.

That wasn't the only loss she suffered. For a while, she could not admit to anyone, or herself, of what had gone from her very being, stripped away from her make-up. It was a realisation brimming with absolute anguish. She could not face it.

By the end of May, and with much encouragement from John, Miriam had finally placed her two feet on the wooden slats of the guest room. Her legs were weak from lack of use, and she would pad around the room like a young animal finding its bearings. It would take another week for her to be confident in her strides and to not crawl back to the safe comfort of her bed.

With this new scope, Miriam could finally wash by herself and get dressed in something other than her nightgown. The first time was supposed to be special. At the beginning of June, with Adelaide's help, Miriam had arranged a special tea for John when he had returned from work – his first day back in nearly two months. Miriam was determined to showcase her progress and her independence. However, she had not expected the impact of opening the wardrobe.

In the light summer's evening, John returned from the hospital to find a fire raging. As he closely inspected the strange occurrence on such a warm day, he found several orange garments in the flames. Still in her nightgown, Miriam pretended to be asleep but could hear the wisps of pity and sorrow on his tuts and sighs. She squeezed her eyes closed, listening to him grab the poker as he stoked the fire further.

Miriam would eventually surprise him two days later. In fact, it was a day where she felt less like a ghoul and more like herself. She awoke with a strange sense of being. Excitement sparked within her. These moments came in fleeting fragments, so she grabbed hold of it eagerly, keen to not let it slip through her fingers. Dressing in a simple white blouse and black skirt, she sat patiently and waited for him to get home.

Then it was as before. They conversed, they laughed, they flirted. John illuminated her with nonsensical hospital gossip and new surgical practices. There was a flicker of normalcy, and both were equally excited that Miriam seemed much better in her mind. They did not talk of the incident, but they did speak of upcoming adventures they could have: Trips to the beach, wine in the country, and more.

When the night drew black, Miriam sensed a long-forgotten urge in herself. She kissed John genuinely and pulled him to the bed with her. He hesitated as she lay down, but gripped with lust, she whispered her permissions.

Upon her word, John climbed on top of Miriam.

This stalled all breathing within her chest. As John leaned down to kiss her, all she could see was that brute. It was as though she were back there on the cold, cobbled stones with every restraint holding her down and every blow raining hard upon her. She could even smell him, that mixture of tobacco, ale, and gin. That overpowering aftershave. It was all around her.

Instantly, Miriam wanted to be sick. Panicking, she cried out for John to stop and, somewhat roughly, pushed him off her. She sat up gasping for air, undoing several top buttons of her blouse and placing a hand on her chest as though she were calming her breathing.

There it was. The other great loss of Miriam's. Harry Wright, in raping her, had taken away her confidence and taken over her cognisance. She could not close her eyes without seeing him first. She could not sleep without visions of him. She could not make love to her husband without being sent back to that dark and dank courtyard.

This was the true gravity of the crime. Harry Wright was right. As long as she lived, he would always be a part of her. That thought blackened her soul. In that moment, she wished to throw herself on the fire like the orange garments from before. She knew she would be more at home within the ash.

For the first time since she returned from the hospital, and, indeed, their whole marriage, John did not sleep in the same bed as her. He did not say a word. He climbed off the guest bed and walked out of the room. Miriam knew he was dejected. The slight slam of the door echoed through her. Could John sense it? That a monster occupied her mind, taking up spots where he used to lay? Was that tormenting him also?

By morning, Miriam was pushed back to her motionless state. For the entire day, she would not move from staring out of the window, even when her side ached, and her mouth was dry. It was not until John came back the next night that she'd even stir from that position. He lay still and waited for her to crawl to him. When she did, he simply kissed her on the forehead. The warmth of his chest and the gentle beats of his heart had become her only security.

Despite taking laudanum for the pain, this position became the only way she could go to sleep, as they did in that hospital cot. Listening the gurgles of his stomach or his heartbeat as he'd sigh were like some sort of lullaby. Miriam wished she could tell him that this was all that was keeping her tethered to this world. That without him, she was sure to unravel and tumble into the night sky, floating forever and ever away. Those words seemed hardest to say somehow.

Miriam would always wake from the cruellest of dreams. For most nights, she awoke in John's arms as he slept enveloping her. In some of the heated nights of July, she was startled awake by nightmares and found him reading or writing by the fireplace. A week ago, she found, again, that he was not there at all. It was curious. Sometimes she was thankful. Sometimes it was good to be with one's thoughts and plans. Sometimes they needed to be alone.

When John returned the next afternoon, he came with grave news. Their friends – Michael and Adelaide Jenkins – had been murdered in the night. A robbery gone wrong, the police said, but they were stabbed so viciously that their housekeeper did not recognise them at all.

The couples had become even closer during these dark days. Michael had been a constant support for John whilst Adelaide had been one of the first to visit Miriam when she was strong enough. Their almost daily chat had become a regular occurrence since Miriam's birthday in early May. Especially since, in recent weeks,

John had become more consumed with his work. Adelaide was one of few people who did not treat Miriam any differently or look at her with pitying glances. They conversed and gossiped like they had always done. Even though Adelaide was heavily pregnant, Miriam tried not to be marred by the mournful echo.

However, the last time, over a fortnight ago, Adelaide had finally brought their newly born daughter Eloise to visit. The hope was to comfort Miriam. As she took the baby into her arms, however, the weight of all she had lost overwhelmed her. In throes of sorrow, she had politely and quietly asked the pair to leave.

Miriam did not cry when she heard the news of their tragic passing. John did. He fell apart in her arms.

Now sitting on the bottom stair, Miriam was caught in the dance that had gradually taken her from the bed to the bedroom to the landing to the stairs. She slowly descended them one by one. It was the day of Michael and Adelaide's funeral. Miriam had promised John that she would go. Now that promise towered over her like the door.

It did not help that Harry Wright had disappeared since the attack, evading police for months. That thought also kept Miriam paralysed to the steps. What if she opened the door and he was there, grinning at her with that yellow smile? Miriam closed her eyes, but his face was still there. She could hear him grunting. She could smell his nauseating scent. She could feel him against her.

Miriam struggled to breathe. Placed her forehead on the banister, she gripped it tight, fearful that if she let go, she would collapse. Tears burned as they ran down her face.

The sound of slow steps descending the staircase she sat on caused her to tense up. She suddenly stood up as though a parent were about to tell her off for being silly. Wiping her tears as she attempted to compose herself, Miriam looked away from John as he stood beside her.

"There is no need to hide your sorrow from me, Miriam. This is a dreaded day."

She breathed out whilst stifling the sobs that were lodged in her throat. She clutched onto the veiled hat, still in her hands, scrunching up the material tightly. "More than I realised."

With a gently stroke of her shoulder, John walked down the last couple of steps to the bottom. He turned to her and stepped in the way of the door. Whether he knew it or not, it was like he walked into the mouth of the beast for her. Extending a hand, John said softly: "I shall not leave your side for the entirety of today."

"John… I…" She sighed. How could she explain this? It was not just the memories and the thought of Harry Wright's bilious smile. No one had seen her since the hospital. She was terrified of their pitiful glances and heated whispers. She was no longer Miriam Bennett – the pushy, big-mouthed daughter of their founder. She was Miriam Bennett – the one who was raped and disgraced. Though John or Adelaide would never have said it, Miriam feared that she was being scorned and whispered about. She could not bear their words for she knew that they blamed her. That being so tempestuous had caused Harry's wrath. That being a cocksure woman was a glutton for this type of punishment. That being who she was had led to her own destruction. For the first time in her life, she feared their judgement. How could they not be thinking that of her? That's what she thought of herself. She sighed again. "John, I am not going."

John blinked. He did not take down his hand. If anything, he leaned it closer to her. "Miriam, fear not, I am here. We shall do this together."

"John, forgive me…" Miriam took a step back up the stairs. "This day… I cannot. It is unbearable."

"Miriam…" Since her incident, Miriam knew that John was keeping a lot of his frustrations at bay. There was an agitation – an anger – within him that he wished her not to see. It was not a wrath intended for her but one that centred around her. He had been so patient and so considerate. However, now as he looked at her, the vexations flashed in his eyes. The last of his calm resting in the palm of the hand that he extended to her. "Miriam, you promised me." Another pitiful beat. "I need you."

"I know, I know, I know." Miriam replied in a flustered whisper. Another step backwards. "But I cannot do this. Please do not make me."

John breathed out of his nose quickly. He put his hand down and wiggled his fingers. It was clear that he could not look at her for fear of what he would say next. Instead, he walked into the open living room beside them, and over to the drinks trolley by the door. John poured himself a glass of whisky. It was gone in a flash. She tentatively hovered on the stairs. "John, do not be mad with me."

"I am not mad with you Miriam." He said, pouring and finishing another glass. "I am not… mad… with… you."

"But you are angry?"

"Of course, I am angry! I am LIVID!" John slammed his fist down on the trolley, causing the bottles and glass to clank together as though they too trembled with fear. Miriam jumped from the sound. It was the first time she had ever heard him raise his voice this loud. It shook through her as well as the house. "Oh, my darling girl…"

"I'm sorry John."

There was a loud, laborious sigh. He walked back to the bottom of the stairs slowly, taking studious breaths to calm himself down. Though he clung tightly to the glass, he looked her deep in the eyes and said, "Oh Miriam, you never have to apologise to me. It's just… it's just…"

"Everything?"

"Yes." He sat, resigned on the bottom steps where she had been momentarily ago. He loosened the black neckerchief of his suit and then ran his hand through his hair. She sat down a few steps above him, placing the veil on the stair behind her. She held onto her knees out of comfort, afraid that she had enraged him too much and that he wanted to be left alone. Miriam almost silently crawled back to her room so he could wallow in his miserable solitude.

"I understand."

Without looking back to her, John shook his head. As he tilted it back, Miriam knew that he was trying to stem his own tears. "This… blasted day."

The crack in his voice was enough to compel Miriam to shuffle down behind him, her feet by his side. Though she knew he was furious and sad all at once, there was a sea of silent feelings flowing through him. At this very moment, he was lost on those waves. In all their love, it was the first time she could not piece together everything going on in his head. Despite this, she placed a hand on his shoulder to let him know that she was there. "It is more than just this day, is it not John?"

Her husband leaned his head into her lap. Miriam instinctively began to tuck his wavy hair behind his ear to calm him down. He gripped onto her skirt with so much need that it ached within her. Through a jilted breath, he whispered: "Oh how I wish it were not so."

"You know you can tell me anything… and everything."

"The things that I wish to tell you Miriam…" The way he said it was as though he was unravelling slowly. Everything he had held from her was on the precipice of his mouth. On the throne of his tongue sat an unkind man with vicious statements, "… are the things that I dare not to."

Miriam prepared to be beheaded by his words. "I fear if we are not to speak of it now, it shall be the poison that kills us." She swallowed as gentle tears came. "Above all things, I do not wish this."

There was a deep and unnerving pause. Then John stood up. She looked at him, somewhat surprised that he said nothing. He did not move from the step. Instead, he downed the remnants in his glass and hesitated. After a second beat, he walked down the rest of the stairs and put the glass back on the trolley. Without glancing at her bewildered face, he grabbed his hat and cape and threw it around him. His cheeks flushed as he said, "I am going to be late."

Miriam stood up. Her heart drummed viciously in her throat. Was he really going to leave her alone like this? The tension that has been created between them descended in the hallway like the thick smog of the city. She could no longer see him. He was clouded in the smoke and noise of the atmosphere. The remnants of what they had said clinging to their skin. Though they were steps apart, she could not reach him. Miriam was frightened that this distance was to become a new hell to face. She said, with a tremor of her heart, "John?"

John froze as he grabbed the door handle. The tension mounting second by second. Without turning around, he said to her quietly; "They were our friends, Miriam."

The door slammed behind him causing Miriam to jump and burst into sobs. She collapsed on the stairs.

And then a book fell from the shelf in the front room.

Chapter Eleven

Sunday 23rd August 1896

It takes a lot to kill a man.

There is so much more than patience and planning. It goes beyond the maniacal need for revenge. There is no rage required – frothing anger that you simply cannot sedate. To murder and get away with the crime, it takes precision and thought. A calm knife that you use to first kill something inside you.

When you decide to kill a man, it starts as a droplet of an idea but grows inside you until you are consumed by the necessity. That goodness you were raised with; the idea of the holy and heaven become meaningless. The part of you that loves the world and wishes to see it evolve for the greater good needs to die. You need to commit a great sin and no matter what reason you may give for your actions; it will always stain you. Like blood upon your fingertips.

Harry Wright had finally killed that part of me. He deserved to die. I could not let another take this man from this world. This was my divine right. My whole purpose. I needed to be the one. No one else.

This world breeds vicious men: rapists, abusers, and murderers all sitting with their unearned power and judgement. I had killed before, but this would take all my strength. Even stepping out of this home to do the deed required a resolve I feared I did not have.

As the night pulled in, I powered myself through the beastly door. I made sure I wore nothing of significance – old clothes and colours that were now baggy on me. I placed make-up on my face to alter my appearance and wore a plain hat. I needed to blend into the shadows. I skulked through the streets of Soho until I faced The Furnace again.

Harry Wright's stench was already in the air. I could smell that wretched scent of gin, ale, and saccharine sweet aftershave. The cold of the night was already settling in for a freezing autumn though summer had yet to leave us. The wind whistled down the alleyways, louder than the chortles and yells of people passing by. The breeze was luring me to him. I kept my movements slow and steady, lest anyone recognise me.

I stood at that pub with a trepidation. The door loomed over me with memories. Did the wood collect history? Did it groan with the weight of its knowledge? Does this entrance know it changed lives and set my world on a path of misery?

I placed a gentle hand on the door and pushed it. I quietly slipped in. I made no fuss. I looked no different from the crowd. I ordered an ale, found a darkened corner, and there, I waited.

I watched him through the bobbing heads. I heard him over the laughter. I felt him through jaunty pub air, through the thick smoke and tinges of alcohol.

Harry Wright.

He who tears people asunder. He sat with new cohorts as though he were untouchable. This wanted man whose previous allies lay six feet under. Dead, because of his deeds. Yet this whole pub protected and hid him. Harry sat in his kingdom with the knowledge that his terror made him invincible.

Not tonight, villain.

My skin itched. I could barely breathe, wishing to strip from these rags and be free of the burden now upon me. I thought about those hands and what they did. I loathed this power he had over me. I shall remove him from this world and my consciousness.

I had to have patience. I nursed my beer and simply watched. My plan required something of me that I feared would be impossible without the libations. See, I had to ignore the hurt and the pain and the demons. I had to infuse myself with an unshakeable steadfastness. I had to become someone new. I finished another beer and stumbled to the bar.

Ordering a round of drinks, I wobbled over to the table holding the glasses in my hand. I bellowed out a jovial cheer and placed the drinks square down on the table. The patrons around Harry matched my jubilant cries. Wright, however, looked me up and down with an unsure gaze. I stumbled as though too inebriated and smiled, saying loudly in toast; "A drunk for the greaaaaaaat Arry Wrrrrrighttttttttt!"

Flashing his foul teeth at me - a grotesque smile that curdled against my resolve - he raised his glass and drank. Then he gestured to those next to him to make room for me. I sat down, delighted. My smile did not waver, even when his arm came around me and pulled me close. "Fanks," he whispered.

I gestured to the waitress for another round for the table. "Drinks are on me tonight boys and girls!!

Another rambunctious cheer! I was one of them now.

Wright had not recognised me. How could he? I was something new to him. I had infiltrated his circle in plain sight. A predator doesn't know when he is being hunted. He is never fearful for his life. He allows prey in without ever thinking that they may too be baring teeth. As long as I paid for drinks...

Over the course of the evening, he drank and drank with me. I'd tell filthy stories and anecdotes and jokes. I even sang a ditty and the pub joined in.

Oh, this deception thrilled me. For I was slowly slipping him his punishment. Second by second, drink after drink, bit by bit, laudanum filled his system.

The night was long. Long enough to test my patience. His friends fell out into the night until it was just me and Harry left at the table. His forehead was buried in his arms in a stupor that many presumed was just the drink. I shook him gently and was met with his grumbles.

The bartender muttered something about him staying downstairs, gesturing with his bandaged hand. I cocked my head from confusion, but the kindly man helped me lift Harry from the table. Together, we walked around the bar, and down the narrow, perilous cellar steps.

The pub basement was nothing of note. Piles of barrels and boxes across blue and white tiles. The walls were covered in light grey bricks. The room itself illuminated only by low gas-lamps. There was nothing to signify that someone lived here. It was cold and damp.

Momentarily, the bartender left Harry leaning against me. The weight of Harry, coupled with his awful stench, made it impossible to breathe. I closed my eyes to strengthen the resolve within me.

I then focused on the other man instead as he walked over to the furthest corner of the room. He then slid over an innocuous barrel and, thusly, revealed a hole and a small set of wooden steps going further down into the basement.

Harry's hiding spot. A rotten room for this rancid rat. It was small, with a rusty, metallic bed, a wooden table that was strewn with papers, and a singular candle to shed light on the hovel. Scum from the streets dripped down the walls. It seemed so simple, yet it had confounded the police.

We threw him backwards against the bed, the springs screaming with his weight. The bartender thought nothing of leaving me alone with Harry. He merely nodded and quickly left the room. Did he know what I was about to do? Or did he think of me as another of Harry's conquests? Even so, I waited until I could no longer hear his footsteps as they walked up the steps and away from the scene.

I took a few deep breaths to rid myself of the fear, then I wandered over to the bed, and climbed on top of him. As I did, Harry grinned and placed his hands on me, without realising what manner of person sat upon him: "My my."

Smiling, I took his hands and forcefully put them back over his head. He giggled as I undid his putrid green necktie, clasped his hands together, before tying and fixing them to the bed frame.

"Ow gerrofme. Whatchadoin'?"

From my pockets, I dug out a familiar piece of rope. Harry groaned as he still struggled underneath me, his eyes flickering from the poison. I held fast and tied his feet to bottom of the bed. He wriggled again but it was no use. This was my realm, and I was the master.

There was a titillation inside me. It mixed with the wrath and shame. Yet it would not stop me. If anything, it added heat that fired through my system. I punched him in the face to stop him from wiggling against his restraints. I then punched him again for myself. Then again and again and again. He moaned in pain.

I grabbed the rest of the laudanum and laughed. I pulled the top off with my mouth. Then I aggressively squeezed his mouth open.

I poured and poured and poured. He spluttered and choked and tried to spit it out. However, I clamped my hand over his mouth and pinched his nose, so he had to swallow.

Flailing his arms, he tried to fight but in his addled state, he was weak. It was an effective drug and he had consumed so much of it already. He fought to no avail. His muscles dead. He was bound to my will. I had stripped him of his power. And I willed him death.

His eyes began to bulge in terror. I removed my hat, and then wiped the make-up from my face to truly reveal myself. I pinched his cheeks as his mouth frothed, leaning down I whispered: "I want you to see this. I want to watch the life drain from you. And most of all, Harry Wright, I want you to know that was I who killed you."

He went limp against me. Dead. I had done it. At last.

Underneath me, Harry Wright looked pitiful and pathetic. How dare this filth occupy me. I removed his restraints, removed myself from his corpse, and removed the control he had on my soul.

For a short while, I stared at him until I remembered myself and staged the crime. I forged a suicide note – a confession, announcing his guilt as the Soho Slayer. I carefully dropped the bottle to the floor, as though it rolled from his cold, lifeless hand.

I took one last look at my villain, decaying in his destitution, before I gathered my things, snuck upstairs, and then ran out into the night.

There is a strange feeling in my gut. A relief. It is as though I have been holding my breath since that fateful night and I can finally let it go. A peace washes over me in a quiet jubilation. Though I am rife with melancholy, and sorrow is still embedded in me, I can at last begin to heal. Without that villain in this world, my spirit can finally rest, and I can take new steps forward. I long to skip away from this tormented, shadowed past.

My goodness, my heart still races within me. This pounding in my chest. A rhythm of fear and exhilaration. I shall not forget the patterns of this pulse. It is almost like I am alive once more. Elated and emancipated from his cruel deeds. I am born again in this moonlight.

Never again shall he bring his violence against another woman. No more shall he stalk these streets. No longer shall he haunt my mind.

Harry Wright has expired.

Yet the work is not done.

Sunday 23rd August 1896

The door had become a beast.

The tinted glass windows shone like the glowing eyes of a demon. John hesitated as he walked up the stone steps to his home. The street around him was quiet as though it were in silent judgement. He heard nothing. No voices came from the homes around him. No laughter from the public houses. No echoes of the night. The world had paused around him; frozen in time whilst he wavered on the steps. For John, it was though he was ascending into the mouth of Hell.

A momentous feeling descended upon him. One he had had before. For it was not a doorway to his home anymore but a precipice. The point of no return. A threshold in which his entire life could unfold and tumble into ruin. As he neared the door, a breath caught in his throat. A blinding fear ripped through him, and he leaned his head upon the wood of the monster which mocked him.

John regretted walking out on Miriam in the manner that he had, but his remorse extended beyond their argument this morning.

After the funeral and the wake, he walked for a long time throughout the city. He retraced old haunts and remembered familiar places; some he had visited long before he met Miriam Clayton. He even visited the hospital when it was cloaked in the dark of a late evening. He slipped secretly through the wards of the wailing wounded, avoided the nattering nurses, and made his way to his office that was now ornery. As he pushed open the door, the hinges moaned with the past and creaked with memories that were as ornamental as the medical bric-a-brac on his walls.

He walked into that office and expected to see Miriam there, her feet perched on the table as she perused through his own medical journal. He remembered the first time he saw her, mightily bounding into a stuffy boardroom with a rambunctious energy as she tried to rally the other men to action. He recollected how her blue eyes sparked with the gaslights upon their first meeting, dazzling with her sordid ideas. John could practically feel her silky skin as he recalled the first time that he ran his hand over her leg.

In his office, he thought of the year that had passed and the way Miriam dizzied him - that rush of air that came with her, whipping around him beautifully. She flew through him like a storm, and he adored the flashes of light and the bellows of thunder. They were more striking than the calm of life he had known before. He reflected on the dull and destitute colours that once decorated his world. How desperate for new ones he must have been.

Now on the doorstep of his home, John contemplated on how the tide had turned. These days of agony and ache burned through him like her eyes once did.

John knew anguish too. For days, he could not help but imagine the hands of that cruel beast, sliding over the flesh of his wife. For weeks, he could not help but be taunted by the child that never was. For months, he watched his wife in a pain that he could not heal. John, too, was defeated and lost in this terrifying aftermath. A shell of himself, yearning for the cure.

How could he tell her this?

It would only deepen her burdens. If Miriam knew he was hurting too, then she would also shoulder that blame. She did not deserve more guilt. But he too had sensed the crack forming this morning, breaking through their once solid foundation. There was a distance between them. They no longer stood on the same side and were chaotically calling to each other across the canyon.

How could he tell her this?

They had both changed so much that their great tapestry had untangled. Their threads undone. There was always a wild darkness rippling through and around them both. Now that darkness had seeped into the streets of London.

Bringing a hand to his mouth, John tried to stifle sobs.

How could he tell her this?

As the summer night produced a cool breeze, and he wavered on the steps of his home, John's thoughts returned to his year with Miriam. He desperately clung onto the moments of their relationship; to their first meeting in his office, to the secrets they shared in the rose garden, to the first time they made love, to their wedding day. He thought on the taste of her lips as he kissed her passionately, the immutable way in which she made him laugh, or the funny manner in which she teased him. He adored their intense nights and bright days. In all his life, John had not felt the strength of love that he had for Miriam. The power of it had unleased something pure and otherworldly within him. Yet throughout it all he still worshipped her – his dark goddess.

Steeling himself, John decided that he would tell her. Everything. Tonight. In hopes that they would cross this new divide together and step forward. Stronger. United. He would tell her everything.

Grabbing the handle and opening the door, John stormed past the beast and entered his home, as he finally was ready to confront whatever hell that awaited.

It had been an hour since Miriam had returned to the armchair in the front room and yet she was still out of breath. Hot and eager with anticipation.

With one hand she clutched a glass of whisky. The other she flexed slowly, trying to quell the pain from her fresh scrapes and bruises on her knuckles. Miriam's eyes were sore as she stared at the fireplace. Yet she did not take her sights off of the flames. She glowered into them, willing the blaze to leap off the wood and finally consume her.

There were many thoughts in her mind, all wayward and wicked. Memories filtered through the heat, taking her back to times even before John, to when she had the ultimate power and control. There had always been a slip of the unnatural about her. Perhaps she belonged in the hellfire to burn forever. A secret emotion settled on her chest and caused her heart to race: Elation.

There was a restlessness in her, and she was eager to see John. Though she was dressed in her cream nightdress and deep purple dressing gown, and had had a few glasses of alcohol, Miriam was not tired. This evening's exultations kept her wide-awake. There was no way she could sleep knowing what she had done. She needed to tell him. Everything. That she was sorry for all that was hurting him so. That she knew what kind of man he had become. That there were dark secrets she also needed to tell. That no matter what happened tonight, she would always love him.

The front door opened, causing her to jump slightly. From her chair, and through the gaping doorway of the front room, she watched him, somewhat hidden. John walked into the hallway and removed his hat and cape. He pinched the bridge of his nose and wiped his eyes as though he had been crying. Taking a long look at the staircase, he breathed in as though he were about to climb a mountain. As he put a foot on one of the steps, she sat up. "John?"

John froze on the step and sighed. Her voice was filled with a heavenly warmth that he didn't deserve. He wobbled before turning to her, brand new tears within his eyes and anguish in his heart. As he faced her, John was surprised that through his sorrow, he was still caught breathless by her beauty. The solitary light from the fireplace fell upon the light brown waves that cascaded beyond her shoulders. The amber tints rolled over her and mischievously shone in her eyes. Miriam looked as she did when they first met, as she did when he first made love to her, as she did before. *My dark goddess.*

Standing up from her chair, Miriam watched as John stayed motionless in the shadows of the hallway. As orange hues of the searing lights reflected in the tears still sitting silently in his eyes, her heart longed for him. She reached out her hand.

Across the darkness, in that timeless space, the pair wordlessly called for one another. In this moment, nothing needed saying. In the beats that ticked between them, they understood each other's torture and torment and trauma. All they wanted was to be united. Forever and ever. Two lovers as one against all of life's cruelties.

John rushed forward; through the threshold, across the precipice, and over the distance that they had created. He ran and embraced her. As he wrapped his arms around her, Miriam sighed softly. She never wanted to leave this moment and urged the night to help her melt into him. John shook and sobbed against her; her husband had come undone. It caused her own tears. He gripped her tightly. As they held onto one another, they ached and feared and cried and moved together. Finally, they were one again, without monster or man, friend or foe, God, or the Devil, tearing them apart.

A freshly found familiar feeling flourished within. Miriam was first to let go but only because she wanted to kiss him. Gently, she lifted her hand to his face and then placed her lips on his cheek. He smiled weakly in the touch. Tears fell, and she brushed them away with her thumb. There was a pause before she kissed his lips, deeply and with all the love that she could muster. John mirrored it and pulled her against him. A refuge in his embrace. It was as though they were kissing for the first time and the last time all at once.

Breathlessly, they stopped, and Miriam took a slight step back. John wished not to let her go, dragging his fingertips down her arm before he took her hand in his. The action caused her to panic, as his quizzical eyes glided over her new lacerations. Yet there were no recriminations, instead he reached into his jacket pocket and removed a handkerchief, licking the cloth, before rubbing against her cuts. He tended to her wounds as though it were second nature, applying the same amount of tenderness and care that he had done these past, terrible months.

This had given time for Miriam to inspect her handsome husband as he dabbed the dried blood from her cuts. She scanned his pale and soft features, noting that he had lost some weight recently. There were new wrinkles that crawled around his bright blue eyes, which in turn shrouded the darkness that flowed through and around them. He still smelled of lavender and mint, with that familiar puff of chamomile wrapping around her. This man exuded a gentle chaos that, in turn, set off a strange calm within her. Never in her life did she think she'd love someone quite like Dr John Bennett.

When John was done, placing the handkerchief back in his pocket, he kissed her hand before letting her go. Then he watched in awe as Miriam slowly removed her dressing gown. She grabbed the hem of her nightie and lifted it off from her. In two simple moves she was naked in the fire's light. He looked over her, swallowing nervously as he hardened. He could see her quivering. It was not from the cold but from the trepidation. His eyes darted over her breasts and belly and thighs and privates and scars and bruises as shades skimmed over her. There was only one word that he could say to her. "Exquisite."

Miriam smiled softly. As John stayed, drinking her in, Miriam tried to squash her fear that was causing tremors within her. She took that step forward again and knelt down before him. Undoing his trousers, she sprung him free. Taking his cock into her mouth without hesitation, Miriam heard him gasp in joy. He nearly lost balance, but he placed a hand upon her head as she wrapped her free arm around his hips. The other hand followed her mouth as she sucked on him. Miriam had missed the taste of him. She wanted to honour him and thank him. He moaned and gulped.

"No, no Miriam." He suddenly said and pulled away from her. Miriam looked up at him, confused and somewhat hurt that he would stop. She did not move. "This is not what I want." He whispered, bringing her up from the floor, "I wish to praise *you*."

He placed his loving lips upon hers to reassure her. Then he quickly undressed himself, wishing to be as nude as she was. He then kissed her fervently again whilst suddenly lifting her up into his arms. She yelped but wrapped her legs around his waist. Walking just a few steps forward, he knelt down with her and lay her gently back on the rug beside the fireplace. Taking her image in, he took his hands and gently caressed her naked body. Miriam instinctively positioned her legs. There was something trapped in her eyes. An uneasiness. He whispered to her; "Are you OK?"

Miriam nodded but an unexpected tear came out. The dark memories loomed in her mind like stormy weather. John leaned down and kissed her cheek where the tear had run down. He then kissed her neck, her chest, her breasts, her stomach - all over until he found himself at home again between her legs.

Gripping onto her thighs, his tongue began to lavish her wanting spot with overdue attention. Slowly, he circled the nerve whilst sucking it in between rotations. Small waves of pleasure began to flow through her, trying to flood the flashbacks that started to seep into her mind. Every time that villain came to her, a small touch from John brushed the image away. John quickened the speed in which he licked at her. Suddenly, Miriam groaned. She had missed this sweetness. This pure joy as it built up inside her. Yet she kept it bridled, caught in her stomach and away from her flesh. As she stiffened, John said quickly, "Let go Miriam."

As he went back to pleasuring her, Miriam heard those words land on her like the smallest feather upon a rickety dam. Its light touch caused her defences to crack and crumble. An orgasm soon submerged her senses. She loudly came against him, arching her back and crying out into the night.

Laughing jovially, John lapped at the new wetness that spread between her slit until she stopped writhing. Then he gently brushed his lips upon her parting once more before emerging from between her legs. She placed a hand on her chest and breathed fast. He leaned over her and kissed her so she could taste herself upon his lips. As he did, his firm penis brushed against her. Despite the ebbs of joy, Miriam suddenly tensed. She closed her eyes and willed the images of that cruel man away.

John kissed her again then leaned his head upon her forehead. "Fear not. It is me. It is John. I am here. I am here always."

Opening her eyes, she saw him. Wholly. The man that she had loved entirely was there - raw and ready to complete her once more. He shone within the fire's light as though he had descended from the heavens to save her. An angel, a saviour, a beacon of hope. She wished to touch his halo and allow him to bathe her in all things divine. The need took over her and fought against the memories. She stroked his cheek as though she were touching the holy spirit.

"May I?"

"Yes John, you may."

John positioned himself at her opening. He entered her steadily as a wordless praise-filled moan fell from his lips. She let out a cry that was both sad and happy, the whirlwind of darkness and light cascading through her mind. His breathing was slow and soft in admiration. This was all he ever wanted – to be inside of her once more, in absolute completion.

In that moment, they stopped together to enjoy this wholeness. Their newly found unison through the distance and the darkness. Enveloping themselves in each other's arms, they were connected by body and soul - just holding onto this moment.

After a few beats, he began to move inside her. To John's surprise, she matched his movements and bucked her hips with his. Making love together beside the fireplace restored a goodness within them. Every thrust into her was a sign of his adoration. Every gasp from her lips was an ode to her worship of him. Their bodies were as close as they could be, their sweat and their skin entangling sweetly.

A switch of electricity rolled through her. Something locked into place. She squeezed her legs against his hips then, using most of her strength, she tumbled them over.

When his back hit the floor, and as he fell out of her, there was a moment of shock. She guided him back in, sliding down on his dick with a glorious whimper. The pair paused for a moment. She giggled and leaned back to the whisky on the table by her armchair. She took a chug. Wincing at the taste, she winked at him, then squeezed his cheeks to pour the liquid into his mouth and down his throat. He spluttered somewhat but she clamped her hand on his mouth and laughed again.

As he swallowed the smoky liquid, John gazed up at her and caught sight of a familiar special bolt ricocheting through her blue eyes. He wished to grab it as he reached up and stroked her cheek with the palm of his hand. She kissed it before she started circling slowly on him, moaning in the motions. Delicately, she glided her hands into his, before she thrust them down on the floor and fastened them tight. She quickened in deep, loving movements.

The queen had returned to her throne again, every action her ruling. She would let no one else take her crown. No one. Not ever again.

This was not going to last as long as they wanted it to. They burned brightly together. John was already building. She furiously kissed him as John began to hasten, deeply pounding up into her. They gasped and gyrated together as he did, moaning and groaning and thriving as one. Ecstasy flowed through Miriam, and she couldn't believe that she was about to climax again.

As she threw her head back, Miriam pressed her hands upon his chest to feel his heartbeat race like hers. John realised that she was as close as he was. Lifting himself up, he wrapped his arms around her, and she wrapped hers around him. Every part of his skin now touched hers and he pushed his eager mouth upon her ravenous one.

They were as united as lovers could be.

In this harmonious rapture, they came together.

As though it were the first time and the last time… all at once.

The morning was beginning to rise. New colours were filling in the day as the darkness was lifted. Miriam had spent the past half an hour watching the robe of night being pulled from her grasp.

No matter how badly she wished the moon to stay aloft her perch or how she willed the sun to stay asleep for a little while longer, the day still came. She had to face the new horrors this dawn would bring.

Spreading her hand out upon the silk bedsheets, happy to be back in her own bed again, Miriam stayed silent for a little while longer and enjoyed the solace of a calm morning.

She leaned her head back against John's chest as he struggled to stay awake. Now reunited, John had lead her up to their bedroom. They did not make love again. Instead of sex, they shared memories and moments over a bottle of expensive whisky. They reminisced on their first meeting exactly a year ago.

They thought on this rampant, fast year with all its fortunes and misdeeds and then looked towards the future. They shared a wish to leave London and to set up a new home in the Manor as their nightmares lay within the city. They spoke hesitantly about future children and how they would grow old on the porch of the refuge, wishing to be buried together in the rose garden. It was silly but, in that moment, their dreams were more important than anything.

Miriam knew better, however. After all, what great tapestry can last in a life like this? What with life's mucky fingers prodding, and poking, and pulling at their stitching? What were they to do with the tatters on the floor? Were they the same threads as before?

What great fire burns forever?

What divine union survives such hell?

By now, they were exhausted and spent like the discarded whisky bottle which had rolled underneath the bed. Miriam turned inwards to him, placing her cheek upon his chest, and sighed. John felt her serrated emotions skim his skin; all that sorrow and joy in that breath… that breath… that breath. But

John could no longer pull his thoughts together. He murmured, disappearing in and out of himself.

As he groaned, Miriam listened to his slow heartbeat, taking in every sense of him. He clumsily placed his arm around her and kissed her top of her head. She lay against him, safe and loved, and whispered, "You were right John."

"Hmmm?"

"I *am* yours." Miriam curled herself further into him. "I will always be yours."

She did not cry, staring into the unknown future that now lay at the end of the bedroom. She said not one word more. Instead, she listened to that beat she had grown to cherish.
That beat.
That   beat.

That   beat.

That   beat.

That   beat

That

Chapter Twelve

Monday 24th August 1896.

I have always been drawn to the fire.

It is the one thing in nature that mirrors me somehow - beautiful and dangerous all at once.

Its power is unlike anything I have ever known. It rampages, destroying nature and humanity. The destruction and devastation that it brings is feared by all. This city - which was built on sweat and flames - was nearly destroyed by the Great one. Fire haunts a good man's soul – fear of eternal damnation in the pits below is always fuelled by the fear of excruciating pain.

The terror.

Oh God the terror.

Yet it is exquisite, is it not?

It practically dances on wicks. It moves with crimsons and ambers and golds. A beacon in the black. The dead of night alive once more. It gives us power, lighting our homes and our stages. It propels our trains. It is magical and bewitching. It is man's greatest discovery.

It also cleanses. A home unduly set alight and consumed by the raging force of fire could be the new beginning one has looked for. It could sterilise the filth and dirt. It could purify a tortured soul.

The duality of the flame. I had this inside me all my life. A powerful horror. A beautiful terror. An engulfed darkness.

It must end. It must. It cannot burn for long.

I know what needs to be done. I know that there is one more person who cannot escape judgement. But I am scared. I do not know if I have the mettle to do this.

Though not innocent, I know this person acted out of fear and pain. My only comfort in this decaying world. Yet their acts are unforgiveable. *To condemn another to the flames - what kind of person can do this? Can I?*

I want to love wholly and keep being loved wholly. I want to step forward in this light. I want to forget the darkness.

But perhaps to do so, I must plunge into the shadows once more.

Perhaps that is the only way to true salvation.

So, I shall face them.

And bring an end to this chapter.

Sunday 30th August 1896

There was a light already ablaze in Marie's new home before she had gotten there.

Hesitating at the end of the alleyway, Marie braced herself. A chilling gust ripped through her, howling off the stone walls and into her soul. She shuddered. A terrible unease kept her locked on the spot. The cool breeze meant that summer was drawing to a close. The long days were turning into long nights. The freeze was about to settle into Marie's bones. She was facing a battle with the night and another scrabble for warmth, food, and shelter. Winter was approaching and it was particularly cruel to Marie.

Yet this summer had brought its own cruelties. Murder stalked Soho and had killed people she had known, Alice and Rose. At a time, they were good friends of Marie's but the act they had all committed together had made Marie sick to her stomach. After her confession, the police had promised her immunity and safety, and she was scurried away from The Furnace, from Soho, and from the life that she had known. With just the clothes on her back, Marie was placed in a room in Limehouse, so close to the docks you could hear the waves of the river crash against the embankment.

Even knowing how far away she was, shrouded in secrecy, Marie knew that when the murders began, terrorizing the poor streets of Soho, the attacker would find her. Most nights Marie waited with a sickening anticipation, expecting the avenging killer to come waltzing through the door to smite her from this earth.

Perhaps the chill that kept her to the spot was not that of the wind. Perhaps her hesitation in going home was the flicker of the flames in her window. Perhaps she knew that someone was waiting for her return with the fury of all hell about them.

Marie clung onto the shawl that was wrapped around her. She thought about running away, which she could do so easily. If someone was truly in her home, then they had no idea that she was coming. The little window had no face in it. No eyes had seen her in the quiet of the night. She could turn heel and escape the city, drifting away with the current of the Thames.

She was tired, however. Four decades of loss and shame and fear clung to her bones like the filthy rags she wore. Marie no longer wanted to run or hide from her acts. She did not want to skulk in these shadows, weary from men who wished to take everything from her. No more. If absolution and judgement waited with a jagged knife and bated breath, then she would face it. If this were her final moment, then so be it. If it should end tonight, then at least she would have finally been brave.

Holding her head up high, Marie walked slowly down the cobbled alleyway to her front door. For a long time, she had suspected who was killing her friends. The papers say Harry Wright confessed to the murders in his suicide note, and the case was neatly packed away. People had moved on quickly – jumping on the latest ghastly bloody news.

Marie knew better. They were all wrong. Harry Wright, though evil, did not have the intelligence for this cold and calculated campaign. The particular targets were so specific and so entwined with the attack that it could be no other man. The police had done nothing; therefore, rage and vengeance took control.

After Harry's death, she realised that she was next. Marie was the final accomplice. Holding her breath as she placed the key in the lock and turned it, Marie prepared herself to face the assailant head on. Swinging the door open, Marie gasped at the familiar figure sat on her small bed.

"Hello Marie," said Miriam Bennett. There was a twisted way in which she smiled, glowing in the amber hues of the fire. She looked like the Angel of Death – dressed in black lace and silk, with a veil over her face. There was an aura around her. It was almost as though she had walked through the infernal flames and emerged an inhuman creature of the night. Miriam looked as though she were ready to consume. She stayed deathly still on the bed.

Marie swallowed, hesitating in the doorway. This was not the face that she was expecting to see in her room. "Miriam!" She exclaimed, wondering if she should run. The vision she saw had put an unruly fright through her. Her heart raced. "You're here?"

"Please do shut the door Marie, it is a rather cold night and I have just warmed the room." Miriam said with a stiff politeness. "There is a pot of tea brewing."

Miriam extended a hand to the fireplace ominously pointing to the kettle that hung over the flames. Marie nodded and closed the door. The last breeze escaped and caused the fire to roar. Softly, Marie said; "It is good to see you, Miriam."

"Is it?!" Miriam replied. "Why yes, it has been too long, has it not? When was the last time we saw one another?" There was a pause that caused Marie's stomach to fall apart like a dagger had already swung and had pierced her belly. "Oh yes... I remember now."

"Miriam, please, I—"

Miriam interrupted Marie with a single slow hand raise. As if by magic, the kettle began to steam and boil. "Oh good, the tea is ready. I shall get you a cup. Please sit."

Although she tapped the space beside her, Miriam leaped off the bed and grabbed a solitary cup. Quickly, she poured the tea. Marie perched awkwardly at the edge of her own bed, almost as though she was afraid that it was going to gobble her up. Miriam walked over and handed Marie a mug - a small white mug with pink roses painted on it. Miriam took her position back on the bed, sitting as close to Marie as they were on the hospital cot together many months ago. "Thank you." Marie nodded, gratefully; "Are you not having one?"

"Oh no," Miriam said, patting Marie gently on the knee. "This is a special brew just for you. Now drink, it will warm you up. You have only just left the cold."

Marie looked hesitantly in the cup. It looked normal; golden brown with loose leaves floating around the concoction. Lifting it to her nose, it smelled fine. Inviting even. With a small, twisted smile on her face, Miriam watched her so intently that Marie took a small sip, thankfully feeling nothing but the heated liquid flowing through her. "You know," she said afterwards, still inspecting the contents of the cup, "when I saw the light in the window, I expected someone else."

The smile on Miriam's face dropped. "Did you expect my husband?"

Shocked, Marie quickly looked up. Through the black lace, she could see that there was flame alight in Miriam's eyes. It was not just from the reflection of the fireplace. This was rage in all its purity, and it was aimed straight at Marie, causing her cheeks to burn and flush. If Marie lived past this moment, she knew she'd never forget the wrath in those eyes that she once knew to be kind and loving.

Grabbing the hem of the veil, Miriam began to roll it upwards. As she did, Marie could see the scar on Miriam's cheek clearer and shame began to swirl with the tea and terror. Miriam sighed: "Marie, my husband is dead."

Whenever someone has died, no matter how little or well you knew them, there is always a strange silence. It is almost as if the announcement takes all sounds from the room. A momentary void is created as your body tries to react. It happened immediately in Marie's room. The fireplace stopped crackling. The drunk echoes of the streets nearby were stunned into stillness. The Thames wasn't even trickling. There wasn't the usual rhythm of breaths and heartbeats. There was nothing. Just the quiet as Miriam observed Marie's reaction.

The only word that Marie could say to break that silence was "How?"

"A fire," Miriam replied with equally hot words. Then Miriam looked away from Marie and stared beyond her, as though the fireplace beside the bed reminded Miriam of those that consumed her home. "It was terrible really. They suspect that he was drinking and was in a deep slumber and did not realise that his dressing gown had caught a blaze. See, I have been sleeping in the guest room, on the floor below, since the attack. I was arisen by the stench of smoke. When I got to our room, it was too late. It was engulfed. John was already gone."

A tear fell down Miriam's face. She did not brush it aside. Instead, she deftly closed her eyes and allowed more to spill. Breathing in deep, she tried to gain her composure. Marie could tell that Miriam was heartbroken. There had been so much loss in her friend's life already, and now she had nothing. "I am truly sorry Miri—"

"My whole home was gone by midday. All my life and memories now smoke entwined with London's smog. We buried John this morning. My great love." Miriam took another jagged breath. "And as I threw the dirt on his coffin, I could not stop thinking about the part you had to play in the destruction of my life."

There was that icy feeling again, clawing at Marie's insides. The pair stared at each other: One out of absolute terror. One out of absolute malice. Marie could not help but envision her death, over and over again. She wondered when her once friend would rip her from this world. In some sort of plea, Marie said; "Miriam—"

"Drink your tea, Marie, it will get cold."

Putting the cup to her lips, Marie took another sip. As she did, Miriam leaned over and pushed the cup upwards so the entire contents would run down Marie's throat. As the older woman spluttered, Miriam took the cup and filled it again from the kettle. Placing a fresh tea in Marie's hands, Miriam seethed with tones of fury and sorrow; "What wickedness had I ever done? To be held down against my will and outraged in such a cruel manner? For my unborn child to be torn from my womb? For my body to be sullied and my mind to be spoiled forevermore? Hmm? What wickedness had I done, Marie?"

Marie tried to conceal her own tears from Miriam, but she couldn't help it. She started to sob into her hand. "Forgive me, Miriam, please forgive me," she said repeatedly through her fingers.

"I have lost my child, I have lost my home, and I… I have lost John." Miriam said, closing her eyes because the grief and sadness had become too much. For the first time, Marie noticed that Miriam had in her hands a navy, silk, neckerchief. She clung onto it for comfort. With a visceral gasp, as though she were pooling what was left of her strength, Miriam continued; "But what is worse is that I lost myself, Marie. Every single component which made me was twisted and reshaped on that ghastly night. My whole mettle destroyed. A pathetic creature crawling in the dirt. No, more than that, I became the ash, yearning to be swept away to nothing. And that was the true crime."

Taking an unprompted gulp of tea, Marie had resigned herself to her fate. She willed herself to stop crying and accept whatever justice Miriam was going to enact. She took another gulp, and the mug was empty.

"Tell me, Marie." Miriam had hushed to barely a whisper as she went and got the kettle, pouring Marie another tea. "Do believe yourself unforgiveable? That you deserve to die tonight?"

There was a beat. "Yes, I do."

"Very well." Placing the kettle on a nearby table, Miriam said; "But before this ends tonight, I wish to tell you a story. It is about a diary. One that I found not too long ago…"

A book fell from the shelf in the front room.

There was a slight bang as it fell to the wooden floor which caused Miriam to jump and immediately stop crying. She leaned her head to see where the sound had come from and saw the black book on the floor.

Miriam had not gone into the living room for four months. She had never passed the stairs. Yet the black book, lying discarded on the floor, called to her. It was an unusual sensation. Perhaps curiosity took over her. There was a gnawing sense that this book was a sign. It was as though the house, which had become her prison, was giving her a message.

In seconds, and without a second thought, Miriam was already walking over to where it lay. Picking it up, she brushed it down. Her heart pounded. This book could tell her secrets that John dared not. As she flipped over the cover, she was sadly disappointed. It was just a medical book. She flicked the pages. It had nothing of note between them. Sighing, she tried to slide it back onto the shelf.

However, she found it did not go all the way back. Furrowing her brow, she slid it back out and tried again. Still, the black book teetered on the edge perilously that it was no wonder it fell off.

"Hmmm," she said with a slight frustration. Her emotions were too spent for her to care about such a trivial matter. Yet she knew that it would nag at her. Peering at the books, she noticed that they all were poking out by a couple of centimetres. She looked within the gap that the black book had created. A red colour caught her eye. It was different from the usual brown wood of the shelves. There was something blocking the books from sliding all the way back.

Soon, Miriam was removing all the books, placing them carefully on the floor so she could put back the secret without rousing suspicion. A foreboding feeling flowed through her, enough to make her forget the argument. Even as the remnants of tears stuck to her face.

The culprit was revealed.

A deep red, leather-bound, book.

Miriam had forgotten about this journal. As she held it in her hands, she remembered how thrilled she was selecting it from the shelves of the stationery store. As the memory filtered through her, Miriam clung on to how excited she was then. The way she wanted to present her gifts to John. The way she wanted to reveal her news. The way she wanted to shower him with adoration. That is what she desperately hoped to remember. The way she was – jubilant and wickedly in love.

She clawed at the memory dreadfully. The rest of the day soon seeped back into her consciousness as though she were not allowed a singular moment to forget. Miriam carried on, in spite of this, and opened the journal to see the front page where she announced…

It was gone. Torn. Viciously. Miriam fingered the tears, wondering how long it took him to rip the page from the binding. Immediately? Recently?

John had still used the diary, however. Without turning the pages, Miriam knew they were weighted with ink. She closed her eyes and wavered. Miriam knew John was burdened with his own loss and pain. He too was so profoundly wounded and hurting. Yet he had not said anything to her. Out of a kindness, she suspected, to not affect her trauma further. A guilt panged inside her. She couldn't help but be remorseful that she was not there for him. In her hands, however, lay all his thoughts. Concerns which consumed him so much, and he was so troubled by them that he hid them from her.

Miriam knew it was wrong, but she wished, more than anything, to lift the fog that had descended upon this house. She started to read:

I write this in the hope that I may be purged of my sins.

A confession before God.

I pray for absolution for my crimes.

For my intent is true and just and that should surely prevail.

This was not the mournful diary of her grieving husband that she had expected. This was maniacal rantings. This was the brutal and bloody admissions of a madman. Each entry revelled in gruesome, gory slayings. As the diary went on, the details became more vicious and crueller. The book described recent murders: Alice Haddon, Rose Steel, Paul Hobart and…

"Oh God! Michael and Adelaide!"

It was all in John's hand. A hot flush pounded through Miriam. Drumming filled her head. She did not know what fuelled it. This was a different kind of dread, a new kind of fright. Her hands were like ice, but her face was on fire with distress. Her breaths were short and sharp.

Had the man Miriam loved, more than anything in this world, truly committed such heinous acts?

In her belly was an absolute fear – pure and naked and wretched. Those words had transformed John from the quiet yet passionate man she knew into something else. The thing about absolute fear in all its splendour is that it came with exhilaration and excitement.

A name throughout the diary was most prominent – Harry Wright. A book of madness all for a streak of vengeance.

As soon as Miriam read the last entry, and realised that her villain had never left London, she dropped the diary to the ground.

When Miriam finished her story, Marie's eyes had gotten heavier. Leaning against the metal frame of her bed, she struggled to stay awake. The vision of Miriam blurred in front of her as her breathing got heavier. At this point, Marie was tired. Too tired to cry. Too tired to scream. Too tired to fight. Too tired. As Miriam grew quiet, Marie sighed and said in a mumble; "So it *was* John after all?"

"Yes, Marie," Miriam said in a matter-of-fact way. "John was the killer."

"I thought as much," Marie replied in a drawl. She closed her eyes, and this time kept them shut. Miriam leaned forward and put an arm around Marie, gently nudging the woman into her lap. In between conscious states, Marie allowed it, curling up against Miriam as a child would.

Miriam began to tuck strands of red hair behind Marie's ear as she did before with John when he lay in her lap. It was all the comfort she could muster. Breathing heavily, Marie had fallen into a deep sleep. Miriam voice broke as she whispered, "I forgive you Marie."

Mulling over her thoughts, Miriam paused. She enjoyed the soft inhalations of Marie and the crackle of the fireplace. Even the distant voices of the streets nearby offered her some contentment. A wind howled down the alleyway, Miriam thought on how autumn was fast approaching. It made her hopeful. The upcoming season meant death and ending but only so new life could blossom from it. The darker nights, the chilling freeze, and the brown leaves all beckoned Miriam to come lay a weary head and purge herself of this life.

Breaking this tranquillity with a momentous murmur, Miriam said, "My John did terrible things and became a murderer. But I killed John. Just as I killed Harry. Just as I killed my uncle so many years ago. A little slip of laudanum in their drink and they all drifted off into a slumber no one could wake from."

Taking a moment to listen to Marie's breathing as it slowed, Miriam stared back at the fireplace and addressed it as though she were confessing to the devil. "See, if there is one thing in this world that I abhor most is entitled men who wield their power ruthlessly against others. I did not shelter blame for anyone but that disgusting creature Harry Wright. Yet John stole the lives of those poor women and even friends we held so dearly. He did so in my name and with my pain." Miriam did not blink, not even as heat and light began to make her eyes sore. "So, I set alight to the life I knew and cherished. I burned my heaven to the ground. I no longer belonged in it. What I wish for you Marie is that you can find your own peace, somehow. Tomorrow, both you and I will be miles away from this terrible place and all its miserable memories."

Miriam inhaled deeply and then listened to the breaths of her

friend.
The breaths
The   breaths

The   breaths.

The   breaths.

The

Epilogue

Friday 3rd October 1896

My dearest

It has been a long time since I wrote you a letter.

Do you remember the notes I used to slide underneath your office door in those first few days? All those cunning details of how we would unite in body and soul?

I was thrilled to have met my match. Someone who would meet my words with similar passions. I never believed in soulmates until you startled me that night.

When we finally united, there was no need to write them anymore. The words you wanted to say clung to the taste of you. The sentences I could sprawl on pages rolled down your back in my wilting breaths. Our bodies spoke the notes – each motion was a verb, each thrust a noun, each calculated movement of pleasure were like sonnets that Shakespeare would be envious of.

No, I had no need for letters, not when I had you most nights and days.

Only a couple of months have passed since I said goodbye to the city that I called home, to all the monsters that still crawled in the thick fog, and, finally, to you - my great love. You.

London had become a tomb long before you died. It could not bring me to life in the same manner anymore. I had to leave it all behind – the world that crumbled to dust.

Yet even now, you followed me home. After all, here in the Manor, so far away from where I buried your body is where I truly found you. Where we united in that unbridled ecstasy. Where we blossomed as one. Where we professed our love for one another and pledged to spread ourselves across eternity.

We vowed ourselves to one another exactly a year ago in this place. Can you remember how much it rained on that day? The way it landed so blissfully on our bodies as we made love in the dark. We joked that the turbulent weather was punishment for our wicked and sordid ways. Yet throughout the thick clouds and thunder roars, we promised that we would walk through Hell's damnation together.

But back then, the fire seemed so far away. Please, please, forgive me for letting you walk through the flames alone. Please wait for me.

I am not a person of religion, yet I can sense you all around me as I walk in my own solitude. I can find your ghosts within these wooden walls and phantoms within the ripples on the lake.

If I were stronger, I would be fearful that you would plague me always. That the grief of your loss and the guilt of my actions would riddle me until my dying day. That I shall never love another for my heart is bound and tied to yours forevermore. If I were stronger, I would want to move forward without you.

Yet I am weak.

The very thought of this world without the wisps of your memory is futile. The ways in which I miss you are endless. With the ache, I am tormented. How can that love for you still pound in my heart with such... bliss? How can I miss you after all that you did? How can I yearn for you after what I had done?

Blood will forever stain our fingertips. The fire was necessary. We had to burn, you and I.

Yet from the ashes of our love, life still blooms darling. I wept for many nights and days at the very notion of it. If only we could've seen what fruits were ripening for us. Maybe neither of us would have succumbed to the darkness. We would have eaten, plentiful, and spent the rest of our days with the glory of this beautiful bounty. We would have been full and content and complete.

I am so frightful that these pages will seep into the soil and ensnare the seed once more. These secrets cannot take root in this home. I fear our acts would poison the flowers that are aching to bloom.

So, I have to bury this final piece of you. Everything you were in those dark moments. Those sickening revelations somehow pulled me closer to you.

And therefore, I shall bury myself with it. At least the pieces of who I was when I was happy within your arms. All the things of which you loved, all the moments in which we shined, and all the ways you made me divine.

In that way, we shall lie together in the dirt eternally.

In that way, I hope, our spirits can be in peace.

In that way, our love will be forever.

Friday 23rd August 1901

A blistering sun stretched the last of the light across the sky, causing the blues to battle with radiating oranges. As they collided, a sublime purple was formed. Miriam stared at the solitary clouds that had become entangled with the colours. She thought about how darkness came into fruition. It did not descend like the robe of a God walking across the earth, it gradually seeped into the world.

Miriam wondered if the same had happened to humanity. That evil and sin trickled slowly into the hearts of man and robbed them of joy and colour and splendour. That we were all destined to become shadows, sucking life from the earth and one another.

It was a terrible thought that ricocheted through her heart. Beginning to shake, she folded her arms as though she were stopping the tidal wave of memories that were about to descend. She closed her eyes and counted aloud things she could hear, smell, and feel. Then she opened her eyes and counted all the thing that she could see. When Miriam did this, her heartbeat began to wane and find rest. A gentle breeze circled around her, and she was oddly comforted by it.

The garden of the Manor lay in front of her. It had not changed much in several years. The land was still long and as wide as the house. Three small stone steps still led to a stone path. The green grass remained with bushes that were trimmed, round, and patterned neatly. The small fountain and small pond had not moved in decades. It was as it ever was; very symmetrical, and beautiful, and well-kept.

Only this time, there were more people to enjoy it. At the end of a pleasant day, a handful of women lay upon the grass. They were of all backgrounds and classes and had all found their way to the Manor through Miriam. In this secret and quiet refuge, Miriam, her father, and Hettie would offer salvation from terrible and violent pasts, with Matron Lockett helping back in London. After all, Miriam too had used the place to escape her demons and start a new life away from the seedy city.

Furrowing her brow, Miriam looked around the garden. She stood on tiptoes and arched her neck and huffed. When she couldn't find what she was looking for, she called out: "John?"

The women went silent, and Miriam heard no voices.

"John?"

Suddenly, there was a small chuckle from behind a hedge.

"John Fredric Bennett!"

There was another giggle, this time louder. Her eyes darted towards a green row of bushes, separated only by a stone pathway. Smiling, she snuck down and crept quietly to where the giggle was coming from. Standing up, she placed her hands her hips and said, "Oh goodness, I wonder where little Jackie is? He simply cannot be here."

"ROAR!" came a tiny voice as a little boy leaped from behind the hedge.

"Oh," Miriam said in a feigned surprised voice before leaning down and scooping up the four-year-old in her arms. Swinging him around, he squealed and screamed. The women on the grass laughed too.

"Stop it Mummy, I am getting dizzy!"

"Yes, I fear I am too." She said before stopping the circles. As she steadied her senses, she held him close, brushing his dark brown hair into place. Tucking it behind his ear, her son giggled from how much it tickled. It sparked a ray of glee in his piercing blue eyes – as bright as his fathers.

Caught in a moment, Miriam gently leaned her forehead against the young boy's and squeezed him close. A month after she arrived at the Manor, she found out she was pregnant. For a while, she did not know whether John was blessing her or cursing her from beyond the grave. She wailed unjustly at the news.

Yet when she first looked at her son, all she saw was love and adoration. He was a gift. The new life and beginning that came in spring as the century drew to a close. When Miriam held the little boy in her arms, she vowed to protect him from the suffering of the world or the darkness that could take hold of men's hearts.

Miriam cuddled him tightly and kissed his cheeks, causing the child to wiggle and exclaim; "Gerrof me Mummy!"

"No, I shall gobble you up, you little monster." She said, pretending to bite his ear and cheek.

"MUMMY!" He squeaked in high-pitched laughs.

From across the garden, where Miriam stood, a familiar voice floated through the air. "Ladies, dinner is up!"

"Oh dinner!" John said excitedly. He pushed against Miriam's arms until she put him down. As the women on the lawn gathered their things, John raced past them.

Bounding to the front door, he ran straight into the arms of Marie, who had bent down to embrace him. Miriam smiled gently at them. The two women had arrived at the Manor together, as Miriam had secretly scurried Marie away that fateful night. Since then, their bond had only grown stronger as they aided one another in healing from their spiritual wounds. Marie had become integral in the running of the Manor and had helped every woman who came through those doors.

It was a wonderful transformation. What Miriam loved most was seeing Marie full of life again: The rounded cheeks blossomed with red, and her eyes sparked with wonder. She also had great stories to tell. Often, the nights would be filled with laughter as Marie and Sir Fredric exchanged jokes or tall tales.

On nights where the Manor had no laughter, where Miriam

would see the ghoulish hands of ghosts that she thought she had left behind, Marie would come and comfort her. Miriam would repay this in kind. After all, recovery was a long, cold path with winding twists and pitfalls when you'd least expect it. Every path, however, is best walked with a friend. Miriam and Marie, through all that pain and anguish, had become the closest friends of them all.

Another wind suddenly wound around Miriam. A chill hit her bones causing her to shudder. At the front door of the Manor, Marie kindly beckoned her, but Miriam shook her head and gestured for Marie to go on.

Turning behind her, Miriam caught sight of something familiar – a stone bench that had stood for longer than she'd been alive. The garden hadn't changed much but there was no longer a thicket of roses at the end of it. Miriam was sickened by the sight of it. As beautiful as it was, it was twisted and dark and full of secrets. She wished for it to be removed.

Instead, she planted neat, short hedges, that ran along like a little maze. The centre, however, could always be seen from the house and the house could always be seen from the stone bench. Miriam sat down as though the breeze had called her here. She closed her eyes and enjoyed the end of summer that howled around her. The night was almost here. It bridled in her.

Miriam thought about her mother in the pictures she had seen. Miriam thought about her own solitary pleasure and discovery. She thought about the gardener's boy and how he was key to her becoming.

Then Miriam thought about John. She thought about the bristles of his moustache as he kissed her. She thought about the taste of whisky on his lips. She thought about his warm hands around her. His kind words and kinder touch. The way his calm would set off chaos within her.

Her great love, her tormented saviour, her dark god.

Miriam was coaxed out of her thoughts by the falling of a tear. She held herself close and wiped her cheek. Standing up, she whispered gently, "I will always be yours."

As the cloak of night came over the garden, Miriam walked up the stone pathway to the warmth of the Manor and left thoughts of the stone bench behind.

A stone bench that had stood there since before she was born.

A stone bench which held all of her secrets.

A stone bench which had buried beneath it a box.

Inside that box lay a diary.

A diary of murders.

Written by two.

Now Dear Reader,

Let us return to happier times with our couple with

this exclusive short story...

The Return to London

Tuesday 3rd September

John Bennett was no stranger to nightmares.

He had known grief and then terror at an early age. Haunting images took root deep within his soul and it was near impossible to rid himself of them. They returned often throughout his adulthood. Usually, he could dismiss the thoughts and swallow them back down to his gullet. Sometimes, they gripped him so fiercely that they hung over his head for most of the day. He'd retreat into his quiet self and mull over the memories as if the moments were alive once more.

This evening, he had only been asleep for a few hours before he was startled awake by images of his dead mother.

It took John a few beats to realise that he was in the safety of his own adult bed in the room at the top of the boarding house. He was no longer a child, trying to shake a corpse back to life, unsure of why she wasn't moving. Immediately, John reached over to his bedside cabinet and turned on his gas lamp, no longer willing to lay in the darkness alone with the thoughts of his mother. He sighed. He picked up his gold ornate watch and found it wasn't even midnight yet. As the hands moved past eleven, he grumbled and fell on his back in bed.

John turned to the window and found it peppered with droplets of rain. There was a mellow roar as a whistling wind rapped against the glass pane. The last days of summer were out of his reach now.

Taking a few deep breaths to calm his pulse down, a longing gripped him fiercely. He was suddenly overcome with both the childish want for his mother and the cloying need for his now fiancé Miriam.

They had arrived back in London only a handful of hours ago. The Claytons took him by carriage to his front door. Sir Fredric had fallen asleep again, this time leaning against his daughter. The newly betrothed pair looked stricken at one another as John took the handle of the cab door to leave. He was suddenly gripped with a fear - would London undo their blissful union?

John kissed Miriam gently on the hand before squeezing it to say goodbye, hoping that the touch would convey what he was feeling; that there was nothing this city could do that would change how he felt about her; that London could billow its smog and he'd still love her with a thousand fires; that the world would turn and spin, but they were bound together - forever. Miriam gently squeezed him back as though she were telling him that she understood.

Then she was pulled away from him. He stood watching the carriage leave, not entirely sure when they would unite again.

Now in the darkness of his room, it felt like an entire lifetime ago. He had nestled quite comfortably in the world of Miriam's body for an entire weekend. Without that warmth, and with the cold cruelty of his mind, it was as though John was abandoned. It was a silly concept. After all, they worked together in the same hospital and were both due to return tomorrow. They lived in the same city, though John was not sure where she resided. They both yearned for one another and had the tools in which to communicate. It seemed easy for them to continue their relationship in this dark and dangerous town.

So why was John so terrified of losing her?

Perhaps the exhaustion from an exhilarating weekend, and the nagging notions of the nightmare, were working against him in this Tuesday evening. John sat up in bed, realising that his pulse was too fast to fall back to sleep. He reached into the drawer and pulled out the journal he had been writing in all weekend, along with the black pen that had helped capture his thoughts.

The hope was to write down his nightmare as though the ink would strip it from his soul. Yet the moment he opened the book, he found her naked body sprawled across the pages. He had forgotten that he had barely written anything whilst at the Manor. Instead, he had crudely drawn her body, over and over again. He outlined her crevices in the pages of the book, capturing her essence in scrawling black lines. The sight of them caused a chuckle to leave his lips.

The drawings were something an adolescent schoolboy would do and yet the sight of them overtook John. The woman he had captured so crassly on the page flowed through his mind like a tidal wave. He'd practically drown if he wasn't so haplessly devoted to each and every sense of her. The taste of her wetness sat on his tongue suddenly and the scent of her flesh whipped and whirled around him. The fire in the lamp danced as a small breeze whistled through his home, causing her shadow to dance upon the walls.

Soon an unexpected moan followed where the laugh had tread.

Hardened at the very thought of her, he discarded the notebook. He reached into this drawer and removed a balm of his own creation – a Vaseline infused with lavender and mint. Often he used it to soften his hands and sooth patients, but he also found it made self-pleasure easier.

Placing the ointment in his hands, John rolled down his blanket, lifted the bottom of his nightgown, and took his stiff cock in his hands. He held himself for a moment, unsure whether to conduct such business with his nightmare still burning in his mind. Yet as he hesitated, he heard Miriam instructing him to caress and touch himself in her absence. He started slowly; up and down on his member as he pictured her commanding sense, willing him to submit to her will. He gasped, wondering on what rulings she could unleash on him now that he had finally given her reign.

The fantasy of the future began to meld into the memories. John had lost count of how many times they had shared in one another over the weekend. It wasn't without its excruciating waits. After they returned, sodden in their clothes after an unexpected dip in the lake, they announced their engagement to her father and Hettie. There were embraces and congratulations that droned on into the night when Aunt Isobel was invited over for supper. There was even a few tears shed. It didn't help that the pair antagonised one another – more Miriam, than John. It marvelled him how she already knew what words she could drip into his ear to almost undo him in front of everyone. Teased and tense, John wished the night away so they could re-join in body when everyone else was asleep.

Of course, Miriam would not make it easy for him. John lay nude in bed, waiting for her arrival. Clayton Manor was steeped in darkness and silence. He tried to listen, hoping to hear the floorboards creak as she padded over to his room. The anticipation rocked through him, turning from feverish excitement into foolish excruciation. John thought of last night, gripped in a similar anticipation as he gasped and groped himself alone.

He had waited an hour, lying in the dark of the Manor before he decided to make the trip to her room instead, too eager to stay still anymore. He put on his nightshirt and quietly opened his bedroom door, only to find Miriam standing right there in the doorway. Her eyes were ablaze with glee, and he wondered how long she had been stood there. Enough for her to relish the agonised look on his face. A sly smile formed on her face. She said nothing but pushed him back into the bedroom and closed the door.

They embraced and entwined in every way imaginable until today's morning rose, and a train beckoned them back to London.

Only when John finally trudged up the stairs of his boarding house, did he realise how exhausted he was. He unpacked his suitcase, sore and spent from a tiring weekend. By all accounts, he should not have the energy or the will for more exertion. Yet now as he touched himself, John wanted nothing more than to complete her once more.

As he quickened the strokes, John closed his eyes then suddenly she was there. Her deep blue eyes peering out at him from the ether of his mind. Her lips touched his as she slid upon his member, the wet warmth of her insides enveloping him gloriously. This fictitious Miriam placed her hands upon his chest and writhed on top of him. He watched as her breasts bounced gloriously up and down as he made love to her.

It all felt real. So real that John eagerly and hungrily pulled at himself faster than ever before, bucking his hips into himself as though he were fucking Miriam once again. Though his haunts lingered in the back of his mind, Miriam thrived in the foreground of it. How devious she was, occupying more and more of his faculties. The very idea of this control built up inside of him and he was ready to let go. He groaned loudly as he released his lust for her, the semen hitting his stomach, warm and plentiful. Breathing hastily, he laid there in the aftermath as a whirlwind of different emotions caught him in this fragile time.

John was no stranger to nightmares, but he found he could finally chase them away. Miriam was healing his nights, even when she wasn't with him. The twilight of her spirit gave him peace at last and he was too alive with the starlight to contemplate sleep. He questioned his sanity over and over again – meeting Miriam was too much like a perfect dream. He dare not wake from her fantasy. He wanted to soar with the darkness forevermore.

Suddenly, John was grappling with yet another urge. The thought of her simply wasn't enough. He wiped off the mess from his stomach with the bedsheet before he hastily started putting trousers and shoes on. He tucked his nightshirt into his waistband before he grabbed a large coat, putting it on before he stormed out of the boarding room.

As John was bounding down the stairs, he tried desperately to piece together her address. He wandered through their conversations as if she may have hinted to her whereabouts with a passing comment. John was crazed to head out into the night without so much as a destination, but his mind urged him to. Perhaps he could head to the hospital and find her address somewhere there.

John knew this sounded maniacal, but he had to try. He was

no longer willing to spend one night without Miriam Clayton. Though he had already told her, countless times, he had to tell her now. He had to tell her all the ways in which he loved her. And the urgency powered him forward out the front door.

Miriam Clayton was no stranger to insomnia.

Lying on her side, snuggled under the blankets, in the bedroom of her family's Clapham Common townhouse, Miriam found herself face to face with it. It curled within her like a sleeping cat, sitting on her chest and purring into her lungs. The feline had always been there, playing with the ball of slumber and batting it further and further from her grasp. The cat had first arrived in childhood and had stalked her through adolescence before Miriam finally allowed the stray to stay from time to time. Tonight, Miriam sighed loudly – accepting that no matter how exhausted she was, she couldn't beat the beast this evening.

Sighing, she stroked at it, and wondered if this time, the creature was here to stay. After all, since she had met John, she had to contend with the idea that she may never sleep again.

The wind howled loudly outside, the rain droplets hitting the windowpane with a ferocious roar. Miriam turned onto her back. She placed her hands on her stomach, then folded them across her chest, then placed them awkwardly to the side. She repeated this routine over and over again.

It was a strange sensation not knowing what to do with your arms but all at once, as the evening's anxiousness rippled through her, they just didn't feel like hers anymore.

She sat up in bed, and threw her hands to her face, silently screaming into her palms. It was useless to deny what she was coursing through her, why the night was somehow out of her grasp, and why she found herself so pathetically alone. She was gripped with the absolute and pure longing for her now fiancé John.

They had only parted a few hours ago. The carriage pulled up to his Camden Boarding House, and Miriam realised that she had spent the journey in silence. Partly because she was memorising the streets which lead to her love, and partly because she was terrified of letting him go. As her father leaned against her, drooling, and softly snoring, she stared at John and willed him not to leave her. This city had a somewhat insidious nature of changing good men and women, breaking their relationships until they were all but shattered glass on the dusty floor. How fragile one is in the looming presence of London. But John made her strong and powerful. This town could be cruel, yes, but it housed a light – a beacon in the darkest of oceans. Doctor John Bennett was the best of men and with his love, Miriam could face anything.

She wanted to tell him all of this, and then impart her rulings to him so that she would never leave his mind, but she couldn't find the right words. Especially not in the presence of her slumbering father. When John grabbed the handle of the door, he turned to her with a face equally aghast at the idea of departing. Instead of speaking, John took her hand to kiss it goodbye, and gave it a gentle squeeze which she mimicked. It told her all she needed to know. That in the silence of this sudden separation, they would still have one another.

Lying alone in her bedroom, Miriam admonished herself that she didn't say these words to him. She wondered if he knew how he made her feel. How that small squeeze reverberated through her even now. How his icy blue eyes captivated her soul. Miriam switched on the small gas lamp by her bed and looked at the small silver clock. It was barely eleven. The night was both old and young all at once. Miriam reached into the drawer. She rummaged for plain paper and a pen, hoping to spill all her secrets onto the page. Removing a small wad, she placed them in her lap.

However, instead of blank pages, she found herself staring at letters. A collection of papers weighted already by the ink. The sight of them caused her to chuckle gently to herself. They were frayed from all the unfolding and refolding that she had done on the day that she had received them. John had passed them to her so slyly after the board meeting. She slipped them into her corset, storing them close to her breast for fear that they'd be found by another. The paper against her skin burned with such lurid temptation that she was quite frightful that they'd etch themselves permanently onto her flesh.

That night she had excused herself early after supper and feverishly read them. John Bennett was quite creative in his wordings. He lavished his longing with loving letters. He scribbled to her salacious sordid sentences. He noted his naughty notions in needful nouns. This man conjured images as wicked as her own. She read them all into the night. When the morning rose, gifting her a whole weekend with him, Miriam wondered if she had finally met her match. This man whom she had met a handful of days ago occupied her mind so deliciously and she was hungry for more. She wasted little time in getting ready to see him, concocting devious games to which to play…

Now as she pawed at the letters again, a similar need growling within her stomach. A small, sigh left her mouth. There was a familiar twinge between her legs as an eagerness bounded through her whole body. She clenched her hands as a rose unfolded on her cheeks. Taking a sharp intake of breath, Miriam carefully listened to sounds of the house. There were several ticks of distant clocks and the soft howl of the lamp beside her, but there was no light, or signs of life. The rain continued outside, the wind whistling with a force similar to Miriam's intent. She was alone in these near-midnight musings.

Quickly, but carefully, she leaned over the side of her bed. Reaching down to the floor, she removed the red rug and wriggled the loose floorboard hidden underneath it. The small pop ricocheted across the room before landing on her in a series of shivers, as it always did. From the hole in the floor, Miriam removed an object hidden in cloth. Laying back in bed, she peered around her bedroom in case someone was lurking in the shadows. Quite assured that she was alone, Miriam unravelled the long, wooden dildo from its sheath.

Smiling at this old toy of hers, she pushed her knees up and positioned her legs open. Before she began with the wooden instrument, she dragged her hand across the neckline of her dress. Delicately, she pulled the fabric up, bunching the material above her breasts. She then threw the blanket from her, allowing the cool night air to hit her almost naked body. With one hand, she squeezed her right breast and fondled her nipple until it was erect. The other hand, clutching the wooden aid, she slithered it down her bare belly and nestled it between her slit. She stroked the thing, cold and hard against her privates. All the while, she suckled her tongue to remember him. The calming scent of his skin that set off chaos within her, the way his lips tasted of peaty whisky, and the way his hands hungrily sought every cell of her flesh. Miriam let out a small gasp as she grew wetter.

Then she slid the dildo into herself, taking a sharp intake of breath as she did. She kept it still there for a few beats before she began to move it inside of her. As she pushed the thing up and down, she thought on how John took her the first time they made love. The thickness of him surprised her and thrilled her all at once. He was a very adept lover, skilled in making her writhe and moan in his arms. He was also willing to submit to her rulings. This quiet doctor who had startled her so in his office had followed her all the way to the Manor and had dropped to his knees before her. Already Miriam Clayton's mind was thinking of new possible scenarios to please and thrill him.

Miriam massaged her breasts with her free hand and bucked her hips into the toy. The fantasy of the future melted into the memories of the Manor. Miriam had lost count in the ways they had shared in one another. Two nights of unadulterated bliss. Of course, it wasn't without its excruciating waits. The celebration of the proposal meant they could not consummate it. The evening's festivities dragged long into the night, causing all sorts of frustration to plummet through her. She didn't make it easy on either of them either – a choice word here or there when no one was looking caused her to also be utterly ravenous for John.

She took her second hand and settled on her aching pleasurable spot and began to rub it whilst moving the dildo faster and faster within her. She thought on last night and how near impossible it was waiting in her room until everyone else had gone to bed. She sat on the edge of her bed, listening to the footsteps of her family as they retired. When all was quiet, she padded over to his room. Despite being ravenous for a taste of him, Miriam lingered by his door for longer than she wanted to, knowing that the anticipation would dizzy him. She listened carefully to him muttering gently to himself. She heard him clamour out of bed. Suddenly the door was open, and his aghast face filled her with glee. Gently she pushed him back into his room so she could have her wicked way with him.

They embraced and entwined in every way imaginable until today's morning rose, and a train beckoned them back to London.

Only when Miriam and Sir Fredric arrived back in their

townhouse in Clapham Common, did Miriam realise how fatigued she was, throbbing from the many ways in which John took her. By all accounts, she should have no energy for such exertions, but the very thought of Doctor John Bennett awakened her once more. She bit her lip, trying not to moan as she pleasured herself.

Twisting over, Miriam knelt and moved quickly on the implement whilst rubbing herself faster and faster. She closed her eyes and suddenly she was upon him, and he was within her. His soft tender touches gliding over her skin as she bounced on top of him. Those bright blue eyes staring up at her with absolute awe. This fictitious John pushed upwards, pounding into her as he gripped her hips and kissed her lips.

It all felt so real. So real that Miriam moved impossibly fast upon the aid and her own hand. No man or woman had yet to occupy the secret spaces of her mind and yet in a handful of days, John Bennett had nestled into her notions so easily. How delightfully devious he was to steal her independence away from her, and she was willing to give him all. Every waking second of her life she wanted to hand over to him. There was no longer a day she could do without him. This realisation struck her so hard and fierce that she suddenly quaked with a tremendous orgasm.

Collapsing on the bed and removing the dildo from herself, Miriam tried to steady her breathing, but she found she was too exhilarated to calm down. Miriam was no stranger to insomnia. But now it was John who was stealing her nights and she didn't care. She wanted to hand over each of her stars and drip her darkness down his throat. She questioned her sanity over and over again – meeting John was too much like a perfect dream. She dared not wake from his fantasy. She wanted to soar with the darkness forevermore.

There was a small clap of thunder, causing Miriam to jump

out of bed. There was another urgency that took hold within her – that the thought of him wasn't enough. She rolled her nightdress down her naked tired body and grabbed whatever boots that she could find. Then she gently padded out of her room, quietly snuck down the stairs, and grabbed the nearest coat.

Miriam cared not that the rain and wind howled outside. She had to tell him how he made her feel. Tomorrow seemed like an eternity away, and she may not have another day to tell him all the commotion that he had caused within her. And the urgency powered her out of the door.

The rain fell down hard upon her as she dismissed the cab. The building where Miriam said her goodbyes looked dark and damning as it neared midnight. She hesitated on the steps, one foot eager to move forward whilst the other wanted to scarper back home. The idea had seemed like such a good one, having memorised where he lived only this morning. Now here she doubted her convictions. After all, she had no idea which room he resided in. Standing just her nightgown, boots, and her father's oversized brown coat, she looked too crazed to knock and enquire with whatever gossiping landlady lived there. For a short moment, Miriam wondered if she should throw rocks at his window but that seemed crazier. Instead, she hesitated as cold, fierce droplets soaked her clothes and skin. Then the door opened, causing her to jump one foot down.

The sight of someone on his doorsteps caused John to startle back into the hallway. He clung onto the doorknob that he had forcefully swung open and tried to make sense of the scene before him. At first he thought he was dreaming, but after a couple of beats, he realised that Miriam was stood haplessly in the rain. She stared at him, flapping open her mouths as though she were trying to explain why she was there, in barely any clothes. Except the words did not come.

It did not matter why Miriam stood on the doorsteps. It did not matter why John was leaving his flat. Because as soon as they realised that they were together again, the pair rushed forward and kissed each other so passionately that the world tumbled away.

John was no stranger to nightmares.

He was startled awake from the most violent of dreams. He did not open his eyes entirely, instead he squeezed them closed as though he were willing away the villain of his childhood. The images that he had seen were so tangible that he was somewhat frightful that he'd open his eyes and be back in the clutches of his aunt. It was a silly notion, but he let out a scared, short breath from his nose to steel himself as he opened his eyes.

John was thankful to be lying in the sanctuary of his own bed.

But he was dismayed to find that he was alone.

For a moment he lay there, watching the fireplace cast light upon his empty silk bedsheets. There was no trace of Miriam. In her clear absence, John wondered if he were so exhausted, and so desperate for her, that he had merely conjured Miriam Clayton. As he reached out across the empty space, however, he found evidence of her arrival. Gliding his fingers across the material produced puffs of her perfume, there were wet patches from their trysts and her rain-soaked hair, and his bottom still stung from where she had slapped it repeatedly. He let out a small groan of remembrance.

It was the first time in their short courtship that he had expressed just how truly dark his desires ran. Soaked and shivering from the rain, John had praised her like the goddess she was. He removed her wet clothes, took a towel, and dried her the best he could. Then he took his special balm and with his soft, warm hands, anointed her skin slowly as the fire drenched her in its orange flame. When he had finished, she removed his clothes and kissed him deeply, pulling his naked body against hers and groaning into his lips. Miriam squeezed and then slapped his buttocks playfully.

John broke from her lips suddenly as his heart leapt to his throat, letting out an unexpected gasp. Miriam scanned his features, trying to discern what emotion he was feeling. Having already been tied up and teased, this was the final part of himself that he had yet to give to her. As she pieced together what he was wordlessly trying to convey, John took a sharp intake of breath before nodding his permission. They settled on a special word between one another to stop the action. A word so key to their becoming – Roses. He then took a position on his bed, leaning on his arms, whilst Miriam gleefully slapped his buttocks until he relented with that sweet word.

John was no fool, he knew that revisiting that damnable wish would perhaps unleash something else. Even though he and Miriam made ardent love repeatedly together after the spanking, it could not dispel the banshee that he had locked in the caverns of his soul. Her presence mixed with the memories of the night caused both shame and excitement to rush through him. He wondered if these two parts of man could run together like the hounds of Hell. As John tried to steady his breath, he sat up in bed and rubbed his eyes in desperation – keen to wipe away the nightmare.

Miriam was no stranger to insomnia.

By all accounts, she should've been asleep by now. Her body was spent – aching and agonised from the enjoyment it had received these few days. Instead, she sat in a brown leather armchair by the fire, reading the most intriguing book, and sipping at a cheap whisky. She had shrouded herself in one of his deep, blue robes. Every so often, she flicked her eyes from the pages to the nude man, lying unconscious in bed.

After sharing one another in a number of different configurations, John had fallen asleep beside her and, instead of joining him, she watched him for a while, inhaling and exhaling the amber hues that covered them. She was griped with a sensational aliveness – strong and powerful like no one else.

That is how John made her feel. Even when she was so desperately afraid of her emotions for him. Doused with the evening's rain, she stood somewhat timidly beside his metal bedframe, twisting with the knob at the very end. She was frightful of the emotion that pushed her into the evening's showers and made her rush across the city to be with him. All at once she felt pathetic and provoked, wondering on the two beasts that ran within her like the hounds of Hell. Her cheeks burned with both the ideas of running back home and staying with this handsome man she knew so desperately well.

Yet this man had not bridled at her hesitation. Instead, he stoked the fire and warmed the room. He reached into a drawer, removed a towel, and brought it over to her. Rolling up her nightgown, he removed her sodden clothes and dried her the best he could. Then he found a soothing balm, one that smelled of lavender and mint, and he rubbed it between his two hands.

Dropping to her feet, he began to caress and massage her like one would do a deity. His soft warm hands travelling over every inch of her body so studiously and loving that she was desperate to sigh from the motions.

Yet she twisted her glee into her lips and held steadfast. For the way he caressed her, praising her body with such precision, made her powerful. He was restoring her authority, pleading for her command with each caress. She was his goddess, and she quaked with dominance.

When he had finished, as a reward for such piety, she removed his clothes quickly and brought him into a kiss as plentiful as she could give. Gripping his buttocks into her hand, she also gave him a playful slap.

The gasp which left his lips was melodious. He broke from her lips to sing it, his eyes alive with such a devilish yearning. She had teased and tied him, yes but this new relationship had yet to indulge in such pain. Miriam wasn't sure if she should broach the question, longing for his skin beneath her hard, confronting touch. Yet the way he reacted to such a gentle touch made her realise that he wanted her to continue. He nodded swiftly to her and bent over the bed to allow her to beat him until he conceded with that special word. Each smack echoed with their gratification. In that moment, they were so wonderfully connected to each other that after, they tumbled into delightful, dark, and delicious lovemaking.

The very thought of it all bounded through her stomach like a joyful kitten chasing after string. She knew that it was quite impossible to sleep with such love and devotion surrounding her. When she was sure he would not awaken, she removed herself from the bed to write the letter that had been sitting on her mind. As Miriam placed her bare feet on the wooden floorboards, she found his journal lying open on the floor. She hesitated, trying not to glance at the pages. This book could tell her secrets that John dared not to. Yet Miriam knew the man that lay curled upon the bedsheet told her much more than the ink sprawled out on the page. She decided to pick up the journal and scurry it away in the drawer. That is until she saw the lurid content before her.

The drawings were rudimentary. Black pen lines like a child would do, if said child were privy to her most private parts. John had drawn her in all sorts of positions – prostrating across the pages in all the many ways they had consummated. Miriam smiled immediately, thinking on all the times she had watched him writing in his journal – on the train, waiting for her in the manor, or in the board meeting last week. She wondered if all that time was spent concocting her body permanently in ink.

She couldn't stop gazing them, not when she found a robe of his to wrap around her nude body, not when she poured herself, mindlessly, the first whisky she could find from his desk, not when she settled into this armchair to study the drawings and the sleeping suitor who had sketched them.

In a moment, however, John was awake – jolted violently from his peaceful sleep. She heard a faint groan come from him, causing her heart to flutter. She watched as he stirred, staring outwards at the empty space that she had previously occupied, his hand skimming the surface of his silk sheets. He grimaced and closed his eyes, pinching the bridge of his nose before sitting up in bed. There was an almighty sigh from him as he leaned his arms on his knees. John's eyes scoured the room for her and as he found her, she flashed a gleeful grin and lifted the book to show that she had found his drawings.

He weakly smiled back before his eyesight drifted away from hers. A frightfulness sunk into Miriam as John's face was pale and uncertain, as though he had been stripped from his very person. He looked scared – terrified of his own being. There were tears in his eyes that he was trying desperately not to show, but Miriam could see them glistening in the fire's glow.

Miriam did not hesitate. She placed the notebook and the drink down on the small round wooden table by the armchair and raced over to the bed. Climbing in, she coaxed him into her arms and held him against her chest, cooing him softly with soothing sighs and tones. How at home she was embracing him, his breath skimming her skin shakily.

John gripped onto her tightly and tried not to cry. Not because of the nightmare, no, but of the overwhelming love he had for this woman. He did not need to speak his distress for her to understand he needed comfort. She did not scorn him for being sad or scared, she took him into her arms and hugged him fiercely. How at home he was lying against her, listening to her heartbeat thud strongly.

The pair fell asleep together in this way, basking in each other's light. John had finally tamed Miriam's insomnia and Miriam had once again chased away John's nightmare. They were shrouded in a heavenly light – one of absolute completion. In this very moment, in this tender support, beyond the looming city and its thick fog, away from the prying eyes of others, there was only one thing that mattered.

Now.

Sign-Up to My Newsletter

For more short stories set within the

wicked world of Diary of Murders

ACKNOWLEDGEMENTS:

I'd first like to thank my father, Steve, who has not only been my greatest cheerleader, supporting my writing career from the beginning, but has helped, in numerous ways, to bring this book to life. Thank you for teaching me about generosity, kindness, and silliness.

Thank you to my mother, Helen, for your undeniable support in everything that I do. Thank you for teaching me about strength, resilience, and the importance of wild, unruly laughter.

Thank you to my eldest sister Louise who will always be the coolest person I know and has supported me in all facets of my being. To my youngest siblings Ollie and Ryan – thank you for helping me grow as a sister and a person. To my immutable niece Kaitlyn – I am so proud to be your aunt. Special thanks goes to Nanny, Uncle Barry, and Dan!

Endless gratitude to Andrew J for your incredible friendship. You were the first person to read this book, you edited countless versions, and your endless belief in my work has made me supreme.

Thank you to Rosie for your unshakeable understanding and the evenings of dancing, laughter, and watching shit fantasy television shows.

Thank you to Cat for your fierce friendship and the calm you bring into my life. Thank you for venturing to musicals with me and our long chats and walks.

Thank you to Clarisse for being such a fantastic person, friend, and one of the greatest writers I know. I've loved all of our adventures.

Thank you to Emily for your greatness and comfort (and pictures of your cat Holmes.)

Thank you to Charis for the parties, the endless support, and being my wife forever.

Thank you to Charlotte for the laughs and the big boys. Thank you to Galia for always supporting my writing. Thank you to the 12 Awesome Film Nerds: Clarisse, Charlotte, Galia, Amanda, Maria, Amon, Helen, Kelechi, Katie, Tom, and Mike!

Massive thanks to my great friends Jess, Kathryn, Ana, Keira, SMK (and Salem & Sheba), Hannah W, Sarah M, Rachel, Andrew P, Robbie, Kayleigh, Ren, Becki, and many more. Special Mention to Mark who gave me advice at the very beginning of this journey.

Thank you to Beth for your exquisite artwork and bringing to life my vision.

Thank you to Miss Walker, my English Teacher who first believed in my writing.

Finally, to my cat Jekyll. I am sorry your contributions had to be deleted. They just didn't make medeouch sense.

ABOUT THE AUTHOR:

Sarah Cook lives with her cat Jekyll in London.

Her poem DIRT was recently published at MONOFiction and she has self-published a number of short stories on this very website. On top of this, she has directed a number of short films including *Toby* and *The Rogue Table*. Her latest short film *Blow by Blow* was featured on the Honourable Mention list at the Women X Film Festival and is available to watch on Youtube.

Sarah Cook is also a prolific media journalist who has had by-lines in websites such as *Movies On Weekends, HeyUGuys, Film Stories, The Digital Fix,* and *Picturehouse Cinemas*. Sarah has established herself as a keen reporter, both on junkets and on red-carpets, interviewing celebrities from Florence Pugh to Minnie Driver.

She works in the art industry as a marketing manager for *UK Jewish Film, Picturehouse Cinemas, Royal Albert Hall*, and *the Albany*, producing celebrated and viral content for their social channels.

In her spare time, Sarah is an active member of the Victorian Society and likes to explore the weird wonders of London.

Follow her on Twitter, TikTok, & Instagram: @sarahcookwrites

If you have been affected by the content of this book, please contact:

Rape Crisis Helpline: 0808 500 2222

National Domestic Abuse Helpline: 0800 2000 247

Thank you.

Proceeds from book sales will go to help Refuge – For Women and Children against Domestic Violence.